FALLING for the CEO

ELENOR POUNTAIN

FALLING FOR THE CEO

Publisher: Elenor Pountain
Photocredit: Deposit Photos
Cover Design, Editor, Formatter: Maria Vickers
Proofreader: Elouise East

Contents

Prologue	1
Chapter 1	5
Chapter 2	9
Chapter 3	13
Chapter 4	18
Chapter 5	21
Chapter 6	23
Chapter 7	26
Chapter 8	29
Chapter 9	31
Chapter 10	33
Chapter 11	36
Chapter 12	38
Chapter 13	40
Chapter 14	45
Chapter 15	47
Chapter 16	49
Chapter 17	51
Chapter 18	53
Chapter 19	55
Chapter 20	56
Chapter 21	59
Chapter 22	62
Chapter 23	65
Chapter 24	67
Chapter 25	69
Chapter 26	71
Chapter 27	73
Chapter 28	76
Chapter 29	78

Chapter 30 81
Chapter 31 86
Chapter 32 91
Chapter 33 96
Chapter 34 101
Chapter 35 105
Chapter 36 109
Chapter 37 115
Chapter 38 121
Chapter 39 124
Chapter 40 129
Chapter 41 132
Chapter 42 137
Chapter 43 141
Chapter 44 146
Chapter 45 151
Chapter 46 156
Chapter 47 161
Chapter 48 166
Chapter 49 171
Chapter 50 174
Chapter 51 178
Chapter 52 183
Chapter 53 189
Chapter 54 194
Chapter 55 200
Chapter 56 206
Chapter 57 212
Chapter 58 217
Chapter 59 223
Chapter 60 228
Chapter 61 233
Chapter 62 238
Chapter 63 244

Chapter 64 249
Chapter 65 255
Chapter 66 260
Chapter 67 265
Chapter 68 271
Chapter 69 276
Chapter 70 283
Chapter 71 288
Chapter 72 293
Chapter 73 299
Chapter 74 304
Chapter 75 309
Chapter 76 314
Chapter 77 319
Chapter 78 324
Chapter 79 329
Chapter 80 334
Chapter 81 339
Chapter 82 344
Chapter 83 349
Chapter 84 355
Epilogue 360

Acknowledgments 363

Dedication

I dedicate this book to those who believed in me. Especially my amazing husband G, without your support this book would probably still be one of the stories in my head rather than being published xx

FALLING FOR THE CEO

Prologue

JESS

I've been here for two years, waiting for the opportunity to move up and gain more responsibility. Working in admin is fine, but I want more. It's been a week since I interviewed for the PA position for our CEO. I should hear back today whether I got the job or not.

Our company consults with other companies to restructure and make them more streamlined. Our consultants are the best in the country, and we are extremely sought after. We have a waiting list that is currently booking two years into the future.

Part of my job is to type up the plans, arrange them into a presentation pack and send them back to the consultants so they can claim all the glory with the clients. I can't say I fancy being a consultant, but I enjoy making the magic behind the scenes.

If I get the job, Kiera, my best friend, is taking me

for a slap-up meal and drinks to celebrate. If I don't, well, we're eating Chinese and ice cream in our PJs to commiserate! Way to live up a Thursday night!

I've maxed my credit card on new outfits for the position. At the time, I felt cocky, but now, I feel as if I should return them. I'm waiting for a call from Carol in HR whilst I tap away at my desk.

Plodding through the same monotonous tasks I do every week, I see Carol's name come up on my phone.

GAVIN

"You've had five PAs in the last year. What are you doing to them?" Paul lectures me whilst I try to go through my emails. Is it so hard to expect someone to do this for me and not quit if I ask them to do other jobs?

I've heard I can be a little demanding, but that doesn't mean I expect more than any other CEO. Last week, I held some interviews; however, I'm not confident with any of them, and Carol has been pushing for a decision for the last two days. I suppose I should take a gamble on the one who seemed the brightest.

"Yes, I've had five PAs. It's not my fault they can't cope with a demanding workload. It's not like I don't warn them in the interview process!" I fire back at Paul. He's my best friend and the finance manager of the company. His opinion means a lot, but sometimes, it cuts.

Carol's name pops up on our messaging system…*again*. Running my hand through my hair, I scan the notes I made during the interviews. Decision made, I ping her the name to hire.

Chapter One

JESS

I ask Carol to give me five minutes, so I could take the call in private and head down to the smoking area with my mobile to find a quiet corner. I wouldn't be able to stomach taking rejection while sitting at my desk.

"Jess, how are you today? Are you free to chat and discuss the outcome of your interview?"

My stomach is in knots.

"Yes, Carol. I'm good, thanks. How are you?" I wait patiently for her to continue and don't realise I am holding my breath until I try to light my cigarette with shaking hands.

"You presented well in the interview, answered the questions with confidence...." *Hurry up!* "Gavin has chosen you as the candidate to fill the position. Congratulations, Jess! I'll email you the details, start date, contract, and salary. I look forward to welcoming you to your new position."

Holy shit, did she just say I got the job? My ears are ringing. It's not that this is the most important career move for me, but it is something that would provide a challenge and change to the monotonous work I do now. I GOT THE JOB!!!!

Not to sound over-eager, I calmly say, "Thank you, Carol. That's excellent news. I'll go through the details when you send them and will speak to Elsie." After saying our goodbyes, I finally manage to breathe.

Smoking the last of my cigarette, I go back upstairs to see if Elsie has time to chat. Elsie has been my manager for two years and is wonderful to work for. She knows I applied for the position, but I don't think she banked on me getting it. I am the best admin on her team, so she will probably be sad to see me go; however, this was the best decision for me.

I head to her desk, which isn't far from mine in the open-plan office, knock on her desk, smile and say, "Elsie, have you got a minute?"

I SIT WITH KIERA AT THE STEAK RESTAURANT SHE managed to get us into, and our waiter brings over a bottle of champagne and congratulates me on my new job. I raise my eyebrow at Keira. "How did he know? We've been sitting together since we arrived." Kiera and I have been best friends for as long as I can remember. We were in school together and clicked instantly. She's one of those natural beauties, with a lovely thin figure but not too thin, with long curly brown hair that requires no effort to look amazing and piercing blue eyes.

She giggles, raising her glass to toast. "I may have booked this the day of your interview and put a note in the 'Special Requests' box to say we were celebrating." I clink my glass with hers and smile. She is always so positive, and she really believed I would get the job even though I was dubious.

"How did Elsie take it?" Thinking back to the earlier chat with my boss, I feel the guilt coming back. "She was okay. She knew I'd be a good candidate but honestly didn't think I would get the offer. She's spread my workload between the others on the team whilst she recruits."

Keira sits back with a frown on her face. "She had no faith! We all knew you were going to get the job, and you were never going to turn it down because your brain would turn into mush if you weren't challenged soon! Now, stop feeling guilty, get drunk with me and eat!" She licks her lips as our food is set down in front of us. I have to admit, I wasn't expecting a good portion of food for the cost, but my plate is full of thick-cut chips, vegetables and a gorgeous-looking steak. My stomach rumbles, and I tuck right in.

After dinner, we say our goodbyes, and then I walk to the station. I don't mind getting on the tube on my own. Some people don't like it, but I enjoy people-watching whilst listening to my music.

Heading down the countless steps to my platform, the train pulls up. I jump on and stand by the door, holding onto the bar. Looking at my phone to catch up with the notifications—*Thank God for underground Wi-Fi*—I feel someone run through the door and onto the train just as the door is closing. The train is always busy on a Thursday night.

Feeling the humdrum of the train hurtling through the tunnels, I lift my gaze from my phone after choosing my playlist and start glancing around the carriage. People are swaying to the movement. Some are reading the papers, and others are kissing and holding hands. Young, old, different ethnicities, and all enjoying their ride home. My stop is coming up, and I can't wait to get home and into bed! I have a handover to prepare, after all.

I got the job!

Chapter Two

GAVIN

Now that I am not being pestered by HR, I can actually get some work done. A lot of the emails on my public address are typical sales pitches, companies wanting to speak to me directly rather than my consultants, etc. Now that I've appointed a PA to handle these, this task can wait, and I can go back to my actual work and my real emails.

As I try to get as much done before meeting Paul for a couple of drinks in the local pub, I notice an email from Carol saying the girl accepted the position. She starts the role on Monday, and I am told I should ease her in gently. *Yes, Carol, because that's how shit gets done, isn't it? Handholding, babysitting and not getting much actual work done!* She means well, but I need someone who can sit, do the job and not ask too many questions.

Whilst I read through one of the finance reports Paul sent over prior to our meeting in the morning, I cast my mind back to the interview. What is her name? I remember she is a curvy blonde who has a nice smile. Some people want thin, model-type people sitting at their desks outside their offices, but I am not interested in that. My assistant just needs to look presentable and do their job. The woman spoke well in the interview, but we'll see how she gets on.

Noticing the time on my laptop, I close it and set off for the pub. Paul will probably be at the bar chatting up anything that looks pretty and doesn't have crooked teeth. Stepping outside the front door, I light up a cigarette and walk the two streets to the pub. It isn't the type of place people would assume I go. It's simply a nice little pub on the backstreets of London, so it doesn't attract tourists. Standing outside, I chuckle, seeing Paul, predictably, chatting up a brunette at the bar. It is seven o'clock, so who knows how long they've been there.

I take the drink he has waiting for me and claim a seat at one of the high tables after I enter. Paul eventually potters over, typing the number of the brunette into his phone from the business card she gave him. He grins like an excited schoolboy as he sits down.

"Another day, another number," he says enthusiastically. Paul has a reputation for being a bit of a ladies' man. He is handsome, I suppose, but it is his charm and character that attracts the ladies.

"Appears so, my friend! Are you actually going to date this one, or will she end up broken-hearted, waiting for the handsome man from the bar to call her back?" He gives me a mocking shocked face.

"Really? You're going to pretend you're shocked?" I tease.

"Well, this one seems quite bright. I may actually take her to dinner first." He grinned into his bottle as he downed his beer.

I can see where this night is going. Thank God tomorrow is Friday.

SITTING IN MY OFFICE, NURSING MY MILD HANGOVER, I massage my aching temples with my fingers. I should not have drunk as much as I did with an all-department meeting this morning. But I have ten minutes before heading to the boardroom, so I once again look over the report Paul sent me last night.

Ding Ding.

Picking up my phone, I check the message. Sacha, again. She seriously doesn't get the hint. We had a good thing for a year until she decided sleeping with someone else was an option. I broke it off four months ago, and she still messages daily to tell me she misses me, regrets what she's done, blah, blah, blah. Sacha is beautiful on the outside, a tall, thin figure with ample breasts. She has blonde hair that comes to just below her shoulders and always wears makeup. I prefer her without too much on, but she likes to cake on her makeup to "look the part."

Although Sacha turns heads when we are out together, she is ugly on the inside. She makes comments about the poor people of the city. She makes fun of women who can't afford the clothes she can and teases them if their hair isn't perfectly styled. It's something I thought I could nurture and change, but apparently not.

Maybe I should change my number. No, that's too much trouble. Ignoring the message, I pick up my laptop and head to the boardroom. Paul is waiting for me as other heads of departments join us. *How does he look as fresh as a daisy?* The meeting is underway in a matter of minutes, and I zone in and out. There are no decisions to make today; it is an information meeting. *Literally, this meeting could have been an email.*

After all of the departments share their stats, I head back to my office. I have the new girl coming to meet me later, so I can set expectations. I really hope this one lasts. I'm getting bored with new names I can't be bothered to remember.

Chapter Three

JESS

Carol pops her head around my desk; she looks different today. Her hair is on point, her makeup flawless, and she is wearing a lot of perfume. I wonder who the lucky man is. "Are you free to meet Gavin to discuss your role that is starting Monday?" *Is she kidding? No!* It is dress-down Friday, and I look like crap.

"Oh, um, yeah, I can pop up to his office. When were you thinking?"

Carol smiles sweetly. "Now? I've cleared it with Elsie already." *Shit!*

We head up to Gavin's office, which is the floor up from admin. *He can't be mixing with the riffraff and all that.* We walk past my new desk. It's empty except for a new notepad, pen, docking station, etc. I'll bring my laptop with me, so that'll be easy. It looks sad, though. I make a mental note to buy a plant for my desk, but nothing I can kill.

Carol straightens out her dress as she knocks on his

office door. "Come in." He sounds authoritative. I am now more nervous than earlier. What is he going to think of me dressed like this? Our floor does dress-down each week. We all bring snacks in on a Friday and have a fun day whilst working. His floor clearly doesn't do this. Everyone is in their normal business clothes. I want to fit in with this floor, and although this meeting is supposed to be quick to fit in with his schedule, my outfit doesn't look as professional as the rest of the team on this floor.

As we enter, Carol smiles and looks at him in a way that suggests she has a little crush. She doesn't look him directly in the eye, and her posture when we were on our own was relaxed, but now she is standing with her hip to one side, which shows off her curves. She also has a slight pout to her lips and bats her eyelashes when she talks. I swear she didn't do that before. The moment he addresses her, she blushes slightly.

Well, going by her extra effort, I would say more than a little crush because not only can I see it on her face, I can tell by her change of attire. When we met previously, she didn't wear much makeup, and her clothes were a typical plain skirt suit with a plain blouse. Now, she's wearing dark pink lipstick, more eyeliner, and I think she might be wearing fake lashes. Her plain suit has been replaced by a figure-hugging dress with a low but still professional neckline.

We stop in front of his desk, and without glancing up from his laptop, he gestures with his hand, indicating the two seats in front of him.

Why didn't I notice during the interview how

handsome he was? His shoulders are broad, his jaw strong, and his arms appear big and muscular in his suit. Why am I picturing him picking me up and swinging me over his shoulder? *Back in the room, Jess!*

Finally peering over his screen, he looks me up and down. He has slight sneer on his lips as he takes in what he sees. It looks like an expression of disappointment. I can feel myself blushing and trying to hide myself. I'm not the most confident person. I am curvy, plus-sized, or whatever you want to call it. But I dress for my size, and it doesn't mean I can't look good. I've always been bigger than my friends, and it took me a long time to try to accept my body. It's still a work in progress.

Gavin gives me a tight smile and goes back to his screen. Carol starts talking about my responsibilities, and I take some notes. Luckily enough, I had the foresight to bring my notebook and pen.

Carol is in the middle of a sentence when he interrupts, "I expect you to be here at seven-thirty and leave when I leave. I need someone who can keep up with my pace, do the responsibilities set out in the job description, and do any additional tasks I send your way without complaint. If I explain something to you, I don't expect to explain it again." He looks up and sees I am taking notes and raises an eyebrow. That must be a good sign, right?

We shake hands after our meeting, and as Carol and I are heading out of his office, he calls out, "Oh, and, Jess, I expect you to be in business attire all week.

This isn't the admin floor." With a blush on my cheeks, I nod and walk out.

This is going to be interesting.

KEIRA SITS ON MY SOFA, LISTENING INTENTLY TO MY drama from today. I am still so embarrassed to go to my new boss's office dressed as I was. Although most of the office participates in dress-down Fridays, the management floor doesn't. I wanted to look the part in one of my new outfits, not head up there in my baggy clothes. I slump further down into my seat, sipping my wine. "Oh, Jess, it can't have been that bad! He had to know about casual Fridays, and it's not like it was a planned meeting. Stop beating yourself up, woman!" I love her. She is fierce, absolutely beautiful and completely honest.

I can't stop thinking about his face. There is something hidden behind those eyes.

I've known Keira since we were in school together. We moved to London around the same time and met up often to discuss our drama. She is one of those naturally beautiful women who could eat what they wanted and never put on weight. She has gorgeous with long, curly brown hair. It takes no effort to look good. All of that paired with light blue eyes, and she is stunning.

I've always been jealous of her figure. She got attention wherever we went. I, on the other hand, have always been curvier. My body is soft and nowhere near as toned. I have scars all over me, and I'm average looking. My blonde hair comes from a bottle. My natural hair colour is a dull, mousy brown. I decided to go blonde when I started working in London. It made me feel a bit better about myself and more confident.

"Keira, I was wearing my proper baggy T-shirt. No shape at all. I'm hoping my new outfits will impress him better. They cost me enough! Why don't thin people's clothes cost this much?" I'm laughing, but having to buy most of my outfits online from shops that offer a plus-size or curvy range meant they cost a bit more. Especially when you need to impress.

We sit chatting for a couple of hours, eat our Friday night dinner of pasta bake, sip our cheap wine and enjoy giggling. After Keira goes home, I jump into bed. I have bought my laptop home so I can clear my inbox and start preparing for Monday. I'm nervous and excited, but overall, I am ready for the challenges and excited to be learning something new.

Chapter Four

GAVIN

After a short message exchange with Elise, she reminded me that I authorised dress-down Fridays last year. That must have been when I was a little less grumpy. I admit my mood isn't as good when I'm not having regular sex. But…work needs to get done.

Ding Ding.

> Sacha: Gavin, baby, I miss you, and I can never apologise enough for the mistake I made. Please have dinner with me. Just drinks. Anything. I need to see you. xx

Urgh! Sacha again. She is really grating on me. I suppose the only way to get her off my back is to meet her for a drink and tell her again that it's over. I was hurt when I found out that she'd been sleeping with someone at work. I didn't think twice about her working late at night or staying over at hotels to get to client meetings early because it comes with the territory of some management roles. I should know since I'm often working late.

I shouldn't have been such a naïve idiot and should have seen the signs, but I was too into her. She made me feel good, but then I couldn't be my true self around her. As soon as people figure out you have money, you are expected to act in a certain way. As with most women, they want things, but Sacha wanted the status that came with being my girlfriend. We were still in a honeymoon phase, and I wanted to let my full self out gradually. I wanted to cook for her, have nights cosied up in front of the TV.... I'm pleased I didn't. It takes a lot for me to be myself around women, and after her, I won't trust another easily.

Me: Fine, seven o'clock at the pub.
ONE drink!

By the time I've got through the last tasks on my list for today, I have enough time to head over to the pub. I'm going to end this here and now. She is bordering on stalker. As I walk up to the bar, she is there waiting for me and has got me a scotch on the rocks. I shake my head and order a beer instead. She doesn't get to pretend to know me that well.

Sacha: So stubborn! You're going to
need that scotch soon!

She launches at me for a hug, and I feel her hips get closer to mine. Her face is leaning in, and those beautiful eyes stare at me through her fake lashes. I know what she's trying to do. "Sacha, I came here to listen and tell you this isn't happening. We will not be together."

Pouting, she returns to her bar stool, takes a sip of her gin and exhales, setting it down. "Honestly, Gavin, I don't know what to say that I haven't said before. I thought seeing me would change your mind. I shouldn't have slept with Tom." Hearing her say his name makes me clench my beer bottle to the point I think it might break. "It didn't mean anything. It was one time, and I thought…." She pauses for too long.

I'm getting bored with this. "No, Sacha, it wasn't one time. You were sleeping with him for months, or have you forgotten that row we had over this? You thought? You thought your indiscretion wouldn't get found out. Enough is enough. Stop contacting me and go back to his place. It's no secret you're seeing him!"

She looks at me, shocked. Like a deer in headlights.

With that, I walk out of the bar. I haven't finished my drink, but I am finished with this conversation. She doesn't bother trying to come after me. I don't want her to.

Hailing a cab, I go home. I need to clear my head. A nice hot shower, dinner and bed sounds perfect.

Chapter Five

GAVIN

Walking into the office at seven-twenty in the morning, I expect it to be empty, but there is the blonde girl at her desk, ready and waiting with two cups of coffee. "Good morning, Gavin. Uh, sorry, Mr Andrews. You have two reports on your desk waiting for your sign-off, and here is your coffee."

How does she know how I take my coffee? She hasn't started yet.

Urgh. She seems like a "chirpy in the morning" type of person, but at least she is dressed smartly and looks a lot better than she did on Friday. I go to my office and motion for her to follow. I'm pleased when she automatically picks up her notepad and pen. Opening my laptop, I see an email from her. I remember her surname but had forgotten her first name is Jess.

"Right, Jess. Unfortunately, due to the haste in which my last PA left, there is no handover. I have emailed you the location of certain documents, but this will be an on-the-job learning opportunity. I have three meetings today, two of which are in my office. I will email you the details and expect you to offer my clients drinks and attend the meeting to take notes. My last meeting is out of the office, and I won't require your attendance. You will be emailed draft contracts that I expect to be typed using our official documentation by the end of the day. I will need lunch to be picked up and will send you a message with my order. Do you have all that?" I know I sounded like a dick, but I needed to know that she could handle me in the mornings and just get on.

"Yes, Mr Andrews. I will await your meeting details and set to work once I receive your drafts." With that, she gives me a smile and heads out of my office.

Setting to send her the details, I raise an eyebrow as she leaves. This one may actually work out.

Chapter Six

JESS

He seems demanding. I knew a CEO would be, but this is my first day. I really hope I didn't show I was intimidated. I don't even get a welcome to your new position, just straight in at the deep end, which is how I actually prefer to work. I don't like my hand being held. I will show him just how amazing I am, and hopefully, over time, he will give me more responsibility.

Just as I glance down at the notes I took in his office, his emails come through. I've been given access to the drives required and set to work, finding the documentation he discussed with me. Luckily, I have seen our contracts before when Elsie showed me a project she worked on, so I know what I am looking for. They are mainly self-explanatory and fill in the blanks.

By lunchtime, I have attended his meetings, taken notes, ordered his lunch, and typed up the notes for me to proofread as I eat lunch. I am heading out when I hear my name. "Jess, have you got started on those contracts yet? When are you getting lunch? I need to leave in an hour for my next meeting." I walk into his office. He hasn't even peered up from his laptop, but I notice his expression is intense, his eyebrows are furrowed, and his eyes don't move from what he's reading. You can almost hear the cogs turning in his head, so I make my response to the point. "Mr Andrews, one of the contracts should be in your inbox, and the others will be completed this afternoon. I'm heading out to get lunch now and will be back in fifteen minutes, so you will have plenty of time to eat before leaving."

Stop ogling the man and move! I can't help eyeing him whilst he works. During the meetings this morning, he was in control, powerful, at ease with his dominance….

He looks like he is concentrating on something. I edge my way out of his office, not entirely sure he heard me. Rushing out the front door, I have time for a smoke before I get to the sandwich bar. This job has a lot less free time than my old one, but it is only day one. I haven't got into the stride of it yet. I pick up our lunch and head back to the office. I knock on his office door when I arrive. No answer. I pop my head in and see his office is empty. *Shit!* He hadn't heard me, which means he's probably looking for me. I leave his lunch on his desk and go back to mine to type up the notes from the last meeting.

He walks past my desk two minutes later and goes into his office. My messaging service pings.

Gaven: Thank you.

Okay, I am doing all right on day one. I don't know what the thank you is for, but I hear praise and appreciation aren't things Mr Andrews is famous for.

After lunch, I'm happy with my notes and ping them across to him. He's sent me more bits to do during the day and has advised me that he would not be coming back into the office after his meeting, so I could leave at five o'clock. Today was a good day. I think I've made a much better impression.

Chapter Seven

GAVIN

She is doing well on day one and hasn't faltered even when I was rude. She picked up my lunch and was back in record time. Not long after she left, I went out for a smoke, and before I could return, she was back. Her work is efficient with no mistakes.

My meeting this afternoon is at a hotel. After my clients leave, I have a drink whilst working. I enjoy the background noise occasionally. I send her the voice recording I did on my laptop from the meeting, and within the hour, she sends me the transcript. With a small chuckle, I decide to send her some praise. I have never said thank you to any of my PAs on day one. She seems different to the blushing, shy girl who was in my office on Friday.

Me: Jess, well done today. You have impressed me with your efficiency.

Jess: Thank you, Mr Andrews. Is there anything you need me to do before I leave for the day?

Me: No, Jess, that's all.

I've never been impressed this quickly before. It is either first-day luck, and it will go downhill from here, or she may be a keeper.

I finish my drink, shut my laptop and head home for the evening. I want to go for a run before I eat and flick through the TV before bed.

I come back from my run, grab a bottle of water from the fridge and search for what I fancy for dinner. Unless I have company, I always cook for one. I got smart and did bulk cooking, so I always have leftovers in the fridge. I opt for the lamb Balti I cooked over the weekend, chuck it in the microwave and head to the shower. By the time I've finished and put some shorts on, my dinner is at the perfect eating temperature. I sit on my sofa and flick through the TV.

It's nights like this I think about having someone in my life. It would be nice to talk about our days over dinner and watch some rubbish on TV before going to bed. Of course, there are women in my phone I can call, but I got bored of one-night stands years ago. Then there was Sacha, the woman I thought I could see a future with until I got suspicious. It took me a couple of months to catch on, but she started making mistakes, like coming home, smelling like another man, and telling me she'd been hugged in a bar. Her bra shouldn't smell like aftershave!

After that, I followed her one evening and saw her having dinner with Tom from her office. I thought he was gay. After chastising myself for thinking she was cheating, I noticed her foot under the table. She had her shoe off, and her toes were circling his crotch. Definitely not gay! *I won't be making that mistake again.*

Chapter Eight

GAVIN

Over the last couple of weeks, Jess has impressed me with her efficiency. I almost feel guilty for assuming she wouldn't be up to the job. She hasn't failed on any of the tasks I've given her. I did notice an email at ten o'clock last night. She shouldn't be taking her work home.

"Jess, can I see you in my office?" I hear her breath hitch from her desk. I shouldn't have said it in my demanding tone, but I didn't have time for pleasantries this afternoon. She bustles into my office with flushed cheeks. "Jess, I know I said I expected you to work the same hours I do, but you are still getting used to the position. I'm not going to force you to work those hours immediately. So, what is the reason you sent me an email late last night?" I can see something flickering through those big blue eyes, but I can't tell what it is. I'm usually pretty good at reading people, especially my PAs.

"I'm sorry, Mr Andrews. I wanted to ensure that I had a clear plate for you today as I knew you were busy with video calls and would need notes typed and contracts prepared."

Well, I wasn't expecting that. She seems too good to be true. I sit back in my chair with my hand on my chin, contemplating what to do with this little wonder that has appeared in my life. I study her for a moment. She is curvy, beautiful and has blonde hair that I can see from the very small amount of roots showing isn't her true colour. She blushes slightly under my stare. I'm not sure why that makes me smile. I lean forward and try to concentrate on my laptop. "Thank you, Jess. I'm emailing you some more contracts to type up. I don't expect you to work from home. Once you leave here, your work day is done." She lets out a breath and leaves my office.

Why am I suddenly curious about this woman? Something about her makes me smile. When she leaves the office, I watch the way she walks. This isn't like me at all. I tell myself I am a cliché to letch over my PA and that it should not happen, especially when she is this good at her job.

Chapter Nine

JESS

I spend the rest of the day smashing task after task. When Mr Andrews goes to a meeting that I'm not required to attend, I take the opportunity to sneak outside for a cigarette. As I stand in the smoking area, I think back to that smile on his face when I was in his office. I thought I was going to get reprimanded for working late. I knew his schedule for the next day and knew I was going to be busy. I haven't missed a deadline yet, and I'll be damned if I am starting now.

He probably thought I was silly for blushing. Yes, that's it. Yet, my mind is going elsewhere. I notice how bright his eyes are when he smiles. I wonder what else will make his eyes light up like that. The way he looks at me certainly makes my body light up! *STOP IT NOW! You cannot have fantasies about your boss!*

I go back to my desk, get comfortable and ready to steam through the rest of my day and start preparing for tomorrow. I enjoy the variety this job gives. There are no two days the same. One day, I'll be taking notes between Mr Andrews and a client, and then in the next breath, it's typing up notes from meetings with potential investors. The business is extremely interesting; I enjoy learning new parts every day.

Mr Andrews also approved a suggestion I made to the templates. I'm excited that I can contribute as I send these off to the legal team to approve then changes on their side.

I felt valued, not because he told me, because that didn't happen, but from his actions. He's letting me grow and change things I think could be improved. We are in the streamlining business, after all.

After a quick text exchange with my mum, who is checking in, I order dinner, setting the delivery time to after I have my bath and am in my PJs, ready for some Netflix and relaxing.

Chapter Ten

GAVIN

It's been a couple of months since the new girl started, and she has done nothing but impress me. She arrives before I do and leaves after I do unless I dismiss her early. I've noted her becoming more confident in my company and have realised she doesn't blush when I stare any longer. Maybe she doesn't even notice? This is stupid! Why do I care?

Thankfully, a knock on my office door distracts me from my thoughts. "Come in," I say absentmindedly whilst looking at my screen at a new proposal.

"Well, hello there, handsome," Lucy pouts as she sashays over to my desk. Lucy is our top consultant, never failing her clients. She is tall and thin with long blonde hair that is often tied up in a neat bun like it is today. She wears dresses that hug her figure. She's a pretty woman but not my type. It doesn't escape my notice she constantly flirts with me.

"What can I do for you, Lucy? We don't have a

meeting scheduled." I'm trying my best to get her to the point. Jess must have been away from her desk when Lucy arrived. She doesn't normally let people in, no matter who they are, without letting me know.

"I thought we could grab a coffee and catch up. It's been a while since we were able to be alone together." She flutters her lashes at me. Based on the length and fullness, I think they must be fake. *What is it with women and fake lashes? Surely they must be heavy and annoying?* She leans into my desk to give me a full view of her cleavage, leaving absolutely nothing to the imagination.

"I'm sorry, Lucy, but I'm tied up right now. Please see Jess outside, and she can schedule something." I'm trying to get her out of my office before I come across harsh. She's our top consultant, and we can't afford to lose her.

"She's a pretty young thing. A tad on the chubby side for your usual PAs, though," she scoffs. Why does she sound jealous? Why do I feel defensive at the negative remark about Jess?

"She's brilliant at her job. That's all that matters. Now, if you'll excuse me?" I motion towards the door. I can't let this emotion, whatever it is, show, especially in front of her.

Thankfully, she leaves my office with a huff. When I hear her leave Jess's desk, I ping Jess a message.

Me: My office, please.

Jess walks in, notebook in hand. "Yes, Mr Andrews?"

Was she wearing her hair differently? A new dress? It looks good on her. A simple black dress hugging those delicious curves. *Alright, stop objectifying her.*

"Jess, please call me Gavin." She nods and gives me a little smile. Her lips look fuller like she's been biting that bottom lip as she works. I've seen her do it when she concentrates, and it's sexy as hell. *Man, I'd love to bite that lip.*

"Sorry, Gavin, how can I help?" Her soft voice drags me from my dark thoughts.

"Yes, I'm having a problem with my files and can't get hold of IT. Could you have a look for me?" She smiles and comes over to my desk.

When she's beside me, I realise I'm holding my breath. What is wrong with me? She leans over, and the scent of her washes over me. Coconut. Either her shampoo or shower gel, or maybe both? She smells divine. I inhale slowly so she can't tell what I'm doing. I can see her breasts hanging over my desk, tucked nicely into her dress. The thought of those swaying back and forth whilst I stand behind her is penetrating my mind. Within a couple of minutes, she's standing again, a slight blush on her cheeks. Am I having an effect on her?

"All done, Mr Andrews. Uh, sorry, Gavin," she says with a sweet smile. She picks up her notepad and pen and stands expectantly, waiting for further instructions. I nod to the door, letting her know there is nothing else for her to do. She turns on her heel and leaves, swaying her hips as she saunters away.

Chapter Eleven

JESS

D*id he just smell me?* I suddenly feel very aware of our proximity. There is plenty of space for him to budge over, but he doesn't. I catch myself glancing down at his thick thighs in his chair whilst I try to concentrate on fixing his files. A simple task, but I take my time so I can smell his manly scent. What is it? It's a mix of citrus and something warm…cinnamon?

After I leave his office, I sit down at my desk and release the breath I don't realize I'm holding. He is one of the hottest men I've ever laid my inexperienced eyes on. There was my ex, Kyle, and he was handsome, but not Gavin handsome! Kyle was my first boyfriend from college. We were each other's first sexual partners—the first time is always a little fumbled, and ours definitely was—but that feeling carried on throughout our relationship. There was no flow, no easiness to us being alone together. We couldn't cuddle up and watch a film. It's like those scenes from *American Pie* where they try to get laid, and it's just awkward all the time. We had no sparks; he didn't make me feel tingly like Gavin does when he looks at me.

Kyle and I split amicably after a couple of years together. We were more friends than boyfriend and girlfriend, and we both knew it. We appreciated what we gave each other, but it never felt passionate. Now, my mind is wandering back to leaning over Gavin's desk, wondering what I would feel like with his breath on my neck. My body reacts to those intoxicating thoughts by sending a warm feeling between my thighs. *Work, Jess, you're at work. He's your boss and is not into women like you.*

That's right. He will be into tall, hot women like the lady from earlier, Lucy. She really is beautiful, but she was off with me when she asked me to book a meeting for her and Gavin. I think she likes him. I can still allow myself little fantasies about him, like him kissing my neck. Oh, that just sent shivers down my spine. Enough! I have work to do.

Chapter Twelve

GAVIN

Getting through the afternoon is difficult because my mind is distracting me, and my cock is pressing against my trousers every time I think about Jess leaning over my desk. I have to get a grip. *You'd love to get a grip on her.*

I chuckle to myself at the thought of bringing her in here again and seeing if I could entice a reaction. Of course, that would be wildly inappropriate. I need to get my mind back on work and off of Jess.

I open my messaging system and type a message.

Me: My office, bring coffee.

Within minutes, Jess is in my office with a coffee, her notebook and a pen. She looks a little flustered. Could it be my short message, or is she thinking of how close we were earlier? I know I am.

I motion for her to take a seat in front of my desk.

She places the coffee in front of me and sits down with grace, her dress riding up slightly as she lowers. Jess blushes when she sees my gaze fall on her lap and covers herself with her notepad. I remind myself I'm her boss and CEO, and she is off limits.

"Jess, I have some important meetings coming up over the next week, and I'll need us to work closely together." Is she holding her breath? "There'll be some late nights. Will that be a problem?" I can see her breathing getting harder. Maybe I do have an effect on her?

"No, Gavin, that's not a problem. I see there's a meeting tomorrow evening. Will this be one I need to attend? How long will it last so I can make arrangements?"

Always so professional. "Oh, it could last all night," I say, smiling inwardly as I hear how it sounds. She flushes instantly.

Chapter Thirteen

JESS

I don't mean for my question to sound sexual, but his response sends a wave through my body. My god, this is going to be a long week if he carries on with that tone. I can feel myself blushing when he says he can last all night. *No, he said* it *could last all night. Mind out of the gutter!*

I AM PREPARING FOR MY MEETINGS WITH GAVIN TODAY. There is one at a hotel in town later this evening. I said I would need to make arrangements, but I'm not sure what for. It's not like I have a social life apart from seeing Keira. She texted me earlier about catching up. However, with my busy week, it'll have to be the weekend. I quickly respond before gathering my laptop for the meeting.

Since Gavin headed out earlier, I have time for a quick outfit change. I have brought in a spare dress to change into and head to the bathroom, giving myself five minutes to freshen up. Exiting the building, I quickly light up a cigarette, savouring the calm feeling that the first drag gives you before heading to the hotel. Earlier, I made sure I had some body spritz in my bag so I don't smell like smoke in the meeting.

I totter off down the busy London streets. I love working in London; the bustle of people everywhere is comforting in a strange way. I barely notice I have arrived at the hotel because I'm that busy watching people negotiate the pavement and walk around each other.

Entering The Langham, I feel really out of place. This hotel is really nice: the building, décor, the feeling as you walk in. Just as I'm about to double-check my calendar for the meeting place, my phone pings.

Gavin: You look beautiful. You didn't need to change to impress.

I redden at the message. Clearly, he sent it to the wrong person, right? But if it is for me, how does he know I've changed?

Me: Where are we meeting the client?

Gavin: The bar. I took the liberty of ordering you a drink.

Tingles are making me shudder. Why is he having this effect on me from just a text? I make my way over to the bar, trying my very best to appear professional and ignoring the feeling that is pooling in my stomach.

"Well, hello, Jess. Don't you look lovely this evening!" He practically purrs the words at me.

My god, it's going to be tough sitting through this meeting feeling like this. "Thank you, Gavin. I thought a quick outfit change would impress the client you are meeting." That's a lie. I want him to notice me. I know I'm not his type, but it's nice to be noticed. *He is just being kind, after all.*

He pats the bar stool next to him and slides my drink over. He's ordered a Prosecco, by the looks of it. Taking a sip, I discover he's actually ordered champagne. Very nice. I can't have too many; otherwise, I won't be able to talk, let alone type. Gavin's phone pings, and he checks the message, smiles and puts his phone back on the bar.

"Well, Jess, it looks like it's just the two of us this evening. My client cancelled. Something urgent came up."

My heart stops. I can't be seen having drinks with the CEO without a client. What will people think? "Oh, I'll leave and let you enjoy your evening at home. You don't want to waste the time with me." I jump down from my stool, thank him for the drink and say goodnight. As I head to the door, I feel a hand on my wrist and spin around to see Gavin staring at me. *My god, his touch is sending sparks to ALL the right places!*

"Stay for a drink. I already have the table booked,

so we may as well have dinner whilst we're here." He says it so smoothly that I find myself following him back to the bar. We make small talk until our table is ready, and then I sit down to peruse the menu and try my very hardest to not appear too shocked at the prices. This is food I can't afford. Although I'm making good money and have money in my savings thanks to my parents' insistent nagging that I save some of my wages each month to fall back on, this wasn't something I would normally budget for a meal. "The meal is on the company, Jess. Please, choose anything you'd like." Clearly, I didn't do well at hiding my shock.

After we order our food and more drinks, we talk with an ease we didn't have before.-"Kiera and I have been friends for many years. We see each other as much as we can, but with our work schedules and living across town from one another, it's not as often as we'd like." I'm prattling on. Damn champagne. "What about you, Gavin? Tell me about yourself."

He sits across from me, twirling the scotch around his glass, staring at me as if he is drinking in every word I say. *He's just being polite. Stop talking so much.* He starts talking about the company, how he started it, and how he and Paul have been best friends for years. It's nice to hear him talk passionately.

Our dinner arrives, and we eat in comfortable silence. Or is it the booze making me feel it's comfortable? The food is mouth-watering, and I hum in appreciation, looking up to see him smirking at me.

"So, Jess, what do you do for fun? Surely you have a boyfriend tucked away at home."

I choke on my drink. Why does he want to know about a boyfriend? He laughs at my reaction. My cheeks are positively glowing by now. "No, no boyfriend. What about you? Girlfriend?"

His lips twitch up to a smirk whilst drinking his scotch. No answer. Interesting.

Chapter Fourteen

GAVIN

She moans slightly as she eats. I can imagine her pretty little lips around my cock, humming. I shouldn't be here; I should have let her walk out and ended the evening. But there's something about her. As much as my head is telling me to go, my gut is telling me to stay.

"No, no boyfriend. What about you? Girlfriend?"

I like her direct question. I smirk into my drink whilst wondering what she pictured my life to be like outside work. It's pretty lonely if I'm honest. "No, no girlfriend. Big penthouse all to myself. Stunning views." She looks so pure, hanging onto my every word. Although if she drinks much more, she will be hanging tomorrow.

I catch the attention of our waiter and signal for the bill. Once I pay the bill, we walk outside of the hotel. I'm a little shocked when she lights up a cigarette. "Oh, sorry. I shouldn't be smoking in front of you. This isn't the professional image I wanted to give off." I chuckle as she sways slightly. I pull out my own pack and light up. Her eyebrows shoot up so fast that I think they'll fly off her head. We stand there for a minute, enjoying our after-dinner cigarettes. I notice she is about to lean against the wall, and I stand closer to her and slide my hand around her waist to hold her steady. Her breath hitches, and I feel her suck in. There is a gentle sway of her body in my arm. Under my hand, I can feel her body. I appreciate a curvy woman. I can't speak for all men, but I love a little something to hold on to.

We stand there for a few more moments whilst we finish, during which I find my thumb mindlessly rubbing her hip. Why does this feel normal?

"How are you getting home? I know you live across town."

She looks at me with a smile. "Oh, I think I'd better catch a bus and then walk the rest of the way home. The fresh air will do me good, I think."

I frown at the thought of her walking most of the way home. It's dark, she's beautiful, and we're in a city with lots of hidden places. Absolutely not. I pull out my phone and order a car. I am making sure she gets through that door safely. "Car's ordered. We have a few minutes before it gets here."

Chapter Fifteen

JESS

H*is hand is on me. He's rubbing my hip. I can't hold my gut in much longer.* The feel of his hand is electrifying, but I can't bring myself to look at him. When I mention getting a bus and walking home, his grip tightens. I know it isn't anything romantic. He simply wants to make sure I get home safely because I'm his assistant. That's all.

"You didn't have to order a car. At least let me pay for it."

"Nope. Already paid for." He is so stubborn and authoritative. I like it. We stand there for a couple of minutes before a Jaguar pulls up. What type of Uber account does he have? I've never had a Jag pick me up before. Is this how he travels? It certainly beats the bus.

He opens the door for me, and I sit in the back. As I'm about to thank him, he puts his hand on my hip to move over. He fails to mention he's getting a ride, too. *Oh, you'd like to take him for a ride.*

I don't realise I'm grinning at my own thoughts until he speaks. "And what has my beautiful assistant grinning?" He said I was beautiful again.

"Oh, nothing. Just making myself laugh. So, um, whereabout is your place? Are we dropping you there first or last?" Please say first. I don't know if I can be in the car with him for very long. My flat is half an hour away. He probably lives in a really expensive part of town. His light touch next to me is dragging me out of my thoughts. Did he mean for his hand to be next to mine? I put my hand on my lap to make sure I'm not in his space because that small touch is making me warm down there.

"I'm making sure we get you home safely, then I'll head home." He's staring at me with those dark brown eyes. I can feel the heat coming from them. Am I imagining it? I smile at him, thanking him with my eyes. I'm not entirely sure I can speak.

Chapter Sixteen

GAVIN

She is absolutely beautiful. Sitting this close to her, knowing we have a good twenty minutes before we get to her apartment, I breathe in her scent. She is truly intoxicating, and I'm not sure she even knows it. A strand of her hair has fallen by her face, and I instinctively tuck it behind her ear, holding my hand by her face longer than I should. My brain is telling me to take my hand away. I'm her boss, for Christ's sake.

Jess has beautiful blue eyes, her blonde hair is down today, her dress hugs her curvy figure, and the smell of coconut….

Fuck it! I lean into her, my lips capturing her soft ones. I feel her breathe in, and then she kisses me back. My horniness takes over. My tongue licks her lips, begging for entry. She obliges, parting her lips. Oh god, she tastes amazing with a hint of champagne still on her tongue. I don't realise I'm pulling her onto my lap until she hesitates, and I reluctantly pull my mouth from hers.

Does she want me to stop? Why am I nervous? I want nothing more than to devour her. She is truly one of a kind. Gorgeous, hard-working, and I can feel the kindness in her heart. *Stop it, Gavin.*

Chapter Seventeen

JESS

Oh my god! I'm on fire. He's kissing me, and my god, I want him! My lower abdomen is pooling with a warm feeling. I was in the moment, enjoying his taste, when he tried pulling me onto his lap. *No, no, no, I'm going to squish him!*

He pulls back from the kiss and stares at me with concern. "I'm sorry. I shouldn't have kissed you. I didn't even ask. This was not professional. I'm sorry." I can't figure out the look in his eye. Regret?

"No, I'm sorry. I can't sit on your lap. I'll squash you."

He throws his head back and laughs. My cheeks flush, and right there, I have ruined the moment. His laugh is genuine and is such a light sound. Before I can process my thoughts, he grabs my hips and pulls me onto him so I'm straddling him. His hand is in my hair and dragging me into a more passionate kiss than before. It feels urgent, needy almost. I give him everything I have. He is better than I imagined. He tastes hot, and I want more.

Before I knew it, the car has stopped outside my block of flats. We pull from the kiss, both of us breathless. I search his eyes for some realisation that he's made a mistake. I climb from his lap, which isn't easy to do in the back of a car, even if it is a big car, and reach for the door handle. I can feel the embarrassment washing over me. I'm going to have to see him in the morning and act like nothing has happened. He gets out of the car with me. Gavin is walking behind me when I go to the main door of the building, assuming he would be happy I got home. I turn round to thank him, right into his chest. He is a huge wall of muscle, and my cheeks flush instantly.

Chapter Eighteen

GAVIN

Ow. Her elbow has just gone right into my side when she turns around. Jess looks horrified. Clearly, she thought I wouldn't be walking her to her front door. "I'm walking you up just to make sure you get in safely." I know I shouldn't be doing this, but there is something about her. I need another minute with her to satisfy my…whatever it was.

She lowers her gaze and keys in the entry code to the door. Walking up the two flights of stairs, I can see her getting her keys ready. She opens the door to her flat, and a warm smell wafts out of the door. It smells like her. "Thank you for a lovely evening, Gavin. I know this wasn't how you had planned your night." She looks at me with those big, ocean-blue eyes. Before I know it, I grab her waist and pin her to the wall, smashing my lips to hers. I can't get enough of her. I want more, so much more, but not tonight. Her hands are in my hair, yanking me in for more.

What am I doing? She is my PA. She's light, warm, sexy as hell and didn't ask for any of this.

I step away from our embrace and kiss the back of her hand. "Thank you for such wonderful company, Jess. I'll see you in the morning." With that, I walk down the stairs, still able to taste her on my tongue, and strangely, I have no regrets.

Chapter Nineteen

JESS

Holy shit, my head hurts. Too much bubbly. As my senses come around whilst I turn on the shower, flashbacks of last night hit me like a bus. *No, no, no, no, nooooo! You kissed him. He kissed you….*

My hand covers my mouth as I remember what happened. I wasn't drunk as such, but I'd clearly pushed those feelings and memories to the back of my mind. How the hell am I going to act normal today?

I have to push back the embarrassment. I walk into the shower, trying to regain some form of control over my emotions. I will be the epitome of professionalism today. I will do my job and then go home. He won't want someone like me. It's probably the scotch and our conversations. Probably?

Chapter Twenty

GAVIN

I can't stop myself from smirking whilst sipping my coffee, the taste of her still in my memory. Teasing her is going to be interesting today, but it will take all my strength not to take her here in my office.

I hear her arrive at seven-twenty, clearly not knowing I'm in yet. My office door is shut. I can hear her humming to herself whilst she gets ready for the day.

A reminder pings on my laptop. *Erghhh Lucy.* I had forgotten she'd scheduled a meeting with Jess. This is going to be hell. I ping Jess a message to make sure she is in this meeting, taking notes. I don't want to be alone with that woman. She actually makes my skin crawl when she attempts to flirt with me. I know she wants to be more, but I have no interest at all. I have never given her any indication that we will be anything other than boss and employee.

At eight o'clock sharp, Jess walks into my office

with Lucy. A flush of rose pink appears across her cheeks. Clearly, she remembers our hot kiss last night. I try not to smirk, but I think my mouth twitches a little, which entices Lucy to look at me with her head cocked. I rarely smile at work.

The meeting is pointless. Lucy has no information to give, and I can tell she isn't happy that Jess is asked to stay for the meeting, as I believe she doesn't want an actual meeting. She merely wants some time alone with me to flirt and try it on. Deciding she is getting nowhere today, she makes her excuses and leaves.

"Jess, can you hold back, please? I have some requests to go through with you." With Lucy sashaying out of my office, Jess sits back down in front of my desk. She can't look me in the eye. Why does that make me chuckle? *Sadist.*

I move from behind my desk to perch on it right in front of her. "Jess, I had a great time last night. Please, don't be embarrassed in front of me." Her ocean-blue orbs peer straight into my soul. She is breathtaking. I can swim in those eyes.

"I can only apologise for my behaviour, Mr Andrews. I had a little too much to drink and—"

"Gavin. Jess, please call me Gavin, and you have nothing to apologise for. If I remember rightly, it was me that kissed you. It was me that pinned you against the wall outside your flat." Her breathing is coming more quickly now. I can see the arousal in her eyes. Hell, I can feel my own!

"I have three long boring meetings today: ten o'clock in my office, two o'clock at The Langham and eight o'clock tonight at my penthouse. I'd like you to be there for all three to take notes. There will be presentations for all of them, so I'll need packs printed before ten o'clock."

"Yes, Gavin. I'll get on that right away."

Eight o'clock in your penthouse? Try not to sound too obvious. Who goes to a CEO's home for a meeting? I roll my eyes at myself as she walks out of my office.

Chapter Twenty-One

JESS

Why does it bother me that Lucy gave me filthy looks during the meeting earlier? I didn't ask to be in there. Reading his body language, Gavin doesn't want her attention and needs a buffer. The meeting wasn't structured, nor did it have any direction, and the way she flirted with him, trying to get near him.... Why does that make my chest clench? Anyway, I have meetings to prepare for. Luckily, I have all my work done already, so I'm not going to be behind. But who has a meeting in their home? Maybe he knows them well?

It is coming up to one o'clock, and my stomach is rumbling. I hope to dear god that no one hears it. I'm typing as Gavin, and his potential investor are talking and negotiating. Having to concentrate is a great distraction from the memories of his mouth on mine last night. The thought of him pinning me to the wall is exciting. My lower abdomen practically vibrates just thinking about it.

The meeting ends, and we have thirty minutes before the next one. That is travel time. I quickly finish my notes to tidy up later, pack my laptop, and glance up at Gavin. I can feel him watching me.

"I'm going to bite that bottom lip for you if you don't stop distracting me during important meetings," he says with a wink and in *that* tone. I blush and murmur an apology, not meaning it because I'd like nothing more than for him to bite my lip.

He has a car waiting for us as we exit the building. The ride over to the hotel is short, but thankfully, I have packed an apple to snack on to stop my hunger. I make a mental note to plan for meals in between his meetings.

Heading into The Langham, my cheeks flush with embarrassment from being a little tipsy in front of him last night. I look at him as he grins. Clearly, he's enjoying this. He places his hand on my lower back and leads me to the seating area where we are meeting his client. When will my body stop tingling when he touches me or even looks at me?

After the gentlemen chat as I type notes, they shake hands and leave.

It's now six o'clock. If I leave straight away, I have time for a quick bite to eat and to freshen up before heading to his place for the next meeting. *His place.*

"I'll text you my address. Be there at eight sharp and wear something nice. Dinner will be served." He does not look up from his phone as we leave the hotel.

He walks off as his phone rings, and that's my cue to leave.

Deciding not to take public transport, I hail a cab, wanting to get home to freshen up and change into something nice. What does that look like? And I'm still going to grab a snack. I've barely eaten today.

After having a bite to eat and a quick shower, I do my hair and makeup and choose a simple but elegant black dress for the evening. The dress has a sweetheart neckline, which can be a bit risqué with my large breasts, but I want to impress, and it's the nicest dress I have. I put on some short heels and head to the door with my bag in hand, ready to head over to his place for the meeting.

Chapter Twenty-Two

GAVIN

I have a restaurant deliver the food at seven o'clock. I could have prepared the salads and sides myself, but I don't have time today. My client will be here at eight-thirty and Jess at eight o'clock. I don't often host meetings in my penthouse, but I want to with this client. He entertains his clients in his home, so I will do the same for him. Pierre is someone I've been interested in working with for a while. He has profitable connections that we would be able to use. Entertaining him in my home shows him the same respect as he would give me.

Just as I look at the clock on the far wall, my phone pings:

Jess: On my way up

Minutes later, I open my door, and my breath is taken from me. She is an absolute vision. She wears a black dress with a neckline I appreciate. I can feel the drool coming from my mouth. When she said she wanted to freshen up, I expected a brush through her hair and some perfume resprayed. It took Sacha hours to achieve this look. Jess must have had, what, forty-five minutes?

"Come in. You look…amazing." Why am I struggling with words?

"Thank you. You said to wear something nice. This is the nicest thing I have. Will it be okay?" she asks, smoothing down the material on her hips. Is she trying to seduce me? It's working.

"Pierre will be here in half an hour. He likes being entertained in the homes of those he does business with. He is going to struggle to pay attention with you looking like that." She blushes, and I sweep my eyes over her. She really does look ravishing.

I walk over to the kitchen and pour her a glass of champagne. I can feel her nerves from here. Jess looks around as she wanders over to me, taking in my environment. I've never invited any of my PAs to a home meeting before. Hell, other than Paul, no one from work has come here. My place isn't well decorated. It's neutral soft grey throughout, with the odd splashes of yellow and green. It is to my taste, and although I'm not sure what she thinks, I want to find out.

I make my way over to her before she walks into the breakfast bar. She jumps when my hand slides around her waist. I put the glass in her eyesight, and she takes it as I bury my nose into her neck, inhaling her scent. It not only calms me but makes me want to take her right here, right now. Completely inappropriate, but the way her body shivers, and the slight moan escaping her lips, tell me she enjoys it.

Before long, there is a knock at my door. I glance at the time. Eight-fifteen. *Damn Pierre for being early!*

Chapter Twenty-Three

JESS

My whole body shivers when his hand slips around my waist and his nose touches the sensitive spot on my neck. I can't help the moan that escapes. It feels amazing and much better than I fantasised.

There is a knock at the door, and I assume it's his client. I straighten myself back up and gulp a large portion of my drink. I've never drunk so much champagne in my life as I have done this week. I have to be careful; otherwise, I may end up tipsy again. A repeat of last night can't happen. I'd lose my job, for sure.

The meal with Pierre is nice. He is charming in a typical French way. I'm not needed to take notes. This is a relaxed meeting. Informal. I'm not entirely sure why I'm here.

We move over to the sofa area, which has a large corner sofa that could easily seat eight people. The TV is on the wall, with a beautiful electric fire underneath with white stones at the bottom and an oval coffee table in the middle, where Pierre sits next to me. A little too close for my liking. Gavin sits on the other side with his hand draped over the back of the sofa. At some point during our conversation, Pierre's hand touches my shoulder. I see Gavin physically tense. He clearly doesn't like the attention the French man is paying me. *You shouldn't have worn this dress. It's literally asking for trouble.*

Pierre doesn't notice Gavin's tension, or if he does, he doesn't let on and carries on trying to charm me whilst discussing a deal they are considering. I peer at the clock above the large stone fireplace. It's eleven o'clock already.

Pierre sees me looking at the time. "Time really does fly when you're having fun," he breathes heavily. His breath smells of red wine and his teeth are stained. I attempt to hide my grimace behind a tight smile.

Gavin stands, motioning that it's time for him to leave. "Can I offer you a ride home, young Jess?" The thought literally has my stomach churning.

"She has some things to finish here before her ride arrives." Gavin's chest puffs out slightly. What is happening? However, I'm thankful for the excuse not to be in the same car with Pierre alone.

Chapter Twenty-Four

GAVIN

I show Pierre to the door, thankful he's leaving. He has given Jess too much attention, which makes me a little jealous. Although judging by her body language, it's unwanted. He's good business. I just don't like the way he behaves around women. With *her*.

How is that any different to what you did? I chastise myself.

As he leaves, I turn to see Jess swaying her hips to the music I had forgotten was on. I couldn't hear it over the rage I felt when he touched her. I lean against the door for a moment, my hand holding my chin and notice my stubble coming through. The way she moves as she tidies the dining table is enchanting.

I move towards her. She stares up at me with those gorgeous blue eyes, almost expecting something, but also seems cautious as I move towards her. She finishes putting the final dishes in the kitchen and turns back around. I'm standing inches away from her. I can feel my breathing getting heavier the more I smell her scent. She is wearing perfume this evening, but I can still smell the coconut mixed with the amazing smell of her. I notice her breathing, mainly because her low-cut dress shows her rapidly rising and falling breasts.

Before I know it, I'm gently lowering my head, my lips touching hers in a soft kiss, one hand snaking around her waist, dragging her to me, and the other going to the back of her head, fingers intertwining with her soft hair. She lifts onto her tiptoes, making the kiss deeper, wrapping her arms around my neck and pulling me into her. Her lips part, letting me into her mouth. She wants this as much as I do. A moan vibrates from her throat, making my cock press against my trousers. My god, she is turning me on so much from just a kiss.

Breaking our kiss, I notice her hooded gaze and breathlessness.

Chapter Twenty-Five

JESS

What is happening? We're kissing again, and my body feels like I've shoved a fork into an electrical socket. Every part of me is vibrating. Why? I mean, yes, this big hunk of a man is kissing me again, but I've never felt anything like this.

His hand is still around my waist, looking down at me with those deep brown eyes. It's almost like he's trying to search my soul. His breathing is as heavy as mine. We stand there, paused in time, staring at each other. I want more, but there is a line that shouldn't be crossed, and technically, I'm working. Aren't I?

He slowly licks his bottom lip, his gaze still locked with mine. It's in that split second I realise a line has already been crossed. My body wants to know what he feels like if this is where it's going. I lift myself onto my tiptoes and kiss him softly.

That's the signal; it's almost like he's been waiting for permission. He grabs my hips and lifts me. My legs wrap around his waist, and my arms go around his neck. I don't have time to think about being too heavy for him. He makes it feel effortless. He takes me to the sofa, and I'm trying with all my might not to be self-conscious, but it's creeping in slowly. He lays me down with him on top of me, his hands beside my head. Lifting his lips from mine, he smiles an oh-so-wicked grin. His mouth kisses every inch from my cheek to my neck, where he bites slightly. My breath catches as a wave of pleasure goes through me. Gavin has one hand on my hip, pushing his crotch into me. I can feel his erection.

My God, I'm turned on. I want this. I love the smell of him, the feel of him, and the way he makes me feel.

Chapter Twenty-Six

GAVIN

Jess is responsive. I can already tell what she likes by the way her body reacts to mine. She likes being bitten on the sensitive part of her neck. She arches her back when I kiss down to her cleavage. Her hips tease me, pressing up against my already rock-hard cock, which is nearly painful from being constricted by my trousers. I can't wait to taste her. I move my mouth back to her lips, kissing her with want and need. Her arms wrap around my neck, dragging me closer.

My hand is on her hip, slowly moving down her outer thigh and across to the inner thigh. I feel her breath hitch when my fingers trail up her sensitive soft skin. I move my mouth to her neck to ease her as I can feel her body tense up. Nibbling, licking and sucking on her neck, she starts melting back into the sofa. I let my hand wander up her thigh, and I can feel her warmth before I reach her knickers. Softly biting her neck, I smile when a whimper escapes her lips. I trail my mouth down, leaving kisses along her chest and down her dress until I reach her legs. My eyes are on hers the whole time, asking permission without speaking as my hands softly push her dress up. Anticipating my next move and giving me permission with a small nod, she lifts her hips.

I hook my fingers into her knickers and slowly slide them over her hips, down her legs and fling them to the floor. The smell of her is turning me on more.

Chapter Twenty-Seven

JESS

This is slightly romantic and amazingly hot at the same time. *Stop romanticising it. It's just....whatever this moment is.*

Before I can go too deep into my mind, his mouth is on my thigh, leaving a trail of soft kisses up from my knee to the top of my leg, and then with his tongue, licking his way down my other thigh. I'm pretty sure I can have a heart attack with how quickly my heart is pounding.

Gavin is between my legs, his hands pushing up the skirt of my dress whilst his mouth is teasing my thighs. He starts kissing higher, pushing my legs wider apart with his hands. I hold my breath. I haven't trimmed, waxed or anything down there in so long. It must look like an absolute jungle. Covering my face with my arm, I try to hide my embarrassment. Gavin doesn't notice at all as he sniffs me. Why is that arousing?

"Perfect," he says in a deep, throaty voice. With his

fingers parting my labia, he peers up at me, and his eyes are ablaze with lust. My whole body tenses. That look is intense, and my want for him shoots up like a rocket. Before I can think for too long, his tongue is on me, moving up and down my lips until he finds my clit. A groan escapes my mouth, and he growls into my pussy, as if eager to make me come.

His tongue is working my clit, circling, flicking up and down, side to side. I'm in pure ecstasy. I can already feel myself working towards an orgasm. My breathing is shallow, my back arches, and I can't stop moaning. Never before have I felt like this. I look down, and our eyes lock. It's as if he's watching my body as I'm working closer and closer towards an orgasm. Then he pushes two fingers inside me, thrusting them in and out, curling them slightly until he finds my G-Spot, and then he gently bites my clit, and I can't help the rush of breath leaving my body in a scream as I pulse around his fingers. My vision blurs. I have never come from foreplay, let alone that quickly, and my god, that is the best orgasm I have ever had.

I lay my head back, my body feeling like it's floating, whilst he moves up my body and kisses me. It's the first time I've tasted myself. It's not as bad as I expected it to be. Kind of sweet. Gavin licks his lips with such a playfully wicked grin on his face that makes his eyes sparkle. He looks very pleased.

I try to disguise my 'you've just given me the best orgasm of my life' grin, changing it to something a little more laid back, but I can't. I'm not sure I can control anything at the moment. I was never like this with Kyle. Ever. At that moment, my phone starts ringing. *Damn!* My ride is here. I didn't think any of this was going to happen, but I really wish, at that moment, I was less organized.

Gavin looks a little disappointed, but as a true gentleman, he helps me off the sofa. I grab my coat and bag and head to the door. I want to say something, but I don't know what to say. "Um, thank you for a nice evening, Gavin, and, um…." My face is on fire.

"Earth-shattering orgasm?" he says with a cocky grin, followed by the sexiest laugh, and with that, he walks me down to the front door and watches me get in the car.

What happened tonight? What does any of this mean? *Stop overthinking it! It was what it was and won't happen again.*

Chapter Twenty-Eight

GAVIN

Jess's car turns up at midnight to take her home. The timing could have been better. I give her what appears to be an amazing orgasm. One that makes her struggle to walk afterwards, so I feel rather pleased with myself. I want to explore her responsiveness more, but this can't be rushed.

What is it about her? I normally don't pursue a workplace relationship, but Jess certainly has something I want.

When I return to my penthouse, I can still smell her, and my cock is already hard from her reactions to me. I start cleaning up more and think a cold shower before bed would be best. As I grab the glasses off the coffee table, I notice something on the floor. I pick it up and realise it's her underwear. I can't help but grin. We were both a little distracted to remember I'd flung them on the floor. I place them in my pocket and head for a shower.

I WAKE UP THE NEXT MORNING THINKING ABOUT HER. I can't get her out of my mind. I go for a run in the drizzle to clear my head. The autumn air is cold, with the smell of change coming.

After my run, I have a shower and something to eat. I still can't stop thinking about Jess. I was adamant I wouldn't want anyone after the way Sacha treated me. I can't trust that someone isn't going to hurt me again. But what is this? I'm so attracted to her, but there is something more than physical attraction. Something about her that I want to protect. An innocence. But I'm not the right man for her. She's light, warm and innocent, and I'm dark, cold and damaged. As much as I enjoy our fun, it can't go on. I'm not looking forward to seeing those ocean-blue eyes on Monday morning.

With that, I push Jess to the back of my mind. I set to work on items from our meeting last night and get a proposal together for Pierre. This is something that I would normally pass to one of the consultants, but Pierre wants to work with me and not one of my staff. He is the CEO of his firm and expects to be dealt with at an equal level. With him on board, we will have access to a wider range of companies to consult with, including some in Europe.

Jess wanders back into my mind. I imagine her in a light dress, strolling down the Parisian streets with a warm, happy glow. *Back to the proposal.*

Chapter Twenty-Nine

JESS

I sit in my joggers and an oversized T-shirt, waiting for Kiera to come over. We've both been looking forward to a catch-up this weekend and decided to spend the day together. As I am in the kitchen, making a coffee and seeing what we can snack on for the day, I remember last night. Gavin made me feel so alive in a way I've never felt before. I'm sure it's something that won't happen again, but I secretly hope it will.

Kiera comes over just before lunch. We order food from the local sandwich shop and scroll through Netflix whilst catching up. I decide I'm not going to mention what happened with Gavin last night as, although it was amazing, there isn't anything to tell, really. Nothing was said, nothing will happen again, and we will go back to normal on Monday.

Kiera leaves in the evening. We've had a full day of chatting utter nonsense, watching films and serial killer documentaries and eating food. It was wonderful to have a day like that. It's as if no time had passed between us. That's what I value most about our friendship; we can speak to each other daily, weekly or monthly, and nothing changes between us. We know where each other was.

I decide it's time for a shower to freshen up and go for a walk. Autumn is setting in, and there is nothing better than a walk on a crisp evening.

MONDAY MORNING COMES INCREDIBLY FAST. I DECIDE I'm going to be friendly but professional. I want to progress my career, and I can't afford any mistakes.

I quickly get ready and make my way to work. I have my earphones in with my playlist on shuffle and a coffee I can sip whilst people-watching on the tube.

By the time I've made my way into the office, I can tell Gavin is already here. I'm not late, so he must have had something urgent he needed to do. I settle myself into my desk, go through my emails and re-read the notes I took on Friday before emailing them to him. I pop to the kitchen to make us both a coffee, and by the time I put mine down on my desk and head into his office, he isn't in it. I place his coffee on his desk, anyway, and decide to do some filing whilst he's out of his office. On the admin floor, we had a wall of filing cabinets for projects. Gavin's filing is mainly projects he's working on, client information and research he's doing on prospective investors.

As I'm pottering about, filing and singing away to

myself, I hear a chuckle come from the doorway. "Well, Miss Freeman, it seems you like to sing as well as dance. Thank you for the coffee. I have a conference call in five, so I'll need my office." I smile shyly and leave. The rest of the day goes by painfully slowly, and since I'm caught up on my work, I message Gavin to see if there is anything he needs to be done that can keep me busy.

Me: Is there anything else I can take on? I'm caught up on everything else.

Gavin: Come in at five o'clock. Bring coffee and your beloved notebook.

Me: No problem.

At five o'clock, I knock on his door with our coffees. Upon entering, his office is dark. I can make him out by his laptop glare and make my way over to him.

"Are you okay, Gavin?" He glances up with bags under his eyes. Where have those come from? "Migraine, but this work isn't going to do itself."

I hand him his coffee and get some painkillers from my bag. "Take these and move over. You shouldn't be staring at the screen with a migraine. Tell me what to do, and I'll finish this up."

Chapter Thirty

GAVIN

I have a blinding migraine, and my angel saves me with caffeine and painkillers. She then gets incredibly bossy. It's a side I haven't seen before, and I like it. I'm not one to be told what to do, especially at work, but I move over to the sofa so she can take my desk. I swallow the painkillers, down the coffee and take my water with me. Lying down with my eyes shut is bliss.

Jess is insistent on helping me. It's not in her job description, but I've spent the last two hours trying to type and am getting nowhere, so I mumble instructions to her and can hear her tapping away. I don't realise I doze off, and yet, when I wake up, it's eight o'clock in the evening, and Jess isn't at my desk. There is a blanket covering me. Where did this come from? My head feels a little better. Slowly, I get up and head to my desk, and there it is. A post-it that makes my heart flutter.

All done, checked twice and saved in your folder.
Left you to sleep. Migraines suck!
See you in the morning.
J xx

I didn't want a relationship. I especially didn't want one at work, but something about her.... She isn't my usual "type"—if you can say I have one—but she's kind, warm, amazing at her job, sexy as hell and knows her shit. She is someone I want to explore more with, and not just in a sexual way. I want to know more about her. I want to head over to her place, but I decide to go home for more sleep. My work is done for the evening, thanks to that wonderful angel. As a PA, she takes care of typing up documents, contracts and managing my schedule. I wonder if she can take on a project. She's a quick learner and is like a sponge when it comes to absorbing information. Tomorrow, I will give her more responsibility as she clearly has more ambition than I gauged at the interview. She really is a keeper.

THE WEEK FLIES BY WITH NO ISSUES. JESS LAPS UP THE extra responsibilities and workload. She is proving to be an absolute gem. I can't let this one leave the company. She's good for us *and me.*

With Jess taking on more of the project side alongside her PA role, I actually have time for the meeting with Paul to discuss the Christmas party, bonuses and plans for the new financial year. This is something I normally leave to him as my Finance Manager, but I want to go through the budgets to give Jess a pay raise and a bonus.

We meet at our usual bar. The waitress shows us to our usual table. It's a nice quiet corner where we aren't disturbed. We go through our reports. I allocate a nice little bonus for Jess's hard work and a pay raise for April. The Christmas party is going to cost a fortune, as always, but we've made a great profit this year, and the staff deserve to be treated. We'll hold it at The Tower Hotel with its beautiful views, good food and rooms for those who want to stay rather than trying to get a taxi home.

"So, my friend, how are things with Jess? She seems to be doing incredibly well, considering you're giving her a bonus and a pay raise." Paul gives me a cocky grin and sips his beer.

"She has surprised me on all levels. I'm not sure how she managed to stay hidden in admin for as long as she did. She has a lot of potential, and if she had a desire, she may be a good candidate to promote within the company. We would have to talk about it, and she will need to be tested and trained, although I don't want to lose her as my PA because she is wonderful."

"She's shown that she can do the PA job easily, so providing her with a project to get her teeth into could be beneficial to her development and could save the company money instead of hiring another body for projects. Could we look at the role and adapt it? Personal assistant is quite dated. We might be able to change the role and give her more. Something like…." He taps his chin excitedly. Paul loves creating new roles. "How about Business Manager? She will still work under you, but as she's taken on some of your work, she's clearly capable of managing more and helping the business. The pay raise will bring her to the bottom of that manager bracket, and she can work her skills and improve both those and the pay in time."

I like that idea. I will discuss this with her before Christmas and then make the change. We sit and chat for a while, Paul telling me about his latest conquests and trying to dig for information about Jess and me. I trust him to keep quiet and tell him how I feel.

"I honestly thought Sacha did a number on you. I didn't think you could feel this way. You seem completely smitten." Paul is pragmatic yet has a huge romantic side. If only he could work on his own relationship issues.

"I know it seems daft, considering how little I know about her personal life, but there's just something about her. I can't stop thinking about her."

We spend most of the afternoon and evening discussing the pros and cons of dating an employee, but in the end, Paul offers a gem of advice, "Being alone isn't making you happy, not really. If you think you can find something with Jess, then go for it. It appears that you can both still work well together, even after things have happened between you. Just don't break her heart. She's a good girl."

After a couple more hours of catching up, I head back to the office to finish a few bits before heading home for the weekend. A lovely redhead catches Paul's attention at the bar. With that, I roll my eyes and leave.

Chapter Thirty-One

JESS

Gavin left a few hours ago to have a meeting with Paul. He won't be back for the rest of the day, so I take the opportunity to tidy up a few bits that I have to do and organise myself for the following week. It's five o'clock on a Friday, so no one else is in the office, and they are probably at the pub. I have my music on my phone and headphones in. I go to Gavin's office to finish the filing I had from the week, and as I'm dancing around, I can feel someone behind me. My heart stops as I take my earphones out and turn around.

I feel all the colour drain from my face when I see it isn't Gavin. "Good evening. Can I help you?" The man looks me up and down with a smile on his face that turns my stomach and makes my heart pound in a bad way.

"Well, good evening. I don't believe I've had the pleasure. I'm Miles Bancroft, one of Gavin's personal clients." He holds out his hand, and I shake it out of politeness. It feels clammy.

"Nice to meet you, Mr Bancroft. My name is Jess. I'm Gavin's PA. He won't be back in the office until Monday. Can I give him a message?"

Miles edges closer to me, and I can feel myself being cornered. Every time I try to move past him, he advances a little more. He places one hand on the filing cabinet I'm working on, pinning me in. He's muttering something, but all I hear is "pretty young thing" over the pounding in my chest. Why won't he move?

"Sorry, Miles. I need to pack up for the evening. Could I show you out?" As I go to push past him, he grabs my wrist and pulls me back into him, his other hand travelling down my waist. When he reaches my thigh, he moves his hand back up, dragging my dress up as he goes. My heart's pounding, my stomach is sick, and I'm frozen on the spot. My brain is yelling at me to move as I can feel his breath on my neck, and tears threaten to spill over.

After what feels like an age of him touching me, my brain and body snap into action. My dad showed me a move when I said I wanted to live in London. I twist my hand and body so that I'm in control of his wrist now and push my other palm into his nose as hard as I can. I hear a crunch as I do. He lets go, screaming and swearing as I rush out of the office.

I'm running to my desk to get my phone when I look up. There he is. Gavin. He's going to be angry that I broke his client's nose.

"Jess, what happened? Why do you look scared? Are you okay?" I can't answer any of his questions.

Miles comes out of his office shouting, "This bitch just broke my fucking nose! Fire the whore now! She tried to seduce me and then cracked my nose. Call an ambulance, for God's sake, you useless girl."

Gavin's face turns from shock to serious in a split second. He calls security from his phone and asks them to come up to his floor immediately. I quickly pack my bag, grab my coat and go to tell him I'm leaving when he grabs my arm and gently sits me down at my desk.

"Jess, can you tell me what happened?"

I stare at him. I honestly think he will believe his client over anything I say. When I try to speak, my voice trembles, my throat drier than a desert. "Gavin, I'm sorry. I was filing and listening to my music. No one else was here, and I didn't think you were coming back. He came in and...." My whole body is shaking at this point. My eyes are prickling with tears. Gavin kneels in front of me, grabs the water bottle poking out of my handbag and tells me to drink.

"Jess, it's okay. I'm here now." Security comes through the office and asks Gavin what the problem is. "I believe this man has harassed a member of my staff, and she broke his nose in self-defence. He needs medical attention, but I want this reported to the police and dealt with immediately."

Miles is more than irate at this point. "Now, hold on. I didn't do anything of the sort. She wanted something. I barely touched her."

Gavin's expression is hard, and a glint of anger

appears in his eyes. "You will never come back to this office again. Our contract is terminated, and you will never touch a member of my staff again."

Security takes Miles over to the lifts to go down to their office. I'm frozen, shaking and can't breathe properly. What would have happened if I hadn't broken his nose? I feel my breathing becoming erratic. Dammit, I'm having a panic attack. The drama of what happened has caught up with me. I don't notice Gavin pick me up and take me into his office. He takes us over to the sofa, sits me on his lap and pulls me close. I feel safe with his arms around me, and I can't help the sobs that come out.

When there are no more tears, I can feel one of Gavin's hands on my lower back and the other stoking my hair. I slowly sit up and have a drink of water to compose myself. "I'm sorry, Gavin. I didn't realise you had a meeting with him. Nothing was on your calendar. I was tidying up after the week and—"

"Jess, stop. You have nothing to be sorry for. I didn't have a meeting with him. I have no idea why he showed up tonight. I was coming back to the office to work on a couple of points when I saw you. I'll be emailing his father to advise of the situation tonight and that I will no longer be dealing with Miles."

Now that I feel better, though, I want to go home, have a nice hot bath and get in my PJs to forget about tonight.

"Where are you going?" Gavin cocks his head. He looks cute like that.

"Thank you for coming to my rescue and sorting this mess out. I'd like to go home if that's okay?"

Gavin nods and insists he takes me home. I'm not arguing. I feel safer with him around. With winter coming, the days are darker, shorter, and after tonight, I need a bit of comfort.

GAVIN DROPS ME AT HOME, AND AS SOON AS I'M indoors, I feel my emotions overwhelming me. The realisation of what could have happened and what did happen hits me hard. Why do men think they can still behave like this? I grab a bottle of beer from the fridge to calm my nerves, go to the bathroom and run a bath. I'm shaking whilst I'm in the bath, too. I have even put nice salts and everything in. Calming affects my ass! Since the bath is unable to calm me, I get out and wrap myself in a towel. Who can I call? Kiera is away this weekend visiting her parents, my parents will be in bed by now, and I don't want to worry them. Before I know it, I'm texting Gavin to ask if he's busy. My phone buzzes immediately.

Gavin: I'm on my way.

Chapter Thirty-Two

GAVIN

I drive to Jess's flat, picking up dinner on the way. I know she probably hasn't eaten. I knew I should have stayed with her. What happened this evening will have shaken her. I have packed an overnight bag but would leave it in the car. If she wants me to stay, I will, but I will leave if she wants to be alone.

I knock on her door and can hear her gasp. "Jess, it's me."

She opens the door in just a towel. If it was any other night.... I shake the thought from my mind. I need to be here for her. She messaged me for a reason, and then I remember her mentioning that her friend was away this weekend. I take the food into the kitchen. When I turn around, she's holding her arms around herself.

"Sorry, you didn't have to do anything. I didn't know who else to call and...and this is silly. You can go back to your evening." Her eyes are focused on the floor, and she's not looking at me.

I move over to her and pull her into my arms. She feels tense, but her body begins to relax eventually. I pick her up and take her to her bedroom. Her eyes are searching mine, wondering what I'm going to do. After setting her down on the end of her bed, I open her dresser drawers and find her some PJs to slip on. "Get dressed, and I'll serve dinner. You'll freeze if you stay in a towel all night." Her cheeks flush.

By the time I've dished dinner, she comes out of her bedroom. "Thank you. You really don't have to stay. I feel much better now."

I take the dishes over to the sofa and place them on the coffee table whilst rolling my eyes at her. "I'm hungry now that I've smelt this Dansak. You're just going to have to put up with me until we've eaten. Unless you really do want to be alone, then I'll go."

She sits down on the sofa and smiles, tucking into her dinner. I have begun to notice the appreciative moan she makes when she eats. I find it attractive when a woman enjoys her food. Sacha never ate anything other than rabbit food. I sit down with her and tuck into my own dinner.

"How are you feeling?" I can feel her becoming more relaxed as we sit and eat.

"I feel better. Tonight shouldn't have happened. I'm angry, scared, sad and just want…." I let her pause, sitting in silence until she's ready to continue. This isn't anything I've been through. I can't imagine how she feels. "I just want to feel safe tonight. You don't have to, but do you think you could stay? I haven't got anyone close to me and don't want to call my parents. If you have plans, you can go, and I'll call them."

"I'm happy to stay and keep you safe." I smile at her.

Jess's shoulders relax from the tense position. She finishes her dinner and relaxes into the sofa, looking a little brighter than when I arrived. "Thank you, Gavin." She smiles up at me.

After dinner, we talk. Tonight isn't her fault, and she needs to know that. I run her another bath, using some of the lavender salts I found in her bathroom, and light some candles. She comes into the bathroom with a beaming smile on her face. She looks radiant, happy, and calmer.

"Thank you. I'd love a bath. I honestly feel much better now that we've talked through what happened. You can go home if you'd like or...." Her eyes are bright, mostly from the tears. She slides off her pyjama bottoms, her eyes not leaving mine, and steps out of them as she lifts her top off. She wears nothing underneath. I can't move. Her body is captivating. There are little scars in some places that I want to kiss. Her curves look delicious. And as I'm standing staring, probably drooling, she gives me a cheeky grin as she gets into the bath.

She's inviting me, but I want to make sure she feels better and pampered before I do anything with her. I move closer to the bath, where she lays with her head tilted back on the edge, letting out a humming sound as she takes in the warmth of the water.

I kneel beside the bath, and her eyes search mine. She starts to cover her body with her arms, but I stop her. "No, don't do that. I'm here to look after you. You are beautiful." I reach over to grab the sponge and add some of her fancy-looking body wash to it. The smell of coconut and shea butter hit me, and my heart beats a little faster. The smell of her is intoxicating.

Starting at her shoulders, I slide the sponge across her collarbone, circle the little sweet spot on her neck and sweep across to the other side. My eyes watch her face. She tilts her head back, breathing gently. She really is beautiful. Moving the sponge down to her ample breasts, slowly circling her now erect nipples, brushing them gently and teasingly with my thumb, I continue to watch her as her breath hitches. Stroking the sponge down to her stomach, I notice her body tenses, so I go to her legs, washing from the ankle up, stopping just short of her now groomed pussy and back down the other leg. Gliding back up, I let the sponge drop out of my hand and feel her soft, warm, wet skin on my palm. Her eyes shoot open, and I can see the desire in those ocean-blues.

Moving my hand slowly, caressing her left leg, I shift a little closer to her warm spot. Her breath is becoming heavier. Keeping my eyes on hers, I cup her pussy with my palm and massage gently. She bites that bottom lip. I can feel my own breathing becoming louder. My desire to feel her is growing stronger. I slip my thumb between her lips and circle her clit. Her moan vibrates off of the bathroom tiles, and I make a mental note to make her come many times in a bathroom just for the sound of her pleasure. I can hear her panting.

Using my index finger, I tease her entrance. Jess arches her back, and I thrust my finger into her, curling to find her G-spot. She's going to come quickly. I can already feel her muscles tensing. Her moans get louder, and her panting becomes faster, so I follow her rhythm. Within minutes, her pussy clenches around my finger, and she relaxes back into the bath. Her legs are still spasming slightly, making me smile. Her hooded gaze meets mine, and without speaking, I dry my hand and hold my other hand out to her. She steps out of the bath, and I wrap her in a towel and lead her to her bedroom.

Chapter Thirty-Three

JESS

I stand there in the aftershock of a darn good orgasm, staring at this handsome man, wondering what he's going to do next. He sits on the edge of my bed and pulls me between his legs. His brown eyes have got darker, not in a dangerous way, but with desire. He tugs me closer and holds my ass with one hand whilst the other removes the towel. With his eyes on mine, he leans in towards my nipple, grasping it between those soft lips, making me gasp as he circles it with his tongue. His hands run over my hips, and before I know it, I'm flung onto the bed, which makes me giggle. Gavin smirks and kisses me. A full, passionate kiss that makes all the nerves in my body stand on end.

With his hands on either side of my head, his fully clothed body on top of my naked one, he kisses me. This situation needs to be rectified. I fumble at his shirt buttons, my hands taking over whilst my body feels his weight, his electricity. By the time I've undone his buttons, his mouth is on my neck. A moan escapes me, and I swear I feel him smile.

I push his shirt down his arms, and he leans back, takes it off and discards it on the floor. His mouth is back on my body.

"Jess, you are beautiful. Your body is so responsive and seductive. I could spend hours pleasuring you."

My head is spinning. Why would this powerful, attractive man want to be pleasuring me? Oh god, my mind can't think. His hands move under me, pulling me towards him. His lips sip at my skin, a wave of goosebumps flowing in his wake. Arching my back and inadvertently pushing my pelvis into his, I can feel him. He's still dressed from the waist down.

"This doesn't feel fair that I'm fully naked and you're not," is all I could manage whilst gasping for air. *Why does he make me feel breathless?*

He chuckles, pushes himself away from me and gets off the bed. I prop myself up on my elbows to take him in. His dark hair, which is normally neat and tidy, is now loose and draping over his face slightly, probably in need of a haircut, but it looks cute. His body isn't typically "ripped" like in magazines, but he definitely has muscle definition. He stares at me and slowly undoes his belt. The button of his trousers seems to take forever to undo. Is he doing this on purpose? A little strip tease?

He sees my smile and pulls his trousers down, kicking them off. He has that sexy V at the top of his boxers. I swear I'm drooling from looking at him. He has shown me a different side tonight. He's kind, sensitive, and, my god, sexy as hell compared to the straight-faced CEO he shows at work.

By the time he takes his socks off, I can feel my pussy throbbing. I desire him. Never have I felt this way before. It's exciting and new. I want him right now. I push myself up and perch on the edge of the bed. He stalks towards me and stands there, smiling down. My hands touch his soft but firm body, moving their way to his hips. Tucking my thumbs into his boxers, I tug on them gently, sliding them down slowly. I can see his breathing getting heavier as I pull them down over his cock. That thing springs free, nearly hitting me in the face. I try not to laugh because I don't want to ruin the moment, but later, I will definitely mention it should come with a warning sign.

I lick my lips at the sight of him, thick, slightly longer than average, with no foreskin. I haven't seen a circumcised one before, and it looks beautiful. My hand automatically goes to the base of his cock, and his breath stops. I peer up into his eyes as I slide my wet lips over the head, and he sucks in air. I love the effect I have on him, and I haven't even started.

I move my mouth down as far as I can to get a feel for him. When I withdraw, I press my tongue to the underside of his cock. I've read this is the most sensitive part. He seems to like it, which makes me more eager to please him. I start a rhythm, bobbing my head up and down as my hand pumps from the base. His fingers become tangled in my hair, not pushing himself deeper. It seems more to steady himself.

He releases a growl, which vibrates throughout his body, and he slowly pulls my mouth off of him and pushes me back onto the bed. "Jess...." is all he says before his mouth is on mine, his smooth hand moving down my body to my pussy. Surely he isn't going to make me come again. Before I know it, he has thrust two fingers into me, making me gasp.

His mouth moves down to my nipple, licking, sucking and biting me with his fingers inside me. I can feel myself about to orgasm again, feeling the pressure build-up. I'm on the edge when Gavin bites my nipple a little harder, and it throws me over.

Just as I'm coming down from *another* glorious orgasm, I feel his tongue on me, lapping up my juices. I'm so sensitive that everything tingles when he licks me. I hear a wrapper open and feel him putting a condom on as he kneels between my legs, nudging me. Gavin is back on top of me, and without warning, he slides right in and pauses, letting me get used to his size. My god, he feels huge, and yet, a perfect fit somehow. He feels amazing!

Gavin lowers his head and kisses me gently, growing more passionate as he withdraws and thrusts his cock into me. "God, yes!" is all I can manage. I wrap my arms and legs around him as he pistons over and over, deeper and deeper. This is pleasure. Moving together, I can feel another orgasm racing towards me. HOW? Before I can think, he lifts my hips slightly. The angle makes my eyes roll back into my head. Fuck, this is...just...amazing! My whole body tenses as I have the best orgasm of my life. It keeps rolling, and it's euphoric.

Gavin's body tenses over mine, and he thrusts faster into me. With a slight growl, he shouts, "Oh god, Jess!" No one has ever shouted my name like that. I feel like I'm on cloud nine, ten, eleven through to one thousand. Panting, he lands a kiss on my lips before pulling out and collapsing next to me.

"That was…that was incredible," I say, panting. He removes the condom, ties it and puts it in the bin by my bed. Then he rolls over and kisses me. There is something in this kiss. It's warm and affectionate. "You are wonderful," he says before getting off the bed and going into the bathroom.

I expect him to leave in a minute, so I sort myself out and put on my underwear and a large T-shirt. When he comes back into the bedroom, he picks up his boxers, puts them on and looks at me with his head cocked to one side. "Where do you think you're going?" he asks with an amused expression. I had been heading to the kitchen to fix a cuppa because I thought he was leaving. He grabs my wrist and pulls me into him. Pushing my hair out of my face, he kisses me and holds me close. "Do you still want me to stay over? If you need some space, I'll understand."

With that, I pull him onto the bed.

Chapter Thirty-Four

GAVIN

When I open my eyes, I feel different, disorientated as I don't know where I am, but I feel different. Lighter? As I'm coming round, I hear a loud noise. What on earth is that? Opening my eyes properly, I realise I'm still at Jess's place. I turn over to watch her sleeping. She snores like a tractor, mouth open, but she is still gorgeous. At least I found the source of the noise.

Leaving Jess in bed, I go to the bathroom and then to the kitchen to find some form of coffee. When I can't see a machine on the worktop, I fumble around in the cupboards. I can't help but wonder how could she not have a coffee machine with the amount she drinks? Finding some instant coffee, I put the kettle on and get straight on Amazon. *It's criminal that she doesn't have a coffee machine!*

With the coffee machine ordered, which will be a nice surprise for her tomorrow, I'm shocked at how much I'm enjoying pottering around her place. After Sacha, I didn't think I'd feel comfortable being with another woman, but Jess is different. At that moment, like a ray of sunshine with bedhead that makes a bird's nest look neat, Jess walks into the kitchen.

We stand and chat casually, the feeling between us light and easy. By mid-morning, we are both showered and dressed. I check that she is okay after everything that happened last night. When she says she's good, I give her a kiss to remember and leave for home. I want to have some alone time to process what happened and give her the same.

By the time I've done my domestics, Saturday night has arrived, and I suddenly feel alone. What has she done to me? I want her to be here to enjoy a night in, watching a movie, but this is new for both of us. I need to tread carefully. I take out my phone and stare at her number. Deciding not to text her just yet, I go about making dinner.

After dinner is made, eaten, and I've tidied the kitchen, I busy myself with anything but thinking of Jess. I open my laptop and start to distract myself with my work, and that's when I see an email from Lucy.

Subject: Let's Get Together
Message:

Hi Gavin,

You seem to be avoiding me since you hired that podgy little thing for your PA. I suggest we have some drinks privately without her tagging along so we can discuss something important.
I look forward to your availability.

Lucy

What is it going to take to get her off my back? I haven't given her any indication that we would be anything other than co-workers. How can I deal with this without her getting upset or angry? What is her problem with Jess? If this carries on, I'll need to get HR involved.

Subject: Re: Let's Get Together
Message:

Hi Lucy,

Thanks for your email. I would like you to familiarise yourself with our policies around discrimination and appropriate behaviour in the workplace. I will not accept any further negative comments directed towards my staff. If this continues, we will need to go down the disciplinary route.

With regards to your invite, if this is work-

related, please email me a summary of the important issues you'd like to discuss.

Regards,
Gavin

I'm crossing my fingers that this will resolve this problem. I don't need any drama. Lucy, unfortunately, reminds me of Sacha, and even if she didn't, I'm not interested.

My thoughts then wander back to Jess.

Chapter Thirty-Five

JESS

Kiera texts me after Gavin leaves, wanting to come over. She isn't staying at her parents' all weekend as planned because they want to go to a garden centre or something, and Kiera just doesn't have the patience for plants.

Whilst I potter around, waiting for Kiera to arrive, I reminisce about last night. It was absolutely wonderful. The caring side of him was unexpected. I'm not sure why. Maybe because he's portrayed as this big, tough CEO, who doesn't take any rubbish when he is actually a ball of mush. Who knew?

The sex…well, that has me blushing just thinking about it. I've never felt so alive. I have no idea what will happen after last night. I want to message him, thanking him for last night, but it feels a little…I don't know. Childish? We're not in our early dating times. We are…. I have no idea what we are.

The intercom buzzes, dragging me out of my

thoughts. I haven't ordered anything from Amazon, and I'm not expecting anyone. When I buzz in the delivery driver, he brings my parcel up, and I put it on the coffee table and open it eagerly. Who on earth has bought me a Nespresso machine? These are expensive. Then I see the note.

Jess,
Utterly appalling you don't have a coffee machine. A gift from me to you.
G xx

He bought me a coffee machine? This is such a wonderful gift. It feels like Christmas morning. I open the box and follow the instructions to set it up. Luckily, it comes with some pods, too. I do love my coffee. After it's all arranged and I've made myself a cuppa, I take a selfie with my cup and the machine in the background and text Gavin.

Me: You really shouldn't have, but I'm so happy! Thank you. x

Shortly after that, Kiera comes up. We sit on the sofa and catch up on our last couple of weeks. With both of us working a lot, we haven't had time for a chat. Of course, the first thing she notices is my "glow."

"You've had sex! Tell me everything. How did you afford your coffee machine? I thought your cards were maxed? What's happened in the last two weeks?"

I laugh, make us a coffee, and go back to the sofa. The one person I trust to tell me their honest opinion is Kiera.

"…then the coffee machine turned up, and that's you all up to date!" I sit eagerly, awaiting her opinion. We have been friends for many years and have been truthful with each other even if we don't want to hear it.

"Let me get this straight. Your hot-as-hell boss flirts with you, kisses you, protects you from a sexual assault, comes over to look after you, knowing you had no one else around last night, gives you the best sex and orgasms of your life, and then he buys you a coffee machine? I want to say, dear God, no, steer clear, but I honestly can't see any faults other than you work for him." I know I like Gavin a lot, but I didn't realise how much until I was talking about us out loud. Kiera's opinion means so much to me; I can't bear it if she disapproves. "I have two questions. One, are you happy? Two, please don't let yourself be taken advantage of. You're such a nice girl, and I know that wasn't a question, but I wanted to put it out there."

"I am happy. I love my job. I've started taking on more project work rather than just typing up notes and arranging meetings. I don't think I'm being taken advantage of. He came nowhere near me in that way until I basically stripped naked in front of him and invited him into the bath with me."

Thankfully, Kiera is easy to read. I've always been able to tell when she is happy about something as her eyes smile, and when she's unhappy, she gets a furrow in her eyebrow. She's never been one to hide her feelings. She isn't controlling like some friendships I've had in the past. Because I'm nice and easygoing, people often take advantage of me before I realise what they are doing. But Kiera is easy, chilled and no drama.

I know she's worried about the whole boss/PA situation, but I honestly don't think it will make anything awkward at work—unless someone finds out about us and starts spreading rumours, then it could be an issue with HR, and I could get fired.

Kiera and I spend the afternoon chatting away, and after she leaves, my flat seems strangely empty. I really enjoy my own company, but I suddenly feel alone. I completely forget I messaged Gavin earlier until I see his reply.

> Gavin: So pleased you like it. If there's a next time, at least there'll be decent coffee. ;)

With a smile on my face, I grab a blanket and sit on the sofa with a nice cup of coffee and Netflix.

Chapter Thirty-Six

JESS

The next week and a half passes by in a flash. Work is busy, and between my parents and Kiera, I'm occupied most evenings. Gavin and I haven't spoken about that night at my flat, but there also isn't any weirdness between us, which is good.

It is a dreary Wednesday; winter is closing in. Christmas is around the corner. We have the Christmas party next week and a charity event in the new year. Lots to plan for, and apparently, more outfits are needed. It's nearing lunchtime when I have a ping on my laptop.

Gavin: My office. Please, bring coffee.

I grab us both a cuppa and head in with my notebook. As I sit down, I can't read the expression on his face, making my stomach tie itself in knots. He glances up from his laptop and links his fingers. This does not look good.

"Jess, you've been with me longer than any other PA now. You've proven yourself to be more of an asset than I could have anticipated from our first meeting. I've already given you extra responsibility and tasks that I wouldn't normally allocate to a PA."

He looks at me as if he's trying to gauge my response to his statement. Very kind words indeed, but dread still lingers in my stomach.

"It's with this outstanding commitment and enthusiasm I've made the decision to change your role."

There it is. He regrets sleeping with you and is now moving you on. You've clearly romanticised this whole thing and are being shoved out of a job you love.

"Mr Andrews, Gavin, I'm sorry if I have offended you in some way. I love my job and don't want to move to—" He holds up his hand to stop me from talking. My stomach is in knots.

"Jess, you misunderstand me. I'm promoting you. You will still work under me, but instead of being a PA, you're going to be a Business Manager. You've more than proven yourself over the last few months with the extra work I've been giving you, and your attention to detail is second to none." I just stare at him. I'm hearing the words, but my brain can't process them. "As a PA, you type up my meeting notes, arrange my days and get my coffee, along with general admin. Our company is projected to grow exponentially within the next three years, more than doubling our size. With that in mind, promoting you to Business Manager would enable you to enhance your skills and knowledge. You've proven that admin work comes easily to you, and it feels like the PA position is holding you back. You've shown me that you can, and have, carried out some of the project work I do, and with you assisting me in projects, I would be able to concentrate more on growing the business."

"Oh." I can feel my face blushing. Why did I assume he wanted to get rid of me? This is an amazing opportunity. When I was in the admin team, I wanted nothing more than to be recognised for my work and what I could do. Gavin has shown appreciation throughout my PA role, but this is an amazing leap in roles. If I'd applied for a Business Manager role in a different company, I doubt I would have got it, but they can see what I am capable of. My whole body is now buzzing with excitement!

"Thank you, Gavin. I honestly don't know what to say."

He chuckles, looking devilishly handsome as he does. His eyes crinkle in the corners, and the smile he gives when chuckling creates creases in his cheeks, which make his eyes sparkle with joy. "Well, Jess, you can say, 'Yes, I'll take the new position.' You'll be in the office next to me, and you'll need to train your replacement. So when you're no longer doing the PA side of things, you'll be working more closely with me on projects." The way he waggles his eyebrows is not helping.

I burst out laughing. I'm not sure if it was the nervous energy I have, pent up from the beginning of this chat or what, but I feel much more relaxed, and I grin.

"Now that all that's cleared up, make some reservations at any restaurant you like for tonight. I'm taking you out to celebrate," he says.

I smile giddily and walk out of his office. My head is spinning. I got a promotion. I'll be doing more project work, and I'll literally be learning from the best as we'll be working side by side on some projects, by the sound of it. The company has many Business Managers, and they all work in different parts of the business, finance, acquisitions, HR, etc. There are a couple that work within projects, but they work with the consultants. I'd be working alongside Gavin, which is a huge leap from PA but a role that is needed considering his workload.

I decide to make a reservation at one of my favourite steak houses and send him the details. This is cause for celebration indeed. I wonder if there'll be a pay raise.

Whilst my mind wanders, I eat my lunch at my desk and crack on with my work for the afternoon. It's gone five before I realise the time. Gavin must still be in his office. I ping him a message to say I'm leaving for the day and will see him later. Before I can shut down my laptop, I have a return message.

Gavin: Pop in before you leave.

Deciding not to close my laptop in case he needs something, I tap on the door and go into his office.

There he is, perching on his desk, staring at me. I close the door behind me and wait for him to speak. Before he does, he stalks over to me, his eyes not leaving mine.

When we are nearly face to face, I feel the door at my back. One of his hands slides around my waist, and his other goes to my hair. He kisses me with such passion my knees actually wobble. I didn't know that was a real thing. I thought it was something they wrote about in books or movies. When he pulls his mouth from mine, I'm breathless and searching his eyes, but I'm not sure what I'm looking for.

"I've been wanting to do that every day. I wanted to make sure you didn't feel you got the promotion because you slept with me because that certainly isn't the case." He leans in and places his lips on mine.

I don't speak. I thrust up onto my tiptoes and kiss him back with as much passion as he gives me. I don't want to admit it, but I'm falling for this man. His tough CEO persona isn't the real him. He's kind, caring, sexy and, for some reason, into me.

"At this rate, we're going to be late for our reservation," I say, coming up for air from an amazing kiss.

"Well, we can't be having that, can we, Miss Freeman? But according to my watch, we still have half an hour before we need to leave." Waggling his eyebrows, making me laugh, he hoists me up so I can wrap my legs around his waist and takes me to the sofa. He sits down with me straddling him.

Grinning, I lean into him and kiss him. Feeling the spark between us makes me hungry for him. As if he can read my thoughts, his hands are unzipping my dress and pulling it off of me in one move. His mouth goes straight to my breasts, biting my nipples through my bra. I remind myself to be quiet since we are in his office, but he's driving me wild. His right hand moves up my body and grabs the nape of my neck, and he brings his lips to lick and nibble that sweet, sensitive spot on my neck whilst tweaking my nipples, one at a time, with his left hand.

I can feel him growing under me, and I grind into him. I can already feel the slickness on my knickers. He leans back, unbuttoning his trousers and sliding them down his hips, freeing that beautiful beast. Gavin slides his hand into my knickers and teases me with his fingers. Grinning like a Cheshire cat, he moves them to one side and positions me on top of him. I'm so ready for him, I can't wait, but I let him guide me and control the rhythm at first. When I can't wait any longer, I set my own pace. Desperate for the orgasm he always makes me crave, I can feel myself getting close when he grabs my hips and thrusts deep into me over and over until I throw my hands over my mouth to muffle the scream, and my body shakes and quivers. He quickens his pace for his own release, and then I collapse onto him fully, both of us breathless but still smiling.

Chapter Thirty-Seven

GAVIN

I'm still getting my breath back as we get dressed again. We will still make our reservations, so I can celebrate with my girl. *Your girl? Neither of us knows what this is, but it feels amazing.*

As we enter the restaurant, I can see people looking at Jess. She's beautiful. She has luscious curves and a smile that can make the world stop. I slip my hand into hers to show everyone that she's taken. She looks at me with those gorgeous blues and smiles sweetly. Why am I acting possessive? She isn't mine? But I want her to be!

We take our seats and set about looking at the menu. I didn't realise that I'd worked through lunch until my mouth started watering as I read what is on offer. Yet all I can think about is this beautiful creature sitting across from me.

"Jess, what's taking your fancy?"

She gives me a devilish grin and flutters those

beautiful lashes at me. "Well, Gavin, I've had a little of what I fancy already this evening, but I am quite partial to a steak, too." She makes my stomach flutter. What is that about? I can feel myself falling for her, and I don't even know her that well. Does she feel the same? Is it too soon to ask?

After the waiter takes our drink and food order, I'm about to test the waters when she pipes up first. "With the excitement of this afternoon, I've just realised we didn't use anything, but I am on the pill, so that should cover that part. I haven't been with anyone since my ex years ago, and we always used protection."

Ah, she's asking if there is any risk of an STD. "I haven't been with anyone since my ex, other than you, and I got tested after breaking up with her. Everything came back negative." I see her body relax, and she takes a sip of her gin. She isn't shy about talking serious stuff, which is good. I don't want someone who won't speak up. I want a partner in everything.

"Jess, there's something I've been meaning to talk to you about. This afternoon, the other week…."

"Gavin, honestly, I understand. You're a busy, successful man who doesn't have time for relationships." Her eyes seem sad as she speaks those last few words. Her eyebrows are lower than usual and slightly raised in the middle, and her usual smile isn't as broad.

"Jess, no. Yes, I am busy and successful. And you are correct that I didn't want a relationship. But you have thawed me. I'm completely taken by you, and if I'm being honest, I'm falling for you." It's my turn to drink. I had decided to try one of these trendy new gin concoctions. Way too much stuff floating in my glass for my liking, but I enjoy the taste.

She doesn't say anything, simply looks at me. I've overstepped. It's too early for this, and I'm clearly about to lose her, not just for me but for the business as well. Before I can backtrack, the waiter brings our food. I'm suddenly not hungry anymore, but we start to eat, regardless. Moments pass in this strange silence. We normally eat in comfortable silence, but I have made things too weird now. My thoughts are dragging me down, and I can feel her eyes on me. She cocks her head to one side.

"Penny for your thoughts?"

"I'm sorry. I shouldn't have said anything." That is all I can muster.

She sits, chewing her food, looking deep in thought. She puts down her cutlery and picks up her drink. Seriously, this is the longest pause. I feel myself sweating. This isn't like me at all. "Why shouldn't you have said anything? You told me that you think you're falling for me. That's definitely something I should know. And just so you know, I feel the same." She smiles sweetly, and before I know it, I stand beside her and bend down to kiss her.

She feels the same! Is this what love feels like? Bubbles and butterflies, smiles, and this amazing feeling of lightness and happiness. I compose myself and sit back down. We are both grinning like teenagers. Once we've finished our main course, we are asked if we'd like dessert. I wink at Jess, knowing full well what I want for dessert.

I pay the bill, and we leave the restaurant to grab a

cab to my place. I can't keep my hands off of her. I have to touch her in some way, whether it be holding her hand, my arm around her waist or my mouth on hers. We walk through the lobby and head to the lift, hand in hand. Luckily, it's empty because I want nothing more than to make her come once before we get upstairs.

When the doors close, I push her back against the wall and kiss her passionately but sweetly at the same time. I'm assuming it's appreciated with the moans vibrating through her. I lift the hem of her dress up and move her knickers to one side. I find her clit with my thumb, roughly circling it, which makes her gasp and pant. This is exactly the effect I want. With that, I thrust two fingers into her, curling them to find her G-spot. I move my hand with no particular rhythm, but I can feel her trembling already. I suck on her neck and bite the sensitive spot where her neck meets her shoulder, which pushes her over the edge. Her moans are not contained and sound amazing. I put her knickers back in place and smooth her dress down whilst I kiss her.

As the doors open, a sense of dread fills me. Sacha stands by my door. I can feel Jess tense next to me. "What are you doing here, Sacha? I thought I made myself clear."

She pushes herself away from the wall she is leaning against and glares at Jess, sneering at her. "Well, I had to see for myself. I had heard through the grapevine something was going on between you and your PA. Such a cliché, Gavin. You seriously want *that* over me? This…." she moves her hands up and down her body, "is much more than *that.*" She spits the last word, which angers me.

"Sacha, leave now. What Jess does is of no concern to you. What I do is of no concern to you. Leave and never come back here." I didn't realise how hard my tone was, but I don't care. She isn't going to meddle in my life. She opens her mouth to say something, and I'm about to shut her down, but Jess speaks first.

"I do believe Gavin said leave now." Jess's arm comes around my waist, and I can feel the tension in her body as she comes closer, and her tone is cold. Sacha looks like she would explode. Instead, she pushes past us and steps into the lift. Once the doors close, I know I have to explain to Jess.

We walk through the front door, the exciting lift moment feeling far in the past. "Jess…."

"Gavin, you don't have to explain. She is your ex. You clearly don't have feelings for her anymore, and you asked her to leave." I'm astounded by her. Most other women would have wanted to know every single detail up to when I last saw her. Before I can get too deep in my thoughts, Jess kisses me with her arms around my neck and her body pressing in on mine. Pulling away slightly, she stares up at me with lust in her eyes. "Now, I do believe we were going to have dessert," she says in a low tone.

I sweep her off her feet, carry her to the bedroom and throw her on the bed. I grab her hips and pull her to the edge, which makes her giggle. I roughly push up her dress and pull down her knickers, kneeling on the floor beside the bed. I push her thighs apart and put my mouth on her, my tongue finding her clit, making her moan and arch her back. I thrust my fingers inside her as my tongue works on her clit. Within minutes, her groans are getting louder, her breaths becoming shorter, and I bite down on her clit, which pushes her over the edge. Lapping up her juices, I move up her body and kiss her so she can taste herself.

Chapter Thirty-Eight

GAVIN

Within minutes, we are both naked. Jess tries to pin me down, making me chuckle. I pick her up and pin her to the bed with her hands above her head. Skimming my mouth over her body as far as I can reach with one hand holding her arms, lightly kissing as I go, Jess gasps with pleasure from my touch. That sweet mouth. I push off of her, shifting over to a drawer. I can hear Jess sitting up on the bed.

"Is everything okay?" She sounds worried. I pick up what I want and stalk over to her. I can feel how tense she is.

"How do you feel about being tied up?" I hold up a length of silk for her to see. Jess doesn't recoil, which is a positive sign. I reposition myself over her body again, and her eyes are on me and full of curiosity.

Moving her hands back above her head, I tie the silk around them. Not too tight, though. "How does that feel?"

She tests her wrists, and sure enough, she can't get free. "Well, you've tied my wrists. What will you do with me now?" The glint in her eyes tells me she's enjoying this. I use another silk piece to cover her eyes. When her vision is blocked, I lightly touch her hip, which makes her jump. Satisfied she can't see, I move back over her. Leaning over, I kiss and nibble her earlobe, her gasps making me eager. I move my tongue down her neck, over her collarbone and right between her breasts.

I move one of my hands under her to grab her sweet ass whilst I kiss her stomach. I can feel her panting. Removing my hands from her fine ass, I lift her legs, placing her ankles on my shoulders. I tease her slit with my fingers, feeling her wetness, and push my cock deep into her. As Jess lets out a delectable sound, I grab her hips and thrust into her at a punishing rate, pistoning harder and faster. She begins to tense around me. Her body shudders as she comes twice, one after the other. I find my release and collapse on top of her.

Kissing her, I untie her hands and remove her blindfold, finding those beautiful eyes staring at me. "That was much better than a sticky toffee pudding." She giggles, rising to kiss me, still breathless.

After spending some time in bed together, we have a nice hot shower and get dressed. I surprise her with some clothes I've ordered. I'd like to say I actually know which sizes she wears, but I checked some of her clothes when we last slept together. Jess is taken aback, but the kiss that follows tells me that I've done the right thing. I've never done anything like this before. I want to give her the world.

We sit in the living room with a cuppa, idly watching what is on the TV. I have my arm around her, and everything feels right in the world.

"I should head off soon. My boss doesn't like it when I'm late for work," Jess says, stretching into a full sitting position.

"Well, you have things here if you'd like to stay over? It's completely up to you, though."

Jess stares for a moment and then settles back into me. "Well, as I'm all comfy and I have some very nice clothes here, I will stay. Thank you again for those. You really didn't have to."

I just squeeze her and smile to myself. This is what I imagined being with someone would feel like. I feel this immense sense of happiness settling over me, and I have to admit, it worries me. I don't want this to end.

Chapter Thirty-Nine

JESS

Waking up in Gavin's bed the next morning makes me happy. This feeling is wonderful. The clothes he bought for me are beautiful. I can't wait to get dressed. When he goes to the bathroom, I make us both coffees and get dressed.

I choose a beautiful black dress that has some burnt orange flowers and hugs my curves, a silky black bra which really boosts the boobs with matching knickers, and some simple black heels. I feel amazing. How did he know what sizes to buy? Leaving for work, we decide it is best to be dropped off a block away from the office, and I'll head in first. We are figuring this out and don't need office gossip getting in the way.

THE DAY FLIES BY, AND AT LUNCH, I EVEN HAVE TIME TO order some outfits for the upcoming events. I do have

Sacha's comment in the back of my mind. "Heard through the grapevine." There is no one else other than Paul who knows about us. No one else has the slightest idea what is going on between Gavin and me.

Deciding to push those thoughts out of my mind, I read through my new contract. I'm getting promoted. So much happened yesterday I haven't had time to call Kiera. With it being busy, I haven't been smoking as much lately either, which is a good thing, but I fancy a smoke and quick catch-up with my bestie.

Heading down to the smoking area, I call Kiera.

"There you are! I was going to give you a message later to see if you fancied a catch-up tonight?"

"I'm free later if you fancy it? It's been busy, but I wanted you to be the first to know."

"TELL ME EVERYTHING!"

"Alright, Miss Impatient. I got a promotion. I've been doing so well, I've been given extra work, and they're making me a Business Manager. How exciting is that? And there's something else I'll tell you about later where the walls don't have ears."

I'm sure the screams coming from the phone can be heard for miles. We agree to meet at our usual bar later and have a few drinks. I feel all giddy with excitement.

When I get back upstairs, I have a message waiting for me on my laptop.

> Gavin: Bring coffee and migraine tabs, please.

I get everything ready and go into Gavin's office, where he sits in the dark. "You should probably go and get your eyes checked. You may need glasses. Or maybe drink some more water?" I place everything on his desk and get a bottle of water. His face doesn't change. "What's up?"

"Pierre is literally giving me migraines. He's sent over several documents that need to be read with a fine-tooth comb, and I do need to get my eyes checked."

"Well, isn't it lucky you've just appointed a new Business Manager? Send them over, and I'll go through them. Take a break. It's cold and overcast outside. Call Paul, and I'm sure he'll come for a break, too."

I go to my desk and start going through the documents from Pierre. These are really tedious, but luckily, I have an eye for detail. Within minutes, Paul is leaning on my desk.

"Congratulations on your promotion, Jess. Well deserved! I hear you're already taking your position seriously and forcing the boss to take a break. I can't believe admin hid you away for so long." He smiles and walks in to fetch Gavin.

The hour or so they are out of the office passes by quickly. I'm immersed in these documents and taking plenty of notes along the way. Something feels off in the few I've been through already. Gavin walks up to me with a coffee from the shop down the road and a little paper bag. My curiosity is piqued.

"I do believe it's the triple chocolate cookies you like? I thought you'd appreciate a naughty snack whilst you work." Damn, he's sweet. Literally my favourite cookie. "You've been scribbling away. Come and debrief me with what you've got so far."

I finish the document I'm reading through, gather my notes and head into Gavin's office. He sits with his hands folded in front of him expectantly.

"I've only gone through three of the ten pages so far, but...." Ten pages seem quite excessive. We normally have two or three at the most. Most of the information is repetitive, and I'm not sure why it has been sent over this way.

"He's trying to swindle us, isn't he?"

"Well, what I've seen so far is that he will invest the amount agreed to a three per cent share in the business, but from what I can gather, when he's made his money back, he will end up with forty per cent of the business. It's not stated as clearly as that. It's worded in lots of paragraphs differently, but that's what I've found so far."

Gavin looks at me, picks up the phone and calls Paul, asking him to come to his office. We then go through the documents I've already been through together, and they agree with my findings. We comb through the documents again and find that it is all worded the same. Pierre is looking to get forty per cent of the business for his small investment, which isn't the agreement.

We come up with a strategy for response. Gavin and Paul think that as I am the one who found this discrepancy, I will be the one to counteroffer. This will be my first official task in my new role, and it is a big one. When we finally glance at the time, it's six-thirty in the evening. I had arranged to meet Kiera at seven o'clock. Once we've been through everything, legal will take care of the rest.

"Gentlemen, I have a prior arrangement for this evening. Would you mind if we picked this up first thing in the morning? Is that okay?" I suddenly feel like I'm abandoning my post.

"That's absolutely fine, Jess. My head is still killing me, and I could do with an early night."

With that, we leave it for now and will pick everything back up in the morning. I head out of the office, excited that I have my first project and excited to see my best friend for a catch-up. I'm dying to tell her about last night and today.

Chapter Forty

JESS

I make it to the bar in time to meet Kiera. Our usual table is free, so we sit down and order our drinks and some nibbles. Kiera is telling me about this guy she's been seeing. Nothing serious, but something seems to be off.

"So, he's asking where you are all the time? That's a huge red flag."

"I know, but the sex is really good! Do you think I should end it? I mean, he's texted me four times since we've been here, asking who I'm with. Now that I've said it out loud, it seems a bit excessive."

"Kiera, yeah. It's a bit much. I'd end it before it really gets too obsessive. That's almost psycho material. Even if you were in a relationship, that's not okay."

We talk about her strategy for ending things with him, and I will be available when she does. I want to make sure it's in a public place so he can't kick off. When she's had enough of talking about her life, we move on to mine. I tell her about Gavin, the promotion, the admission of feelings for each other, and the ex that turned up. Everything.

Our nibbles turn up with our second round of drinks, and we tuck right in. I have a message from Gavin.

Gavin: Are you ok?

Me: Yes, in the pub with Kiera. You ok?

Gavin: Just checking. Today was a big day. Don't get too drunk, Miss Freeman. You have an early meeting tomorrow ;)

Chuckling, I leave it there, making a mental note not to get too carried away with the gin tonight.

I don't realise I have a goofy grin on my face until Kiera pipes up, "I'm assuming that's Mr Handsome texting you."

Giggling, I take a sip of my drink. I suddenly feel uneasy, but I'm not sure why. Swiping that feeling to one side, we carry on putting the world to rights.

"I knew he'd end up falling for you. You are literally the best person. I know I'm biased, but I don't care. So, when do I get to do the whole 'if you hurt her, I'll hunt you down' speech?" Kiera is literally beaming. I am ecstatic that I have someone in my life I can share my news with. She's excited about my role. I don't tell her the particulars of the project, but she can tell I'm enjoying it already.

"You are biased. I don't think I'm the best person. There are many more people better than me, but I'm not going to lie. I'm currently on cloud nine."

"For someone who's on cloud nine, you have one hell of a frown on your face." Cocking her head to one side, her smile disappears as she frowns and looks concerned. "What's up?"

"I'm not sure. I feel uneasy, and I have no idea why. We're having a lovely time, and I'm in a really good place mentally. I'm not sure what this feeling is. You ever get the feeling that someone is watching you?" I look around, and everyone is enjoying their night. Not one person is peering in our direction, but I can't shake this feeling.

"Maybe it's because you're in a good place that you're expecting something to go wrong? But it won't. You're smashing life right now." Kiera always tries to put me at ease. She's probably right. Hopefully.

We carry on talking, and I try to forget the feeling in the pit of my stomach. Then suddenly, time jumps, and it's last orders. I want to get home to rest before our meeting tomorrow. We say our goodbyes and head home.

Whilst I'm waiting for my Uber, that feeling rises again, and then I feel a sudden pain going through my head. Before I know it, I'm hitting the floor and hearing Kiera scream my name. Everything goes dark and cold.

Chapter Forty-One

GAVIN

After work, I go out for a run, shower and go through more of the documents from Pierre. I can't believe he's trying to get a bigger cut of my company in such a sneaky way. Well, I can believe it. He's a slimy bugger, but this is underhanded.

After an hour or so, I shut down my laptop and make a coffee when my phone rings—a number I don't know at this hour. "Hello?"

The other end of the phone sounds busy. I can hear lots of people in the background, and the person on the other end sounds panicked. My whole body tenses.

"Hi, is that Gavin?"

"Yes, who's this?"

"This is Kiera, Jess's friend. We were out this evening, and there's been an accident." He can tell by the wobble in her voice that she's holding back tears. What's happened to Jess?

"Kiera, where are you and Jess? What happened?"

Kiera explains that Jess was waiting for an Uber whilst Kiera was walking down to the tube station, and someone hit Jess on the back of the head and ran off. There were plenty of witnesses, and police were taking statements, but Jess was being taken to hospital because she was bleeding quite heavily. Once I've found out where they are taking Jess, I grab my coat and rush to the hospital. My emotions are reeling, but I have to stay calm. I will speak to the police when I get to the hospital. Kiera told me Jess had a police escort in the ambulance with her.

Rushing into Guy's Hospital, I find the ward where they have Jess. She has been checked over. The bleeding has stopped, and there are no fractures to her skull, but she's still out and had a concussion. I speak with an officer who points me in the direction of the police officer who accompanied her. "Good evening. I'm Miss Freeman's boyfriend. Can you tell me what happened?"

The officer takes my name, address and number for their records and starts talking. "Good evening, Mr Andrews. Miss Freeman was attacked outside of a pub this evening. We initially thought it was a mugging. However, nothing was taken. Eyewitnesses state that they saw a blonde woman running away from the scene. We found a beer bottle that had blood and tissue on them. We believe this was the weapon used, and we have sent the samples to the lab for testing to confirm they are Miss Freeman's. Can you think of anything who would want to harm Miss Freeman?"

My whole body freezes. Who would want to harm Jess? She's so kind, sweet and innocent. When the officer mentioned a blonde woman, my thoughts immediately went to Sacha. Could she do something like this? She's unhinged, but this is another level.

"Do you have a more accurate description of the blonde woman?"

"Do you have someone in mind, Mr Andrews?"

"Yes, Sacha Jackson. She's my ex-girlfriend. We split a while ago, and she's still holding out hope. She turned up at my place the other night and was angered by Jess's presence." I feel sick to my stomach. I gaze through the window into Jess's room. She looks so fragile lying there with her head bandaged. I need to be beside her. I need to tell her everything is going to be okay. My emotions are bubbling to the surface. I'm cool, calm and collected in most situations, but someone hurting the woman I love…I'm no longer falling. I'm fully in love with Jess.

The officer takes down Sacha's details and calls the officer in charge to dispatch someone immediately. Whilst we are talking, the doctor who has been in with Jess comes out. "Good evening, Doctor. How is she?"

"Good evening. Are you family?"

"I'm her boyfriend."

"She's had a lucky escape. There are no fractures. The bleeding has stopped, and we've glued her wound. She has a concussion and will be very foggy when she wakes up. We just have to wait for her to regain consciousness."

Thanking the doctor, I walk into her room. I stroke

her cheek with the back of my hand. She feels warm. Her skin is soft and delicate. I lean down to give her a kiss on her forehead and sit down, holding her hand.

Stroking her knuckles with my thumb with one hand, I grab my phone from my pocket. I call Paul to advise him about what has happened. Obviously, our meeting will be delayed, but we will deal with this in Jess's absence tomorrow afternoon. I then dial a friend who owns a security company. "Dave, how are you? Yes, it's been a while. I need a favour."

If it wasn't Sacha, then someone was out to hurt Jess, which I'm not going to let happen. Within the hour, Dave sends a security guard who will be stationed outside her door at all times. I want to ensure her safety, especially when I'm not here. I stay for a couple of hours and then go home. I ask the nurses and the security officer to call me if there are any updates on Jess's condition.

On my way home, I receive a call from the detective investigating tonight's incident. "Mr Andrews, we have been to Miss Jackson's house, and there appears to be no one in. If she is the one who attacked your girlfriend, she may be lying low. We have stationed an officer at the hospital alongside your security guard to ensure another attack isn't attempted. I would suggest you stay alert in case she comes to you."

I quickly call Dave to see if he sent the other officer I requested to my apartment. The guard had been there for ten minutes, had heard someone inside and assumed I was back from the hospital. When Dave realises I'm driving home, he calls the security officer to ensure the person in my penthouse doesn't leave, and I call the detective in charge so he can send police officers.

By the time I've pulled into the car park, police are everywhere. I take them up to my apartment and open the door.

Chapter Forty-Two

JESS

My God, my head hurts. Where am I? I can hear beeping, talking, phones ringing.... What happened?

As I try to open my eyes, I feel something squeeze around my arm, and my body freezes. What's going on? Blinking away the bright light, I realise it was a blood pressure cuff around my arm and nothing to be scared of. But why do I have a blood pressure cuff? Looking around, I realise I'm in hospital. Panic rises within me. I have no idea how I got here.

A nurse bustles into the room to quiet one of the machines that is now beeping really loudly. "Hi, there, Jess. I'm Betty, your nurse this evening. Do you know where you are?"

Betty seems nice. My panic is slowly dying down, but I can't remember what happened. Why am I here?

"I'm assuming I'm in hospital, but I don't know why." My voice is hoarse, and Betty grabs me some water, telling me to sip slowly through the straw. She makes me more comfortable, adjusting the bed so I'm in a sitting position, and whilst she's taking down all the numbers on the machines, she gives me an update.

"You, my dear, are very lucky to have such a good friend. You were attacked outside a bar, and your friend got an ambulance and the police straight away. She's been calling every half hour to see if you're okay. I'll call her shortly to give her an update. Your boyfriend came in. Very handsome chap! Had all the nurses swooning! He's got someone stationed outside your door." Betty points to the young man dressed in a smart black suit. He nods to the nurse and makes a phone call.

Who would want to attack me? Betty leaves the room, and I sit with my thoughts. My head is killing me. I can see out of the window there's a police officer and security outside. Was it really bad? Before I can spiral into a panic attack, a police officer comes into the room. "Hi, Miss Freeman. How are you feeling?"

"I'm in a bit of pain and very confused. Why would someone attack me?"

"Can you tell me everything you can remember, from being in the bar to waiting outside?"

I recount the night's events and tell him I felt uneasy, which is unusual. I can't see any significance in what I'm telling him. I didn't see anyone, or hear anything, just the uneasy feeling that was out of place for a usual catch-up with Kiera.

"Thank you, Miss Freeman. We are investigating

and will advise if there are any updates. If you do remember anything else, please let us know."

As he leaves my room, Gavin flows in. He looks worried. *Of course, he does. You're lying in a hospital bed after being attacked, and he's falling for you.*

"Oh, Jess!" He swoops in and kisses me gently. Before sitting down in the chair beside my bed, he makes sure I have a drink, fluffs my pillows and holds my hand. He is handsome and kind.

"You've been telling everyone you're my boyfriend." I chuckle, trying to lighten the mood a little. I can see there is something going on other than me being in this bed.

"Is now the time to have that chat? You're recovering."

"I don't see why not."

"Jess, I'm not falling in love with you." My stomach lurches so hard that I think it's going to escape my body. "I am head over heels in love with you. When Kiera called me, I couldn't get here fast enough. I want to be with you. Whatever label you prefer is what we'll use."

"Kiera called you? How did she get your number?"

"I got it from your phone, silly. Don't you EVER scare me like that again!" Kiera strolls into the room and sits on the end of my bed. I smile at her, and she reaches for my hand. I have no idea what time it is, but considering we left the pub at closing time, I'm assuming it's very early morning.

Kiera and Gavin introduce themselves to each other, and the three of us compare notes on what happened this evening. The feeling I had in the bar was completely justified. Someone, potentially Gavin's ex, attacked me and fled the scene. When Gavin left earlier, there was someone in his apartment. By the time the police got there, there were no signs of them or how they left. Gavin, the security officer and the police stayed outside for an hour after searching to see if anyone would come out. They weren't confident that the person had left. They did another sweep, and nothing. Gavin's friend sent over another security officer to stay outside the apartment whilst another stayed inside with him. Sweeping the home every hour just to make sure no hiding place went unchecked.

This is all a bit scary. I feel drained, which is understandable considering the concussion. Betty comes in, making sure I'm okay and takes my observations. "Right, you two. It's four in the morning, and Jess needs some rest. I'm sure you two do as well."

Kiera gives me a kiss on the cheek and leaves, telling me she'll be back tomorrow. Gavin stands, kisses me and heads towards the door. "I'll be back later. Rest and try not to worry. The police are searching for her."

I watch as Gavin and Kiera leave. Gavin is taking Kiera home as it's late. He's such a good man. With that thought, I drift into an unsettled sleep, surrounded by beeping and the hustle of the busy hospital.

Chapter Forty-Three

GAVIN

By the time I've dropped Kiera home, had a shower and looked at my clock, it's already five-thirty in the morning. I text Paul to tell him I'm going to get a couple of hours of sleep before heading back to the hospital. The good friend and colleague he is, he has already rescheduled my meetings for the day, and we are going to discuss this Pierre business when Jess is out of the woods.

My mind is reeling as I lay down in bed. If it was Sacha who attacked Jess.... Why? Why couldn't the police find her? Who was in my apartment when I got back? Where did they go? I have two security guards with me. One in the apartment and one stationed at the front door. The one inside, Jack, is sweeping every hour or so. He isn't convinced the person John heard earlier has actually left. There aren't many hiding places in here. They checked all the other cameras in the building, and there is evidence that someone was in the apartment, even if nothing is actually out of place. Everything has been checked, including the vents, walls, crawl spaces, cabinets and closets. Nothing has been found. They cannot find anyone, but they can't shake the feeling that if the person found a way in, they might still be here or return. And that is why there is a guard inside and outside.

Pushing those thoughts to the back of my mind, I try desperately to shut my eyes and rest. I need some sleep to spend the day with Jess and, hopefully, speak to the detective in charge to sort this mess out. As I'm drifting, I hear footsteps. They didn't sound like Jack's. Sitting bolt upright, I see someone dash from my bedroom door. I shout out to Jack, who sounds like he's already on it.

Jumping out of bed, I put on my clothes and go see who broke in and why. Walking into the living room, I see Jack has restrained someone, and John has come in with a police officer who must have been stationed outside. When I walk around to see their face, emotions flood over me. Anger the main one.

There she is. Sacha. How on earth had she gotten into my apartment? "Sacha, what on earth do you think you're doing?" She looks a wreck, not her usual spotless self. Her hair is messy. She clearly hasn't changed since the attack. There is a speck of blood on her face still, which makes my fury boil. That is probably Jess's blood.

Sacha doesn't say a word. She can't even look at me. The police officer cuffs her and escorts her from my apartment. John goes back outside, and Jack does another sweep. After a few moments, Jack comes back. "Mr Andrews, a unit has been moved in your walk-in wardrobe. I didn't think to check the safe room as it needed a combination to open. I apologise that I didn't check it properly."

"Thank you, Jack. No one else knew the combination other than myself. She must have found it in my study." There is no way I can sleep now, knowing Sacha had been here hiding all night. I make a mental note to change the locks and the combination to the safe room.

I text my cleaner and ask her to do a thorough cleaning today. I want every trace of that woman gone by the time I come home.

Running my hands through my hair, I make a coffee and text Jess to see if she's awake. I want to be with her, to tell her that Sacha is now in custody, but I also want her to rest. I speak to Dave to see if he knows of any nursing aids that can be here when Jess is released. With his experience in security, he knows all the right companies to use. She isn't going home alone. She will be looked after until she's fully recovered.

I GET TO THE HOSPITAL AND SPEAK WITH THE DOCTOR to check on her progress. She's showing good signs and will be allowed to go home later today. When I peek into Jess's room, her face has more colour. She has her laptop open and appears to be working away. I have two questions: who bought her laptop in, and why on earth is she working?

Before I can question it further, Kiera arrives with coffee. There's my answer. "Morning, Gavin! How are you today? Did you manage to rest?" Kiera is naturally beautiful. She has no makeup on, and I can tell she hasn't slept either, but here she is with her best friend.

"Hi, Kiera. Not much rest but refreshed. How is she this morning? I'm assuming you bought her laptop for her?"

Kiera laughs. "You know what Jess is like. She is a workaholic and wanted to distract herself from the fact she was attacked by your crazy ex." Guilt floods over me. It's my fault Jess was attacked.

We both walk in. Jess looks up, sheepishly closing her laptop. She greets me with the most radiant smile, even as she absently rubs her forehead as if she has a headache. Even though she is bandaged up and looks like she hasn't slept, she still looks like a vision. I sit back, letting the girls chat over their coffees whilst going through my emails. I have a nursing team in place to start later today. They are a great company that offers a variety of services with the highest discretion. I will be keeping the security team in place for both of us for the time being as well.

When Kiera stands to leave, I take her place by Jess's side.

"I bet I look an absolute vision. I have glue in my hair and a graze on my cheek, and I'm sure this gown does wonders for my figure." She giggles, trying to lighten the mood. I don't realise how tense I am until her laugh literally melts it all away.

"You look beautiful no matter what you're wearing. You'll be able to wash your hair tomorrow and feel a bit more normal. You're being discharged today, and I'd like you to stay at my place so I know you're safe."

She cocks her head as if she is pondering my request. Gulping the rest of her coffee, she nods and smiles. "As long as you're not hovering over me. I had a bump to the head, and they say I'm absolutely fine. Talking of which, any news on Sacha?"

I give her a breakdown of the events that unfolded earlier this morning. I haven't heard from the detective yet to see what is happening with Sacha, but I'll hopefully hear soon.

Betty, Jess's nurse, comes in to see how we are. "Considering you haven't slept, Mr Andrews, you're still looking handsome." I like Betty. She is an older nurse with a great bedside manner. She makes me laugh as Jess has her observations checked. I notice Jess can't keep her eyes off me whilst smiling. There is something in her eyes that makes me feel warm. She is truly gorgeous.

I want to keep that look in her eyes forever.

Chapter Forty-Four

JESS

I've spent the afternoon speaking to doctors and signing discharge paperwork. By the time we get back to Gavin's, he's filled me in on the nursing team he's hired. Completely unnecessary, but I can't help but feel the swell in my chest with how protective he's being.

The detective calls Gavin shortly after we get back. Sacha has admitted to attacking me. According to the police, she's obsessed with Gavin and can't let go. She's been stalking him for months after they split and has been to his apartment a few times without his knowledge to feel like she's still part of his life. She slept with one of the concierges to gain access to his apartment and got a key cut. Part of me is angry and upset with what she has done, but part of me feels sorry for her. She needs help, and now she's going to get it after she has been charged.

Hopefully, with that drama over, we can figure out

our relationship and how this will work. We've only just discovered our feelings for each other, and part of me thinks it won't last. I mean, he's a successful man with an empire, and I'm just a girl. Granted, a girl who is kick ass at her job to get a promotion so quickly. I'm well aware of how much he's out of my league.

Gavin makes me dinner, and we sit on the sofa, scrolling through Netflix. I don't realise I've fallen asleep until I feel him carrying me to bed. He lays me down, and I drift into a comfortable, deep sleep.

THE FOLLOWING MORNING, I WAKE UP FEELING refreshed. The nurses come in to check my bandages and tell me I can shower and wash my hair. I feel elated to be able to scrub the grime from my body and hair. I walk into Gavin's en suite and turn on the shower. Stepping into the hot stream of water and letting the water fall over me, I'm overcome by my emotions. I don't realise that I've been holding back until I slide to the shower floor, sobbing. The realisation that someone wanted to hurt me because I was with Gavin and because Sacha couldn't have him anymore makes me angry, sad and scared that she wanted to take me out of the picture. If Kiera hadn't have been close, if I hadn't had an Uber turn up minutes after, it could have been much worse.

I don't hear Gavin come into the bathroom. The shower is turned off, and I'm wrapped in a towel and carried back to bed. I sob into his chest. When there are no more tears, I look up at him with blurry eyes. His face shows a concerned expression, but he just holds me.

"I'm sorry," is all I can muster.

"Don't ever be sorry. I'm sorry. If it wasn't for me, you wouldn't have been attacked." We sit there in silence for what feels like forever. *Enough now, Jess. You've been through something, and now it's time to pull yourself together. Sacha is being charged. There's no longer a threat. Be with your man! Pull yourself together, woman!*

"Right!" I announce as I stand up, trying to shake off the anxiety that is mounting. "I'm going to shower properly, and we're going to have something to eat." I manage a smile as I walk to the bathroom again.

After a successful shower with no melodrama, I go to my drawer, where I remember he has spare clothes for me. Whilst I'm getting dressed, Gavin stands in the doorway, arms folded, watching me. His eyes have so much emotion behind them. He's different from the man I first met, who had been hard to read. He has lines between his eyebrows, making him appear worried, and I want to change that. I'm not some damsel in distress. I'm a strong, independent woman who knows what she wants.

Him!

Dressed just in my underwear, I walk over to him with a sway in my hips that I hope will entice him. A smirk appears on his stubbled face. I like the roughness of the hairs on my palm and in other places. I stand close to him, slowly wrapping my arms around his waist. Raising on my tiptoes, I kiss him. I can feel him holding back. I pull away, gazing up at him.

"Jess, you're recovering," he says in a flat but warm tone.

"This is recovery." I smile at him.

I pull him into a kiss that he can't refuse. He grabs my waist, dragging me towards him so hard that I lose a bit of my breath. *This* is what I need! I wrap my arms around his neck and jump to wrap my legs around his waist. I can feel him responding. He carries me to the bed and lays me down gently.

All I want is him, but instead, he kisses me and covers me with a blanket. He chuckles as I roll my eyes at him. "The doctor says you need to rest, so rest is all that's on the agenda, no matter how much you wiggle those hips at me." Defeated, I raise myself up on my elbows and kiss him on the cheek.

"Thank you for taking care of me. I think a rest sounds just what I need, although…." I waggle my eyebrows, even though my head hurts. I lay back down as Gavin tucks me in.

"I'll go and make us something to eat. Close your eyes for a while, Jess."

I wake up what feels like minutes later to the smell of tomatoes and garlic coming from the kitchen. My head is feeling a little lighter, but I can still feel the pain in the back of it. I slip on some comfy clothes and head down to the kitchen. Gavin smiles at me, and as I look at the clock, I realise I slept for just over three hours.

Gavin has cooked me a lovely lunch of lasagne and garlic bread. We sit and eat at the breakfast bar and then head over to the sofa. I put on the TV and notice the glare still hurts my head. Gavin turns the brightness down and chooses a film. I curl up and fall asleep, listening to *Aquaman* in the background.

The next couple of weeks consist of me resting, slowly regaining my strength and stamina when it comes to screens, and at the end of the two weeks I've been signed off work, I feel much better. Gavin has split working in the office and at home during this time to keep an eye on my recovery, which is so sweet. I feel guilty for not doing anything, but at the same time, it's nice to relax and be looked after.

Chapter Forty-Five

JESS

After a couple weeks of relaxing and recuperating at Gavin's, I'm back in the office on Monday morning. Gavin left before me, wanting to catch up. I walk into my office and see flowers on my desk and Paul leaning against it with a coffee from my favourite shop.

"Good morning, sunshine! Nice to see you're recovered and back to work," he says with a big grin on his face.

"I was off for two weeks. It was a nasty bump on the head, but I managed to finish the documents from Pierre." I give him a grin whilst taking my coffee and sitting at my desk. "Well, I'm ready when you are. Gavin has had to go out for a meeting, so it'll just be us going through this, if that's okay?"

"Absolutely! We need space. Boardroom?" After a few hours of showing Paul my findings, he sits back and lets out a deep breath. "Even in this cutthroat world, this is underhanded. How do you propose we respond then, Jess?"

I show him my revised documents to send over to Pierre and suggest we have a meeting to discuss further rather than waste time and energy checking all documentation with a fine-tooth comb. I want the opportunity to prove I can handle this, but I also know Pierre would only work with Gavin. The legal team has approved my amendments. Once we've gone through the details, our legal teams can draft the contracts.

"Right then. I'll leave this with you. You are more than capable. I would suggest taking either myself or Gavin to the meeting with Pierre, though. Not because I think you can't handle him, it's more that I don't trust the slimy guy."

I sit back, satisfied. I email Pierre the revised document and suggest some dates to meet. Walking back to my office, I sit down and look around. It's still so new to me, having my own office. It needs some decorating. I put a note in my calendar to look at paints and maybe add some plants that I'll forget to water.

As I start going through my emails and looking at CVs for my replacement, my phone rings. My mum. Crap! I didn't tell her I was in the hospital. I didn't want her to worry. "Hey, Mum! How are you?"

"Hello, dear. We're heading into town this evening and wanted to meet for dinner if you're free?"

"Sounds amazing. Text me the details, and I'll be there."

Mum sends through the restaurant booking half an hour later, and my mouth starts watering. How is it nearly lunchtime? I pick up my bag and wander down to the local sandwich shop. I really fancy a ham salad sandwich. Boring, but it's tickling my fancy.

On my walk, I feel eyes on me. It takes me back to the night I was attacked. Panic is rising within me, and I duck into the sandwich shop and look out to see if there's anyone following me or whether it's my imagination.

The lady behind the counter makes me jump when she speaks to me. "You okay, love? You look like you need to sit down." She comes round and sits me at a table. I say I'm okay and just felt a panic attack coming on. She takes my order and brings it over to me. "On the house, love. Take care of yourself. You're always welcome to stay in here until it passes." As much as I want to just sit there, I can't let the fear consume me.

It's then I clock him. Jack, Gavin's security officer. He's following me. He catches my eye and hangs his head. I walk out to him and whack him on the shoulder. "What are you doing? You made me feel like I was being stalked!"

"Mr Andrews didn't want you to know we were still around, but we're here to ensure your safety. I'm sorry I made you feel worried. Can I escort you back to the office now that you know I'm here?"

On our walk back, Jack explains about Sacha being in Gavin's apartment. He says he and John are always around to be on the safe side. Walking into my office, I tell him to take a seat.

"Well, now that we're both on the same page, we may as well come up with some ground rules. Let me know when you're around. That goes for John, too! I don't want to feel paranoid. If you're hanging around the office, you may as well sit somewhere comfortable. How long will this 'protection' be going on for?"

"Noted, Miss Freeman, and I'm not sure. We have an ongoing contract with Mr Andrews."

After Jack leaves my office, I decide I'll text Gavin to see how he is. I haven't seen him since this morning.

Me: Out getting a sandwich and I spy with my little eye, somebody resembling Jack.

Gavin: Crap, he was meant to keep out of sight.

Me: Well it's better I know rather than feeling paranoid that someone is watching me.

Gavin: Sorry, I should have told you.

Me: You ok? Not seen you all morning.

Gavin: At the police station. I will update later.

I leave it. It sounds like there is more drama to do with Sacha, and I don't want to think about all that right now. I have a response from Pierre and agree to a meeting on one condition: I go to Paris this time. A shiver of excitement goes through me. I'm going to Paris! Eek!

I message Paul to let him know. He clears his calendar for those dates, and I book our tickets and hotel rooms. I think it will be a good opportunity to get to know Gavin's best friend better, and with how Pierre was last time, I don't want Gavin going all alpha in a meeting.

I'm going to Paris. I start making a note of everything I want to take and make sure I have some free time to shop whilst there.

Chapter Forty-Six

GAVIN

Sitting in the police station being interviewed or rather interrogated by the detective isn't my idea of a good Monday. I was called in to discuss my past with Sacha. I explain everything down to her cheating on me and me breaking things off, then our last encounters in the bar and her turning up at my apartment. I'm questioned about our relationship, how it ended, had I ever abused her mentally or physically, and the list goes on.

In the end, I advised them she manipulated a concierge in my building to gain access to my apartment, found my safe room code, and physically attacked my current girlfriend out of jealousy. The detective explains the questions are a mere formality. I'm asked if I have any idea if Sacha is mentally ill. I say no. I honestly don't know. She has always been dramatic, moody, and obsessive in our relationship, but she is the one who cheated, and I have no tolerance for that.

During an interview break, I receive a message from Jess. Guilt flows through me as she's discovered I've kept security on without telling her. It wasn't my intention. With everything going on, I did forget to tell her, but that's not an excuse. She was clearly panicked by it, and I'm not surprised after the attack. I say I'll update her later on the police investigation.

When the detective comes back from our break, he advises that there are no further questions. They will be pursuing a guilty verdict on the attack, which they have in spades as she confessed, but they will need to tread carefully as the psychiatrist that assessed Sacha advises that she's mentally unstable. This could mean that she would need to get treatment and have a reduced sentence.

When I leave the station, I feel deflated but happy this ordeal is being put to bed. I message Paul to advise I'm driving back to the office so we can catch up. The last few days have been hectic, and I need some normality. When I arrive, he's sitting at my desk with lunch and a couple of coffees. What did I do to deserve such a good friend?

I update Paul on the latest events and what happened at the police station, and we get to talking about work. Normality. "So, we need to get together to go through the Pierre situation and our strategy," I say, eating my meatball sub.

"Well, we don't, actually. Jess has finalised the documents. We've discussed everything this morning, and she's come up with a strategy." Although I knew she was good, this is outstanding; however, I still feel a little putout. "We're heading to Paris to meet with Pierre next week to discuss further. He seems more than happy to meet with Jess."

"We? You're going to Paris with my girlfriend?" I laugh. "Surely I should be accompanying her?"

"You could, but could you keep your cool in the meetings and meals with him letching over her?" Paul's eyebrows are raised, mocking me, but I know he's right. Paul going with Jess gives her the backup if she needs it, and he is the Finance Manager, after all. This is a game of figures, and his game to play.

When we've finished going over their plan, I'm satisfied everything has been covered and under control. It's Paul's turn to update on all personal matters.

"You remember the redhead from the bar last month?" I nod, sitting back and drinking my coffee. "Well, we've been seeing each other for a few weeks now, and I think I might be catching feelings."

I lean forward and spit my coffee across my desk, laughing. "Catching? It's not a cold!" I'm laughing so hard my stomach hurts, although I feel guilty for laughing at my friend who is trying to open up. It feels good to laugh.

"Oh, Paul. I'm sorry, man. But the way you worded it was hilarious. Tell me about her." I sit back again and put my coffee down, just in case.

"Well, thank you for making me feel welcome to open up to you," he jests, but I can tell that stung a little. I let him continue. "Red's name is Sophie. She's an architect for a company in town. Funny, intelligent, beautiful and fantastic in bed, but the thing that's surprised me the most is she makes me laugh. We can chat for hours, and it doesn't feel like a chore. I've not had this before. It feels...I don't know, strange, exciting. I feel like I could spend eternity with her and not get bored. You know?"

I listen to my friend, who has indeed "caught" feelings. Strange for him. He is a proud bachelor, but this is wonderful to hear. He sounds happy. He's telling me about their date nights. He's cooked for her, which is a miracle in itself as he's a terrible cook. But he bought one of those boxes that send you all the ingredients, and he's learning. I'm not going to offer any form of advice, considering my crazy ex has just attacked my girlfriend, but I'll listen.

"She, naturally, wants to meet you, being my best friend and all. I've met her friends, and they seem lovely. I'm nearly a hundred per cent sure they all went to the bathroom to discuss me, but considering that was last week and we're still seeing each other, I must have made a good impression. So, when are you free?"

I raise an eyebrow. It's been a long time since I've been a wingman of any sort. "How about we make a date for after Paris? I can bring Jess along and make it a double date."

He nods and gets out his phone to text Sophie—I assume. All this talk of 'catching' feelings makes me want to go and see Jess. I ping her a text to see if she's busy in half an hour so we can meet for a coffee. I get an instant reply, saying she's free as she's caught up. This girl. She's going to be taking over the business in no time!

After Paul goes back to his office, I call in on Jess to take her down the street for coffee. To my surprise, Jack sits in a nice comfy-looking chair that has appeared outside her office door, reading the paper. Not quite out of sight, but this has Jess written all over it.

"Mr Andrews." He promptly stands. "There was an incident earlier where Miss Freeman saw me and requested I keep in sight. I believe she may have had a panic attack when she felt she was being watched." I nod in agreement. Jess will undoubtedly have anxiety after the other night, so she can handle security however she sees fit. My attention goes to the chair. Where did that come from? "Miss Freeman also ordered a chair for me so I could sit outside her office." Chuckling, I go into her office.

And there she is, sitting at her desk, deep in thought about something. I would rule the world with this woman.

Chapter Forty-Seven

JESS

Gavin and I go for a walk down to the local coffee shop for some air and for him to catch me up on today. I'm not shocked Sacha is mentally ill, but will she try to turn it around to blame Gavin? I don't want to entertain that thought for long. We then get chatting about Paris and how he originally felt shunned from the project but then proud that I'd done everything in such detail.

Whilst we are out, I would have loved to have held his hand, but we are still being careful around the office. I'm pretty sure people will guess if they look close enough, though.

I catch him up on my day and my plans for the evening. My stomach rumbles, thinking about dinner tonight. I look at Gavin, wondering if he'd like to join or whether this is all too new for the whole "meet your parents" thing. He doesn't really speak about his parents. Before I allow my brain to take over, I ask him, "Would you like to join us tonight?"

At the same time, he says, "Jack will be there. I can make sure he's out of sight so your parents won't worry." Gavin doesn't want to come. That's fair enough. I mean, it's not even been a week. I still feel a little sad.

He stares at me with those beautiful brown eyes, boring into my soul. "I would love to come and have dinner, but you haven't seen your parents in a while, and it would be good for you to catch up. And honestly? I'm exhausted and could do with a nice hot shower and an early night. Jack can bring you back to mine afterwards if you like."

And with that, everything feels better. Smiling at the thought of going back to his apartment again, it feels more like home than my own flat does. But then his penthouse is a thousand times bigger.

I MEET MUM AND DAD AT WAGAMAMA'S IN SHEPHERDS Bush. Jack comes in behind me and has a seat to himself, making sure it doesn't look like he is with me. I feel safer knowing he's there, but it feels a little ostentatious having my own security.

Mum is full of news of the family, neighbours, those aunties and uncles you have growing up that aren't related but just good family friends that you barely remember. Dad sits there, trying to make sense of the menu. Knowing his tastes, I recommend Katsu to him. Mum orders Ramen, and I decide on the Teriyaki Soba. We also order some dumplings, sides and drinks before the conversation turns to me.

"How's life as the tough CEO's PA? I hope he's treating you well and not having you work all hours," my dad asks, straight to the point.

"I'm not the PA anymore." Before I can finish my sentence, he's ranting on about work/life balance and men thinking they can treat young women a certain way. I love my dad to pieces. He always wants what's best for me and doesn't want me treated unfairly. I take a sip of my drink and go about setting this record straight.

"Well, Dad, I was a great PA. So great that the CEO and Finance Manager decided my talents were wasted and promoted me to Business Manager. I'm now in charge of the company projects. My first one is underway, and I'm travelling to Paris next week to deal with a dodgy client." It sounds so matter-of-fact, but actually, that's the way it is.

My parents are beaming. My mum is practically squealing in delight. "Oh, my clever daughter! You'll be running the place in no time. Are you happy? It's not too stressful?"

"No, Mum. I'm happy. I'm doing something I really enjoy, and I'm good at it."

We talk further about my office, pay raise, and how well I've been treated. My parents are proud of me, and I feel a huge swell of emotion.

"So, any man in your life?" *Subtle as a brick, Mum.*

"Well, actually…." I think she's going to fall off the

bench; she reacts that fast. After Kyle, I wasn't really interested in relationships. I wanted to progress myself before falling in love.

My dad puts his hand on her arm. "Now, dear, how about you let your brilliant daughter talk and not start planning grandchildren just yet." He chuckles, but I know she's already picking out nursery colours.

"His name is Gavin. He's smart, successful, kind, caring and makes me happy. It's all new, so there are no 'labels' yet, but I'm excited about where this could possibly lead. Things seem to be falling into place." I don't mention he's my boss; I don't want that conversation just yet.

Mum shoots a million questions at me, most of which I answer simply without too much detail. Not avoiding the conversation, but I don't want to jinx what has just begun. She asks about the bruising on my face. Not wanting to tell them about the accident, I spin a story about being clumsy and falling in the bathroom. Thankfully, this is accepted.

Satisfied that their daughter is happy in life, progressing in a career she enjoys and has the possibility of love on the table—I don't want to let on that I've fallen hard for Gavin—they don't ask for more. Dad talks about the gossip at the golf club, Mum carries on talking about the new neighbours across the street, and we finish our meal.

I try to pay for dinner, but my dad, being proud, wants to treat me for doing well at work, which is lovely. When we are outside, they flag down a taxi and head home. Both ask how I'm getting home. Luckily, my friend Jack is in the area and is going to give me a lift, saving me from getting a taxi on my own at this time of night. They don't need to know the drama. They are happy knowing I'm happy.

On our way back to Gavin's, Jack comments on how nice my parents seem. I ask him about his life. Since we're spending a lot of time together, I know nothing other than his name. Jack has a fiancé, George. They're going through the adoption process so they can have a family. Both sets of parents are supportive of their marriage and adoption. They live in Surrey and recently bought a nice house with a garden for their family to grow in. It all sounds beautiful.

Time goes by quickly, and before I realise it, we are pulling into the car park for Gavin's place. We go up in the lift, and John takes over for the night. I bid Jack a good night, say hi to John and go in. When I open the door, it's eerily quiet. Normally, there's music, the TV or something in the background. I take my coat and shoes off and head into the bedroom. There he is, looking handsome and fast asleep. He is exhausted. I go into the bathroom to brush my teeth, slip out of my clothes and get into bed.

Within minutes, he's wrapped around me, and I fall asleep.

Chapter Forty-Eight

JESS

Paul and I are on the plane heading to Paris. Since the company is paying, Paul insisted on getting first class tickets. It's lush, sitting up front. This is definitely how the other half lives. I have my earphones in, listening to a true crime podcast whilst tucking into the meal they provided.

The flight is lovely. I feel very posh sitting in first class. I could get used to this. When we land, a car takes us to our hotel. We check in and go to our rooms to freshen up before meeting in an hour for dinner. We aren't meeting Pierre until tomorrow, so it gives us time to relax and enjoy a bit of the city.

I walk into my room and am immediately taken aback. It's beautiful. The decorations, the furniture, the view…I'm sure it's the same size as my flat. I place my case on the floor in the dressing area and explore. Walking into the bathroom, my eyes fall on the gorgeous bath. I'm so happy we're here for a couple of days. I don't want to leave this room.

After unpacking my suitcase, I make a coffee and have a quick shower to freshen up for dinner. There is a knock at the door, which makes me jump. I wrap my robe around me tightly and peek through the spy hole. Room service? I haven't ordered anything.

I open the door a little, and the older gentleman smiles at me. "Good evening, Miss Freeman. I have a delivery for you." He comes into the room and places a vase with roses on the coffee table, a box of fancy-looking chocolates, and a dress box that's placed on my bed. I give the nice man a tip when he leaves and go to see who they are from.

The chocolates are a gift from the hotel, the roses are from Gavin, and the box has no note on it. I open it to find the most beautiful dress. It's a classic little black dress with beautiful floral detail down one side. A note inside tells me everything.

A powerful dress for a powerful woman.
Knock 'em dead, beautiful.
~G
xx

I hang the dress up in the wardrobe, admiring it whilst getting ready to meet Paul. How did I land such a thoughtful guy? Smiling, I walk out of the room and meet Paul for dinner.

We eat at a little restaurant near the hotel, chatting

comfortably about work. Paul tells me about Sophie, who I'm apparently meeting next week. I'm excited to meet her. She sounds nice. Walking back to the hotel, I can feel he has something on his mind. "Okay, mister, out with it," I jest, but I want him to feel comfortable talking to me.

"You and Gavin fell so fast, but you both know it's right. How? I need a woman's perspective on this."

"I can't describe it. You just know. You want to spend all of your time with them. They make you feel safe, happy and, as cliché as it sounds, whole!"

He nods and keeps walking. I think he's falling hard. I'm not going to push for more details. When we get back to the hotel, we decide on a time to meet for breakfast, and the hotel books our taxi for the morning. All that's left for tonight is sleep, and I literally can't wait to jump into that bed.

We arrive at Pierre's office at nine o'clock. I feel confident in my new dress. I hold my head high, ready to smash this meeting.

We meet Pierre in his boardroom, which has a stunning view of the Eiffel Tower. Paul wants me to lead the meeting, and he will chip in with his parts. After we sit down and are bought our coffees by his PA, we start.

"Young Jess, you are looking more radiant than ever."

I try to hide the shiver that goes through me. This guy gives me the creeps. "Thank you. Did you get my revised documents?" I want to remain professional as possible so we can get through this. I plan to look in the shops after this meeting to find a nice gift for Gavin, and Paul wants to get some nice jewellery for Sophie.

"Firstly, congratulations on your promotion. Well deserved! I did see the revised document. You can't blame a man for trying to gain more of a company he's investing in." He doesn't even look sorry or ashamed that he'd been caught trying to gain more shares.

We sit through the meeting, and I'm on fire. We agree on the terms I had written out, and when all done and dusted, we stand to leave. I'm starving and want lunch before shopping. We are heading back tomorrow.

Pierre comes over to me with a greasy smile on his face, puts his arm around my waist and pulls me closer to whisper in my ear, "If you want a tour guide on your last night, I can show you a night you won't forget."

I pull out of his hold in disgust. "Thank you, Pierre. However, I have a boyfriend and would like to get back to him without your scent on me."

He chuckles and shrugs his shoulders. With that, we leave.

Shopping with Paul is fun. We have a lovely lunch in a quaint French café and walk around the shops. He finds a beautiful necklace for Sophie, and I'm stumped about what to get for Gavin. What do you get the man who has everything?

Walking back to the hotel, I feel deflated. We then walk past a lingerie shop, and I have an idea. I dive in without Paul and find something completely outside of my comfort zone. The ladies in the shop are more than happy to dress me up in their expensive lingerie. After spending a small fortune and feeling rather happy with myself, I go back to the hotel room for a nice hot bath and relax before dinner.

That evening, after climbing into bed, I text Gavin.

Me: Can't wait to see you tomorrow. xx

Chapter Forty-Nine

GAVIN

Jess has been away for a couple of days, and I've missed her. Tonight, I'm going out with a friend for dinner, and when she gets home, I want to make our relationship official so the world knows she's mine and I'm hers.

I'm just about to wrap up for the day when my phone rings. Mum. "Hi, Mum. How are you?"

"I'm well. Thanks, Gavin. How are you? Paul rang me last week. You know, he calls me more than you do?"

I chuckle. Paul has always been my mum's favourite. I'm an only child, and yet, my friend has a better relationship with my mother. But then, I don't always make an effort to call her. Or see her. And she's only an hour's drive away.

"I'm okay, Mum. I've actually been meaning to call. I have someone I'd like you to meet."

The line is silent….

"Mum?"

I hear her sigh. "It's not that god awful Sacha girl, is it?

I laugh. One of the problems with being successful is everyone wants to know your business. According to some sleazy magazine, I'd run away to get married last year. I had a very angry mother on the phone with that incident.

"No. She's sweet, kind, beautiful, and I'm completely and utterly in love with her."

I can hear my mum getting choked up on the other end of the phone. "Mum, I'll bring her down in the next couple of weeks to meet you and Dad. How's that?"

"It's about time, Gavin. Are you going to marry this one and *finally* give me grandbabies?"

I laugh hard. *Straight to the point, as always, Mother.* "We'll see. I want to spend the rest of my life with her and give you a whole rugby team of grandbabies."

Her excitement emits through the phone with her voice raised and chattering in happiness. We catch up over the trivial stuff and end with me promising to call her with a date soon for her to meet Jess. I can't help but smile. She's going to absolutely love Jess.

I WALK INTO THE RESTAURANT ACROSS TOWN TO MEET an old friend. We haven't caught up for years. Sarah is successful, the CEO of her own care company, and beautiful. There's never been anything between us.

We're like brother and sister. We met at a bar one night, chatted for hours and kept in touch.

We catch up on each other's lives, and just like my mother, Sarah is ecstatic to hear about Jess. She wants every single detail. When it comes to ordering drinks, I find it odd that she just orders soda water with lime. Sarah has always had a drink when we catch up.

"What's with the boring juice?"

She laughs whilst sipping it. You can tell the drink isn't great by her grimace.

"Well, Gavin, I have a little secret. I've been seeing this guy for over a year. We're really happy."

I raise an eyebrow. I'm ecstatic for her, but something else is going on. Then her hand goes to her stomach.

"Oh, Sarah! I'm so excited for you!!" I grab her hand, squeezing it tight. Sarah was told from a young age that she wouldn't be able to get pregnant, so this is the best news ever.

Chapter Fifty

JESS

When we are on the plane home, I sit in my own thoughts, and I know I'm completely in love with Gavin already, but it's too soon to tell him. I must have fallen asleep as, before I know it, we're landing.

I'M STANDING IN MY FLAT SURROUNDED BY CLOTHES. I've chosen a black lace body suit with a matching garter belt and stockings, one of the few sets I bought in Paris. I've got my nice new heels that make my legs and ass look amazing. Now for the dress. I can't go like this.

I choose a dress that's red in the middle and black panelling on the sides that gives the illusion of an hour-glass. It's apparently meant to make me look slimmer. I do my hair up with some curls hanging down.

Feeling satisfied with how I look, I order my Uber.

If you'd told me a few months ago I'd be dressed like this, I wouldn't believe you. I live in baggy clothes to hide my size, but I have a man who makes me feel like the most attractive woman on the planet, and I'm starting to feel it a little myself.

When I arrive at the office, I head up to our floor to see him before the party. I've missed his face. I notice his door is ajar, and I begin to step in but stop when I hear him on the phone. I knock on his door and open it a little more.

"I'll call you later," he says and hangs up. Gavin's eyes are full of fire as he gets up and walks over to me. No words, just staring into my eyes with such passion. He pushes me up against the wall hard and kisses me. His hands roam over my body, and I want to ask him questions, but oh my god, this man makes me melt.

When we finally come up for air, he stands back and looks me up and down. "My god, Jess, you look…." I smile when he can't finish the sentence.

He leads me over to the sofa and catches me up on what happened whilst I was in Paris.

"My friend Sarah wants to meet you. She practically screamed the restaurant down when I told her how I felt about you. I'm completely head over heels in love with you, Jess. I know we have not been together long, but this…." He moves his hand between us. "This is something real, and I want to spend the rest of my life with you."

Holy fuck! Don't just stare at him. Tell him you love him back! I can't move. I'm just gaping at him. He loves me? He fucking loves me. Within a millisecond, I close the gap between us, lift my dress and straddle him. Grabbing his face in my hands, I kiss him with everything I have. I can feel his reaction. He's already getting hard. He pulls me closer, grabs my hips and grinds me against him. His hands are roaming all over me until he unzips my dress.

I finally come up for air, drop my feet to the ground to stand on my own and let my dress fall to the floor. His jaw falls so fast that I'm concerned he dislocated it. Exactly the reaction I want. He stands, locks his office door and stalks over to me. His hands and eyes are everywhere.

"Jess, you look phenomenal." I can't help my big, goofy smile.

"Well, Mr Andrews, this is one of three I bought for you."

"Good job. They won't fit me. They look much better on you." He laughs but can't stop staring. He's now moved back from me, and with a hand on his chin and a smirk on his face, it looks like Gavin is enjoying the view.

I can see his trousers tent and am surprised he's not in pain. His eyes go deliciously dark as he unbuttons his shirt. I strut over, feeling like a million dollars, undo his trousers, and as they drop to the floor, I push him back onto the sofa.

Kneeling between his legs, I spread his thick thighs. I pull down the waistband of his boxers to free him. Gazing into his eyes, I lick the precum off the top of his cock and take him into my mouth, my eyes not leaving his. He slides his fingers into my hair and grips my head, guiding the pace with his head thrown back. His moans make me want to please him more. My head bobs up and down. I take more of him until he holds my head still.

"Up," he commands. I stand as he slides my body-suit to one side and inserts two fingers. The roughness and urgency of it make me gasp and grab his shoulders. I can feel my legs wanting to give way already. "Oh my, Miss Freeman, you are wet and ready for me." And in one swift movement, he grabs my hips and yanks me down on him.

Oh god, it's only been a couple of days, but I feel like it's the first time with him. He pauses whilst I stretch around his size.

When he feels I'm ready, he bucks his hips and thrusts deep, My head is thrown back, and pleasure is coursing through my veins. Within minutes, I'm convulsing around him. He pulls me down rough and hard, over and over, until I feel him come inside me. When his cock has finished twitching, he grabs the back of my head and kisses me with everything he has.

"I love you, too," I breathe, resting against his body.

Chapter Fifty-One

GAVIN

After the mind-blowing sex in my office, we head down to catch a cab to the Christmas party. I don't normally stay long at these things, but this year is different. I want to be here with Jess.

She loves me!

We arrive at Tower Hotel, making it look like we arrived separately. I mingle around the room, chatting with the staff, and my eyes keep drifting to her. I'm sure someone will notice, but at this moment, I didn't care. I'm talking with the HR crowd, and Carol's getting a little too tipsy and a little too close. She keeps brushing my arm and giggling at what I'm saying. I'm not trying to be funny. I can see Jess's amusement from across the room whilst she catches up with the admin team.

The evening is going well. I'm standing near the bar when Carol approaches me, slurring, "Mr Andrews, it really has been a pleasure working for you all these years." She takes a moment to steady herself. I chuckle at her attempt at flirting. She then brushes her hand against my leg, which is certainly inappropriate. "Mr…Gavin, I'm going to be straight with you. You are foremost the most handsome man I've ever laid my eyes on." She's now swaying. I put my hand on her shoulder to steady her. "I think we could have sooo much fun." Her drunkenness is a little worrying. The party only started an hour ago.

"Carol, thank you for your kind words. However, I'm taken." She steps back and nearly knocks the beer bottles to the floor. I get her a glass of water and walk her over to the seating area. "I think you may need a few glasses of water to sober up and maybe something to eat?" She looks at me sheepishly, and one of her colleagues comes over to take over the babysitting.

By the end of the night, everyone is very drunk and singing Christmas songs at the top of their lungs. I'm getting a headache. I sneak off to a quiet seating area in the corner to take some painkillers and have some quiet time before the party ends. I'll be taking Jess home tonight and giving her many orgasms for wearing that underwear.

I'm sitting in the quietness of the corner when I hear footsteps. They don't sound like Jess's, but then again, she is wearing ridiculously high heels today. As I glance towards the footsteps, I see Lucy. As if my headache isn't bad enough.

I know I'm blessed in the looks department, but it gets really tiresome being hit on all the time. Especially when women don't accept no for an answer.

Lucy walks over to me and perches on the edge of the chair I'm sitting in. "Fancy meeting you here, Gavin."

"It's the Christmas party, Lucy. Why aren't you in the bar?"

"You've avoided me all night, and now I get a chance to have you all to myself." She leans over to close the gap between us.

A shadow appears in my peripheral vision, and I see a pure vision of power and beauty. Holding herself in a strong, powerful position, Jess saunters over, stopping behind my chair and placing her hand on my shoulder, sending a strong signal to Lucy to back off.

"I'm sorry, but Mr Andrews isn't available for private meetings." I can feel her nerves through our touch, but damn, my girl is holding strong, defending her territory.

Lucy's face is an absolute picture of shock and horror. "My apologies. I didn't get the memo," she says, struggling for words before she gets up and leaves without looking back.

"Take me home, Gavin." That look is one I will never disobey.

THE NEXT WEEK ROLLS BY QUICKLY. JESS IS RUNNING around, trying to figure out what to get people for Christmas. I'm lucky on that front. I treat my mum and dad to concert tickets every year, although bringing my girlfriend to visit my mum this weekend will be the best thing in the world for her. I am struggling with ideas for Jess, though. She doesn't want for anything.

Jess is doing fantastic in her new role. She sorted out the Pierre issues without a blink of an eye. I've passed her a few more projects. Her keen eye for detail is invaluable when looking through contracts and negotiating. I'm pleased we created this position. I would continue being overworked and not trusting anyone to help if we hadn't. I'm also so proud of how far she's come in a short time. I still can't believe admin hid her for so long.

Paul strolls into my office with ruffled hair and his tie loosened. "Mate, what's wrong?" I ask, and he flops down in front of my desk. Now, I'm worried.

"I think I love her, and I have no idea how to tell her. This is bullshit! I enjoyed sleeping with a new woman every night, but this is one I want to keep forever. I have no interest in anyone else." He rubs his face and looks me dead in the eye. "What do I do?"

We met Sophie last week, and she is wonderful. She's good for him. He's eating and sleeping better. He's happy and oh so smitten. I can tell she feels the same about him. "Tell her."

"Have you told Jess you love her?"

"Yes, when she was in hospital. I couldn't not tell her any longer, and luckily, she feels the same. So, tell Sophie how you feel."

This is a big thing for Paul. He's always loved women but has never been in love. We sit and discuss tactics as if he's going into battle. Deciding that tonight is the night, he plans to order Thai, her favourite, and tell her over dinner at home, in his comfort zone. There's no way she doesn't feel the same.

Later that night, as I cuddle up with Jess on the couch, I receive a text.

Paul: I did it

Me: And?

Paul: She just stared at me, fork mid-air, mouth open…

Me: …

Paul: After the session we just had, she admitted she feels the same!!!

Me: Thank fuck for that! Couldn't stand you being a miserable sod over Christmas!

I'm happy, my best friend is happy, and tomorrow, I'll be making my mother's entire year by taking Jess to see her.

Chapter Fifty-Two

JESS

We're going to Surrey to meet Gavin's parents today. I feel so nervous. He barely talks about them, and I have no background to go on. I'm being chucked into the deep end, and we'll see if I sink or swim.

On the drive down, I admire the countryside, absentmindedly thinking this is the place I'd like to raise children, out of the city. That thought shocks me. I've never thought about kids before. I wonder if Gavin wants kids. He probably wants someone to take over the business when he retires, not that I can ever see him retiring.

We pull up to what looks like a mansion. The size of this house is out of this world. I didn't know we had houses this big in England. I thought it was an American thing to have the house and the land. A lot of houses in England, especially in London, are terraced houses and look packed together like sardines in a tin. It has metal gates, a long gravel drive.... *Who weeds this? It's spotless.* The manicured lawns go on forever.

Gavin parks the car, and the butterflies are playing dodgeball in my stomach. "You'll be fine. My mum is excited to meet you. Don't worry." My nerves calm a little as he takes my hand and leads me to the front door. *Jesus Christ, this house is the size of a village!*

We step into a foyer, which looks like a hotel. There's a centre table with immaculate flowers, the walls are a neutral cream colour with expensive-looking art hanging on them, and the floor has some super shiny massive tiles. This place is pure wealth, and I'm reminded that I'm not only dating and in love with a CEO but someone who comes from money.

The butterflies are back.

We walk into the kitchen, which is the size of a football field. The space is huge but feels warm and welcoming. A lady is standing in an old-fashioned apron. She dusts her hands as she turns. "Gavin! Come give your mother a kiss!" When she pulls him in for a cuddle, she's a good half a foot shorter than Gavin. She looks elegant and classy but also warm and loving. Julia is a curvy woman with warm brown hair and those lovely brown eyes that Gavin has. She's wearing a flowing flower-patterned skirt and a white blouse tucked into it. I smile at their embrace, especially as he now has flour or something on his jeans.

Dusting himself off, he turns to grab my hand again. "Mum, I'd like you to meet Jess. Jess, this is my mum, Julia." She looks at me with warmth in her eyes and hugs me. She's nice. "Jess, welcome to our home and family. I can't tell you how happy I am to meet you."

Julia continues to talk whilst she cooks. Whatever she's making, my stomach is rumbling for it. She brings out snacks and drinks, sits us down and talks nonstop for almost half an hour. "Jess dear, tell me about yourself. Gavin has been very quiet on that front."

I tell Julia about my family, my work, and how Gavin and I met. I practically tell her my whole life story in twenty minutes. She smiles throughout and asks more questions. Gavin is sitting there smiling and running his thumb across my knuckles. As we're talking about favourite holidays as a child, I can hear the door open, and a man walks in. I'm assuming this is Gavin's dad as he looks exactly like Gavin, just older and also very handsome. I can see where Gavin gets his looks.

"Gavin boy!" Gavin stands and embraces his dad, and I smile. I don't know what I imagined, but the amount of warmth in this house makes me feel relaxed. "Dad, this is Jess. Jess, this is my dad, Daniel." His father brings me in for a strong hug. They are a huggy family.

"Take a seat, dear. I do hope you bought something more sensible to wear for dinner." He laughs as I look down at my jeans. Now I'm worried that I'm underdressed. "You'll be waddling out of here. Should have worn something stretchy. Julia's a feeder."

I giggle, surprised at how relaxed I feel around

them. They don't come across as people who have lots of money. They're not intimidating in the slightest. They're warm, loving and relaxed.

Daniel wasn't lying. My stomach feels stretched to capacity. I'm so full I feel like I could slip into a food coma. The day is wonderful. We talk, sit and watch a film after lunch. *Probably because no one could move.* After, we go for a nice walk around the grounds, where I discover they have a duck pond. I have no idea why that makes me so happy, but it does.

On the drive home, I feel like I've been a part of the family for years. "Your parents are lovely. Thank you for taking me to meet them." Gavin smiles proudly as he drives us back to his. "Why the huge house? There were just the three of you there?" Whilst I was given a lot of the family history, I can't help but wonder why they have a ten-bedroom house.

"Mum wanted a big family. There were complications during my birth, and she had to have an emergency hysterectomy and couldn't have any more children. They looked into adoption and fostering, but they didn't go forward with it. It makes me sad knowing they wanted more children, but now that Mum's met you, she'll be expecting grandbabies to fill that big house." He laughs, but I have a feeling his mum may have mentioned wanting grandkids a few times whilst they were talking alone. I smile at the thought of having children with Gavin. I know his mum will be a doting grandmother. Mine will also be, but something tells me Julia craves having kids in the house again.

By the time we get home, we are both too full for any kind of shenanigans. His mother really is a feeder. I text my mum to arrange a day with her and Dad so they can meet Gavin. I've not told them much about him yet. It's been such a whirlwind. I've gone from not wanting a man in my life and trying to progress my career to having the most amazing man and having a new job. It's unbelievable that this has happened over the space of a few months.

I've changed within myself. I'm no longer hiding my body in baggy clothes. I'm buying nice clothes that suit my figure. My hair is even brushed every day now and not shoved up into a bun or ponytail. I'm taking better care of myself, and I have Gavin to thank for that. Firstly, for giving me a job that required me to look better, but then for falling hopelessly in love with me for being who I am.

Sitting beside him with a goofy grin on my face, he looks at me. "What's making you smile, Miss Freeman? Puppies on Facebook again?" He chuckles, and I do happen to have a video of puppies open.

"You, Mr Andrews. You make me happy." I sound soppy, but I don't care.

"How do you feel about announcing our relationship? I want to announce to the world that you're mine."

His.

"I don't know. I've never had to make an announcement before. Does this mean I can't go out to the shop for ice cream in my joggers anymore?" I laugh, but then it hits me. Announcing our relationship publicly means I'll be in the media's eye as well.

"We'll go over the details tomorrow, but now that my stomach has deflated, I'm taking my woman to bed." With a devilish look in his eye, he grabs my hand and leads me to the bedroom.

Chapter Fifty-Three

GAVIN

Christmas is in two days' time. I have wracked my brain about what to get Jess, and I think I know what I want to give her. She's had my heart, so I want to give her keys to my penthouse, hoping she'll move in with me. Part of me is saying it's too soon, but I know I want to spend the rest of my life with this woman. When you know, you know, right?

I finalise the announcement for my solicitor to go over and release to the press. I don't want speculation in the press about us; I want to set the record straight. Miss Jessica Freeman is mine.

We're spending Christmas with our families, and then I'm going to be meeting her family on Boxing Day, and the day after, we're at my parents, and then I get her to myself for a couple of days before New Year's. I'm not sure why, but I feel a little nervous about meeting Jess's parents. They are regular people, and I am a good man. They should want the best for her.

I've done my research and found her mum's favourite flowers and her dad's favourite scotch. I want to make this woman my wife; therefore, hitting it off with the parents is a good idea.

When I head out for my morning stroll with Paul, I go into one of the gift shops and find a keyring for Jess's present. "You're really only getting her a key for Christmas? No bracelet or something to go with it?" Paul laughs.

"You should know Jess doesn't do much jewellery. Showering her with expensive stuff isn't going to impress. She did see some nice earrings the other day, though. I might get her those to go with the key."

Satisfied with the simple diamond earrings I thought she'd like and her keyring of the London skyline, I pop them in my pocket to give to her later. Walking back to the office, I see Paul eyeing up the jewellery shops. "What are you getting, Sophie?"

"I have no idea. She doesn't need or want anything. What can I get her? I don't want to keep buying her jewellery." I can't help but laugh. He's right. It's so hard to buy for women, and yet, they say it's men who are hard to buy for.

"When we met her, Jess noticed her laptop case appeared a bit tired. How about getting her a new one? Aspinal is just down the road. They have some beautiful stuff. I bought Jess one as a congratulations present."

We walk into Aspinal of London, and he finds a beautiful burgundy leather case. He ends up buying a matching notebook and a nice pen with it, too. You can never buy too much stationery for a woman. Happy with his purchases, we walk back to the office with Starbucks in our hands and smug expressions on our faces. I drop Jess's coffee into her office and see she's not there. Her phone and laptop are on her desk, so she can't be far.

It's then I notice a message on her phone. I shouldn't have looked, but I can't unsee it.

Jess: I love you more than I ever thought possible. This day and forever, I'm yours. xxx

What the hell have I just read? My stomach feels knotted, and I am hurt. Has she been sending other people these messages? I walk out of her office fast, nearly knocking her off her feet as she walks in. The worried expression on her face hit my heart harder.

I shut my office door and sit staring at my laptop. What am I going to do? I was about to ask her to move in with me. Seconds later, there's a knock at my door, and she enters. I can feel the tension in my body, and a migraine is threatening to appear.

"Are you okay, Gavin?" She seems concerned but doesn't show any guilt at all.

"Fine, just busy. So, if you don't mind…." I sound cold.

"Well, I wanted to thank you for my coffee, and I can assume you saw my phone? Going by your body language and tone...." She raises her eyebrow and sashays over to me with her phone in hand.

I can't say anything. I stare at her. She shares her screen with my laptop from her phone, and I feel ashamed that I had thought the worst.

"And there you have it, you big lug. You've ruined your Christmas present. I am not declaring my love for anyone other than you." She kisses my forehead, stops sharing her phone and walks out of my office. She knows I have trust issues after Sacha. She has given me no reason to doubt her, and yet, I assumed she was cheating.

I dial my counsellor and have an emergency session. I don't want this wrecking my life with Jess. But I know what she has got me for Christmas. Nothing you can buy off the shelf. Something handmade, which is why she was texting the person her inscription. I'm such a fool.

Over an hour later, I feel better after speaking to my counsellor. Now, I'm going to speak to Jess. I walk to her office with my tail between my legs. I knock lightly and head in. She's just finishing a phone call and glances up at me with a beautiful smile. God, the guilt is horrendous.

"Hey, handsome!" She beams at me. I walk around her desk and kiss her. I can't find the words, but I feel them. "You don't have to apologise. I know how it looked, and with your history, I can understand how you felt." Her words are like a blanket around me. This woman is amazing.

"I don't deserve you. Most women would have flown off the handle because of how I reacted."

"Well, luckily for you, Mr Andrews, I'm not most women!" She stands and kisses me. I wrap her in my arms, never wanting to let her go. She peers up at me and grins. "If you're okay, I have a meeting in five minutes. Want to go to lunch at one o'clock?"

Looking back at Jess as I walk out of her office, I feel nothing but love and pride. This woman is amazing on every level.

Chapter Fifty-Four

JESS

Christmas morning at Mum and Dad's is the usual. Bucks fizz, toast and marmalade, coffee and then presents. Mum and Dad bought me some new shoes, a new handbag and a nice coat. They are pleased with their presents. I got them a night away in a nice hotel and tickets to Phantom of the Opera. One of their favourite musicals.

Kiera facetimes me, absolutely loving her new boots. She got me a new notebook and pen from Aspinal. She knows I love my stationary.

Gavin and I are exchanging presents tomorrow when he comes over. I text him to wish him a happy Christmas, and he says he'll call later as he's helping his mum in the kitchen. I chuckle at the thought of him in a frilly apron.

After lunch, I lay on the sofa, nursing a Christmas lunch bulge in my stomach. My god, there was so much food. My mum does love to cook. Over dinner, we talk about Gavin and me, how we met, and how it's going. Mum then starts talking about hearing wedding bells in the air. I laugh it off but really hope that one day I will be fully his.

Gavin calls just as I'm about to slip into a post-lunch nap. "Hey, beautiful. How's your day? I hope you've been spoilt?"

"Hi, handsome. I'm currently in the most unattractive state, lying on the sofa after Mum's lunch. I've had some lovely gifts. How about you?"

"Naturally, Mum bought me some socks and a jumper and happened to leave some knitting patterns about for baby clothes." His laugh is wonderful and cheery. I have a feeling Julia has already started converting one of the bedrooms into a nursery.

We talk for a while, and Gavin says he'll be driving up tonight because he can't bear another night away from me. My heart swells. This man makes me happy. I have a few hours to grab a shower and freshen up before he gets here. I let Mum and Dad know he's coming up tonight instead of in the morning. My mum starts bustling away in the kitchen to make some dinner for tonight.

"Honestly, Mum, leftovers are a tradition. He'll be happy with that."

"But this is the first time we're meeting your boyfriend. He can't have our leftovers! He's an important man in the city. What's he going to think?"

"Mum, pop some half bakes in the oven, and we'll have leftover rolls for dinner like we always do. He likes tradition and would love to be a part of ours."

She puts her hands on my shoulders and smiles. "You, my dear, have found a very good man. We've not met him yet, but I've got a good feeling about him."

Gavin arrives at just gone six o'clock in the evening. He comes in with my mum's favourite flowers and chocolates and my dad's favourite scotch. I have to pick my mum's jaw up from the floor when she sees him. I don't think she believed me about how handsome he is.

"Gavin, this is my mum, Alison, and my dad, Trevor."

"It's very nice to meet you both." He shakes hands with my dad and kisses my mum on the cheek. Things are going well so far.

We spend the evening eating, drinking and laughing. My parents have really taken to Gavin. They haven't grilled too much and are relaxed around him. I feel much better now that they've met and get on. I don't know what I'd do if they hadn't.

I nip into the kitchen to put the kettle on for a cuppa, and Mum comes in behind me. "Oh, Jess, sweetheart, he's wonderful. I'm so happy for you!" I smile warmly at her as she hugs me. "He's easy on the eyes, too!" We burst out laughing. Kyle was ordinary, nothing like Gavin at all. But she's right. Gavin is very easy on the eyes.

We spend Boxing Day playing games. We go for a nice walk after another mammoth lunch from Mum. What is it with mums and wanting to make us eat too much? When we get back in the afternoon, it's time for more presents. I sit, eagerly waiting for Gavin to open his. I didn't know what to get him. He saw the message to the inscriber but didn't know what the actual present was. I'd found this beautiful watch. He probably has loads of watches, but this one looked timeless.

Gavin finally gets around to unwrapping his present. His eyes are full of emotion when he sees the watch. It's a simple platinum strap with a skeleton watch face. There are black sapphires within the mechanism, subtle and not blingy, and of course, the back is inscribed with, '*I love you more than I ever thought possible. This day and forever, I'm yours. J xxx.*'

He leans over and kisses me. "I love it, but not as much as I love you." He puts it on and admires his new timepiece. My dad smiles at me and looks impressed with the detail of the watch, too. "Your turn!"

Gavin hands me a box with a pretty ribbon around it. I don't recognise the name on the box, but I assume it's expensive jewellery.

Opening the present, I see the stunning earrings—the ones I pointed out a while ago. Simple, elegant and breathtaking at the same time. I immediately take my current set out to wear these. I don't normally wear a lot of jewellery, but earrings are a must.

When I take out the soft sponge they were set in, something else catches my eye. A London bus keyring? Why on earth would he hide this in here? I pull it out of the box and notice it had a key on it and a fob.

"Jess, I can't stand us being apart for even one night. Move in with me?"

My breath catches in my chest. I don't know what to think. Is it too soon? But then we've barely been apart since we started seeing each other. My head is saying take it slow, but my heart apparently overrules it. "Yes," I say, slightly shocked at my answer, but his face lights up like the Blackpool Tower.

Mum goes into the kitchen to grab a bottle of champagne to celebrate our news. I can't believe I'm moving in with him. After our celebrations, we go to bed. Gavin hasn't been able to wipe that soppy grin off his face all evening.

"Are you sure this isn't too soon?" I can't help but feel pensive about it still.

"If you feel it's too soon, keep your flat, and then you have the option to go back if you need space. But honestly, Jess, my life has been turned upside down by you. You make me happier than I ever thought possible, and I'd love you to live with me. We can redecorate so that it's *our* taste and not just mine. I want us to build a future together. It's your decision, Jess. It could seem too soon by other people's standards, but we're setting our own rules here."

"Well, if I do move in, then we split the bills fifty-fifty. You can't pay for everything."

He raises his eyebrow at me. Clearly, I'm missing something. "There's no mortgage. I own the whole building. The bills are paid for with the profits from the rent I receive from other tenants, with plenty left over. There's nothing to pay for."

It suddenly occurs to me that I have no idea how rich he actually is. "Well, I'll buy the groceries then. Unless you have secret people who do that for you?" He chuckles and cocks his head. "Oh my god! You actually have people who do your shopping?" I laugh. I can't help it. This isn't something I'm going to get used to quickly.

"Jess, move in with me. You can run the house how you want to."

After a moment's thought, I wholeheartedly know my answer. "Yes, I'll move in."

Chapter Fifty-Five

GAVIN

Cloud nine doesn't have anything on how amazing I feel. It's been a week since Jess agreed to move in with me. She's moved some of her stuff and will be moving the rest this weekend. We go through the particulars of how I currently run the house. I think she forgets my wealth, which is the best thing. I know she's not with me for my money. She's with me for me. I do laugh when she realises that I have a cleaner, security in addition to John and Jack, someone who does my shopping, dry cleaning, and the list goes on. But when I've been busy running the company, the last thing I want to do is go to the supermarket for food.

Knock, knock. I'm pulled out of my head and back into my office. Paul strolls in. "When does Jess's replacement start? I'm missing having someone to talk to before I come and see your face." He laughs as he sits down in front of me.

"She's starting next week. Jess will be training Anna, and you'll have someone to talk to before bugging me. What's up, anyway? We didn't have anything scheduled for today, did we?"

"I wanted to congratulate you in person for Jess moving in and want to go for a drink tonight. Up for it?"

"It's Tuesday. Nothing on tonight, so sure. Usual place at six?" Paul grins and nods before he walks out. I wonder why he wants to go for drinks suddenly. He's been so smitten with Sophie that he's not been out in ages.

Me: Going for a drink with Paul tonight. Depending on his mood, I may not be home until late.

Jess: No worries. I'll start unpacking unless you have someone to do that for me? ;-)

Me: Haha. Well, now that you mention it…

Jess: Seriously! How many people are on your payroll? You're like a mob boss!

Me: How do you know I'm not? ;-)

Jess: Well, I best start dressing to impress your clients then! ;-) Catch ya later, handsome. x

I can't love this woman more. With that thought, I set to work, my mind wondering about what's going on with Paul.

"So, what's up, mate? You've not been out in a while since you've been with Sophie. Is everything okay between you two?"

"Honestly? She's away tonight with work, and I realised we've been together pretty much every night since we met, and I didn't want to sit at home missing her."

I throw my head back, laughing. That's insensitive, but I feel better knowing he is all right!

"Seriously? I thought something was wrong. It's okay to miss someone, you know?"

"Coming from the person who asked his girlfriend to move in with him because he couldn't stand being away from her?" He raises his eyebrows as he drinks his beer. He's right.

"Ask her to move in then. Or at least tell her how your feelings have become much stronger and that you miss her when she isn't with you."

Paul nods his head, clearly in deep thought. "I was actually going to ask her to marry me in a couple of months. She's the one, Gav. I don't want her to get away."

It's my turn to be shocked. I never thought I'd see the day when Paul would want to marry anyone. I pat him on the back with a huge grin on my face. "I'm ecstatic for you! I can't imagine you with anyone else. She is the one for you."

We drink the night away, two happy men with the right women in their lives. Something neither of us thought would happen.

I tiptoe into the penthouse as quietly as I can. We had way too many whiskey chasers tonight. I slip into the en suite to wash my face and brush my teeth. Feeling a little better, I go into the bedroom, and there she is, sleeping peacefully in my…no, *our* bed, looking sexy as hell. I know it would be rude to wake her, but I just want a little taste.

Walking over, I move the duvet from her legs and gently tease them apart, moving between them. I slip her knickers to one side and lick her slit. She tastes amazing. Wanting a little more, I part her lips and lick her up and down. She starts moaning in her sleep and widens her legs for me. I move my tongue to her clit, watching her reaction. She's still sleeping, but her breath is quickening, and her body presses into me. I slip a finger into her, wishing to make her come. Her moans are getting a little louder. I can tell she's close. Another finger in whilst my tongue is on her clit, working her until suddenly, she contracts around me, coming hard.

Her breathing is harsh. "Gavin?"

"Hey, baby. I couldn't resist you whilst you looked so sexy in *our* bed."

She smiles at me. "Pervert!" She reaches up to kiss me. I grab her waist and bring her on top of me. Jess grinds down onto me, making me harder for her. She reaches down and takes me out of my boxers, moves her knickers to one side and slides onto me with her hands on my chest and her head thrown back as she stretches around my shaft.

"Oh, baby. You're tight!"

She moves slowly at first, and then as she gets more comfortable, she quickens her pace. Her moans are delectable. I sit up so that we're face to face, one hand around her waist and the other steadying me on the bed. I know what she wants, and I'm going to give it to her.

I start pumping hard and fast, just how she likes it. I can feel her arousal. She's getting close. Her lips find mine, and as I'm about to come, she comes around my cock and squeezes me tightly. I come with her. Her body fully relaxes against mine as I lean back onto the bed.

"Well, I certainly wasn't expecting to be woken up like that when you came home. I more expected you to be tripping over stuff and stubbing your toes!" She laughs.

"You looked good enough to eat, so I did. Now, you may go back to sleep, my love."

She snuggles into me, and I hear her breathing even out.

Before long, I can feel myself drifting off with my woman by my side.

THE NEXT COUPLE OF WEEKS FLIES BY. JESS FULLY moves in and gives her notice at her flat. We are looking at redecorating, and life feels good. Our announcement went out earlier this week with no negative media surrounding it, and tomorrow, we have our charity event.

We host an event every year to raise donations for local charities. This year, it's going to be Great Ormond Street Hospital. Our staff put in their suggestions, and this place has heartfelt meaning for our employees. One of our employees in the IT department has a child being treated by GOSH for cancer. It's important to support this cause.

I'm sitting at my desk, writing my speech for tomorrow night, when Lucy walks in. "Hi, Gavin. How are you today?" She's changed. She's not trying to hit on me.

"Hi, Lucy. I'm well. Thank you. What can I do for you?"

"I saw your announcement, and I'd like to apologise for coming on too strong the night of the Christmas party. I didn't know you were dating Jess; otherwise, I wouldn't have acted like that." Who knew she had morals?

"Lucy, don't worry. Thank you, though. Is that all?"

"Well, there's one thing. I've been asked to take on a project, but I'm not sure if you'll allow it."

Chapter Fifty-Six

JESS

"You're joking? Miles still wants us to work with him after everything he has done?" I stand in Gavin's office, not knowing what to say. It's his business, but he's asking how I feel about taking on this project.

"Jess, if you're not comfortable, then we'll reject it. I did say we would no longer work with him after what happened."

"Can I think about it?"

"Of course. Let me know. I've got a few calls to make. I'll take you out to dinner?"

Agreeing to dinner and heading back to my office, I decide to call Lucy to gauge her opinion of Miles after the incident. His company is good business, and it will be a good project for Lucy, too. When Lucy doesn't answer, I don't know whether it's because she's busy or because of my relationship with Gavin. But I decide to send her an email to outline what I want to discuss and wait for her to call.

The day goes by in the blink of an eye. I check my phone and emails for Lucy's response and nothing. I shut down and go into Gavin's office to find him already gone, which is strange since we have plans. I ring his phone, and it goes to voicemail. I have an uneasy feeling in the pit of my stomach. Something isn't right. I decide to head home and freshen up for dinner. When I get home, Gavin isn't here. I send him a text to tell him I'm home freshening up and ask where to meet him for dinner. Those three dots come up to tell me he's responding, and then they disappear. What is going on?

After my shower, I stand in my towel and check my phone. Nothing from Gavin. I text Jack, his security, to see if he knows where Gavin is and wait for a reply whilst I dry my hair. My phone pings instantly.

Me: Hi, Jack. Do you know where Gavin is?

Jack: He's in a meeting and won't be home for a few hours.

Me: He didn't have a meeting booked. I'm assuming we're not going to dinner?

Jack: It was last minute. He didn't seem happy about it. I've just asked, and Gavin said he'll take you to dinner tomorrow. Sorry.

Putting my phone down, an uneasy feeling rises. I put on my comfy clothes and go into the kitchen to make a coffee. I stare around the vast penthouse; the space is overwhelming when I'm here on my own.

When nine o'clock rolls around, I still haven't heard from Gavin. I also haven't eaten. The anxiety is making me feel nauseous, but I need to eat something. I opt for some sourdough toast with smashed avocado and prosciutto ham. Something I didn't think I'd ever eat, but it's tasty. Polishing off my dinner, I try to call Gavin. Straight to voicemail again. Jack's phone is also going to voicemail. Something does not feel right.

Me: Gavin, are you ok? I'm starting to get worried.

I wait an hour for a reply and nothing. I call John, the other security officer we have. "Hi, John. It's Jess. Do you know where Jack and Gavin are? They're not home yet, and I'm starting to get worried."

"They left the meeting two hours ago. Let me try to contact them. They should have been back at yours over an hour ago."

"I tried both phones, and both are going to voicemail."

"Let me get some scouts out to see what's going on, and I'll call you back."

"Thanks, John. I appreciate your help."

Now, I really am starting to worry. It's gone eleven o'clock. He was meant to be home over an hour ago. Where did they get to? Why aren't their phones connecting? Neither let their phone go below fifty per cent ever. Just as I'm about to leave to join the search, he walks through the door, looking like he's been dragged through a hedge backwards.

"Gavin!" I run over to him, searching for signs of injury, and then stop abruptly when I smell the scotch on his breath. "Where on earth have you been? I was worried!"

"Oh, here we go. I went out for a drink after a difficult meeting." He wanders over to the sofa and flops down on it.

"What do you mean, 'Oh, here we go?' You could have texted me to tell me you were going to a meeting and would be late. I wouldn't have worried. I'm not saying you can't go out. Just let me know. We had plans." I'm starting to get frustrated. How dare he! I'm at home worried sick, and he's off drinking god knows how much without even an 'I'll be home late, don't wait up' message. He's lying on the sofa half asleep, and I'm too angry with him to argue, so I storm off to bed.

One o'clock.

Two o'clock.

Three o'clock.

I'm still wide awake. I'm furious with Gavin, but

now, I'm concerned. I've not seen him drink this much before, not that we've been seeing each other long, but still. Who called a late meeting? Why did it go so badly?

I get myself out of bed and decide to check the notebook that he takes to meetings to see if I can help. Nothing in there? That's odd. I check his phone calendar, and nothing is in there either. The anxious feeling is coming back stronger and won't be easy to shake off this time. Seeing as I'm wide awake, I want to go for a drive. I pick up a set of keys to see which car I will be driving. Gavin has six cars ranging from an Audi R6 to a Range Rover Vouge. All sporty and high class.

Jackpot! I pick the R6 keys. With the music up, I cruise through town, driving with nowhere to go. I start to get peckish, so I pull into a McDonald's drive-thru. I can eat some nuggets to quiet my feelings. Bad habits and all that. I carry on driving after my nuggets and banana milkshake and realise the sun is coming up. Shit! Best get home and get ready for work. I want to go in before he wakes up. I'm still a little mad at him. When I get home, he isn't on the sofa. I go into the bedroom and hear him moving around.

"Where the hell were you, Jess? I've been out of my mind! You left your phone here, so I couldn't contact you."

"That's rich! I went for a drive to clear my head. I couldn't sleep. Where were you last night?"

"I had a last-minute meeting called, and it took longer than I thought it would. I'm sorry I didn't message or call. I wasn't in a good frame of mind. Can we talk about it over breakfast? I need a shower."

Gavin looks a lot better after his shower. I have mine, and we go to the kitchen for breakfast and a lot of coffee.

Chapter Fifty-Seven

GAVIN

Jess makes the coffee whilst I make us a small fry-up. Both of us are in the kitchen, and the silence is deafening. I'm not sure how to word what happened last night. I finish plating up, and we both sit to eat breakfast. After missing dinner last night and drinking a lot, I'm absolutely starving. I shovel the food into my mouth as Jess pushes hers around the plate.

"Jess, please eat breakfast. We've both had a bad night's sleep and need to eat."

"Gavin, where were you?"

I look at my beautiful woman sitting in front of me. She's wearing her insecurities, and her eyes are blood-shot and dull, not the beautiful blues I'm used to looking into.

"I had a call from my solicitor. They are admitting Sacha into a hospital to get further help for her mental illness. Her one request was to meet with me one last time to talk." Jess's face drops, but I sense a bit of relief coming from her as well.

"How did she seem? What did she want to talk about? Why didn't you tell me last night instead of me sitting here, worrying where you were?" She's angry, and I understand why. Thinking for a moment, I take a drink of my coffee. If the shoe was on the other foot, I would be out of my mind with worry. What if something happened? What if she was with someone else? I stand and go over to her.

"Jess, I want to make it very clear that I would never cheat on you. Ever." Tears fill those beautiful eyes.

"What did she want?"

"She wanted to know why you. What was so special about you that I fell hopelessly in love with you and not her? She wasn't sorry for attacking you. If she hadn't been interrupted, I fear it would have been a lot worse. There's something wrong with her."

"What did you tell her?"

"I told her you felt like home. You make me feel, you make me happy, you make me laugh. There's nothing fake about you, and the moment I started to recognise my feelings for you, I saw a future with you: kids, a big house, dogs, the lot. She wasn't happy and went into a rage. She had to be sedated to calm her down. But she won't be a problem for us, Jess. The way she verbally attacked me last night bought back the feelings of when we were together." Her eyes start tearing up again. I grab her hands to reassure her. "Nothing like love. Trust me. The feelings of doubt, constantly wanting to know who she was with, and all those negative feelings hit me like a ton of bricks. I didn't want to call you and tell you where I was. I didn't want you to worry. But I should have texted or called you to tell you I would be home late. For that, Jess, I am truly sorry."

She stares at me, taking in everything I said. Her expression goes from her poker face, showing little emotion other than anger and frustration, to a softer look of concern, and her body stops being so rigid as she visibly relaxes in her chair. She grips my hand tighter. "Gavin, yes, you're a twat. You should have told me you wouldn't be home until late. I didn't think you were cheating on me. Well, it wasn't my first thought. But it's good to know you wouldn't do that. We're meant to be partners. You need to tell me these things. Especially when they make you feel like that. I'm here, always and forever."

With that, I scoop her up and hold her. She's everything to me, and I couldn't be happier than I am with her. "Right! I think we both deserve the day off. We've got to go shopping to get you a dress."

"Why do I need a dress?"

"It's the charity ball tonight. I want you walking in with me on my arm."

"Oh, crap! I completely forgot with everything that's been going on at work and last night."

We put our *out of offices* on and change our clothes to go shopping. I want to buy her something stunning to match how I feel when I see her. We stroll through the streets of London hand in hand, chatting, laughing and browsing through the shops. Jess is conscious of her size, and a lot of the shops don't cater for anyone over a size ten, which is disgusting. I send various emails to owners during our shopping trip.

We are walking through a little back street, and Jess sees a quaint shop whose window pops with vibrant colours. The next thing I know, I'm being dragged through the door.

"Good afternoon. Can I help you today, or are you just browsing?" The lady greeting us is older, in a beautifully cut, classic style dress, which has stunning patterns on it.

"Hi, there. We're looking for a knockout dress for my beautiful girlfriend here." I smile over at Jess, who is glancing around the shop. "That's something I can certainly help with, dear. What colours are we looking at?"

"I'm not really sure. I tend to wear a lot of black."

"Well, lovely, with your complexion and hair, we've got a wide range of colours we can look at. You really are a beauty. My name is Audrey. Let's get you measured, and we can look at what we've got in for you." Audrey leads Jess to the back as a young assistant shows me to the seating area and brings me a cup of coffee. I've been in shops with Sacha before, but this is a nice experience rather than exasperating.

After half an hour, Jess comes out of the changing room in a beautiful floor-length midnight blue dress with a low back, sweetheart neckline, and the most wonderful smile on her face. The dress has a slit down her right leg, which is detailed with a lace pattern and some delicate sparkles. She looks absolutely stunning.

"What do you think?" she asks, twirling around.

I stand and go over to her. My hands go to her hips, which the dress hugs perfectly. "You look amazing, Miss Freeman."

Audrey comes over and starts talking about accessories that would look perfect with the dress and recommends a shop about a five minute walk away. When Jess is happy, I hand Audrey my credit card and pay for the dress.

An afternoon of buying the dress and accessories and choosing a hairstyle for Jess made me hungry. We stop in a little café for a late lunch before heading back to our house to get ready. It still feels strange saying "our house" when it's only been me in there since I bought it. But it's actually starting to feel like ours, and I love having Jess there with me. Even though she leaves hair ties and grips on every countertop in the place.

"Thank you for a wonderful afternoon, Mr Andrews. I love the outfit for tonight. Although I do wish you'd let me pay—"

"Nonsense, you're my girl, and I can treat you to nice things."

As the bill comes for lunch, she grabs it out of the waitress's hand and smiles. "I'm at least paying for lunch." She grins widely, and I sit back, sipping my coffee, grinning back at her.

Little does she know she has another surprise for later.

Chapter Fifty-Eight

JESS

I have Anna messaging me most of the day for advice. She's been in the job for a week, and I feel guilty leaving her to fly solo, but it should have been an easy day, considering her boss is off today. She is doing well, not quite up to my speed, but then again, I can't expect that of everyone.

I stand in front of the mirror in my new dress and shoes. I have my hair curled slightly and put into an updo. There's no point in curling it properly because it's so fine. I'm trying to find some jewellery to go with my outfit. I don't have much as I rarely wear it, so it's slim pickings. As I'm rooting through my jewellery box, Gavin walks in dressed very sexily in his tuxedo.

"Look at you, handsome."

"Look at you. Just look." Gavin takes me over to the long mirror and stands behind me. His eyes are roaming my body hungrily.

"There's something missing from this outfit." He

gently puts his hand around my throat and slides it down slowly over my chest. I'm getting so turned on by the way he's looking at me and touching me.

"I've got a couple of necklaces to choose from, but if you carry on looking at me like that, we're not going to make it tonight." I chuckle, but I wouldn't mind spending the night in bed with him.

He steps back, admiring my body from behind. I watch his every move and look in the mirror. He reaches into his jacket pocket and pulls out a black box. There is gold writing on it, but I can't read what it says from the image in the mirror.

He opens it and takes something out, comes up behind me and places a beautiful necklace around my neck. A thin platinum chain with a single black pearl encased in a swirly platinum cage. It's absolutely beautiful.

"Oh, Gavin." My hand reaches up to it. "This is beautiful!"

"Not as beautiful as you," he says smoothly. I could have swooned. He kisses my neck whilst his hands roam my body. "We've got half an hour until we leave." He winks at me in the mirror, which makes me giggle.

I spin on the spot, throw my arms around his neck and kiss him, craving his taste. He grabs my hips and pulls me harshly into his body. I can already feel how hard he was.

He pushes me away slightly and stares at me. "Dress. Off."

He's breathless and needy. I slip the straps of my

dress off and let it slide to the floor, leaving me in just my knickers. With a backless dress, I can't wear a bra, after all.

His eyes light up, and he licks his lips, stalking over to me. He slides two fingers straight inside me, making me catch my breath. His mouth goes to my nipples, devouring one at a time. Oh, this man knows all my buttons. My hands rest on his shoulders to steady myself as I come embarrassingly quickly.

"A little worked up, were we?" His sexy chuckle makes me smile even more.

"Well, you will walk in being all sexy and with a look that made me weak at the knees." I try to shift the blame, but the truth is, I want him all the time. I drop to my knees and undo his trousers, longing for his cock in my mouth. Pulling down Gavin's boxers, his cock springs free. Generally, I don't like the look of them. Let's face it, they're not pretty. But his is one to be admired. It's perfect as if crafted by the gods themselves.

Before I can taste him, Gavin pulls me up and swings me face down on the bed, pulls my knickers to one side and thrusts into me deeply. He's as hungry as I am. He grabs my hips, almost painfully, and slams into me. I can feel him getting closer with every thrust. He pulls me up so our bodies are flush with each other. He's staring at our reflection in the mirror, watching me. His hand wraps around my throat firmly but gently, and I have no idea why it turns me on so much, but it pushes me over the edge, and I come hard around him. He grips me a little firmer as he comes inside me. We both stay there breathless, watching each other in the mirror. Nothing needs to be said. It's all felt.

STROLLING INTO THE BALLROOM, I CAN'T HELP BUT admire the beautiful high ceiling, the pictures on the walls, and the decorations tastefully placed around the room. It's stunning. Tonight, we are raising money for GOSH, an amazing cause. This is the first time I've been to one of these events, even though I've been with the company for over three years. I never felt comfortable coming to one. Especially since there are silent auctions to help raise funds for the charities. I don't have any real money to play with. But since moving in with Gavin, I've let go of my flat, have more spare cash and loads more in my savings.

Gavin introduces me to some important people. I feel nervous. I'm sure I'm not the type of woman they're expecting to see with him, but they are all wonderfully polite, and I don't feel like they are judging me. We stroll up to the bar, and my heart skips a beat. Miles stands speaking with Lucy. They stop talking when we reach the bar.

"Miles, Lucy," Gavin says curtly.

"Oh, Jess. I'm so sorry I haven't returned your call. It's been a crazy busy week, finishing a project." Lucy smiles, and I can't detect any ill feelings. Is she over her Gavin crush?

"Jess, it's nice to see you. I'd like to formally apologise for my actions the other month. I was...." Miles glances at Lucy, and she nods. Is something going on here? "I was in a dark place, and I cannot tell you how appalled and disgusted I am with myself." He seems genuinely sorry, and I believe him when he says he was in a dark place.

"Honestly, Lucy, don't worry. I understand. Pop in for a cuppa on Monday morning? And, Miles, thank you. It's all water under the bridge." I smile, and we stand chatting over a couple of glasses of champagne. When they walk off, Lucy takes Miles's arm. If they are a couple, they look quite cute.

"That was all a bit odd. Do you really forgive them?" Gavin stares at me questioningly.

"Them? Lucy had a crush on you and backed off once she knew we were an item. There's nothing to forgive. And Miles, honestly, yes. You can tell that something has happened. He's punished himself enough, and I have no reason to hold this over him. Nothing actually happened. It could have, but it didn't. I don't like holding onto negative energy."

He smiles and kisses me on the cheek. "You are seriously one wonderful person, Jessica Freeman."

The night goes spectacularly. We dance, eat some tiny fancy food, and drink, and I even put in a bid for a weekend away in the Cotswolds! Someone has donated their holiday home for a weekend. The little cottage looks beautiful, but I doubt a £1,000 bid is going to cut it. However, the money is going to a good cause, so my savings can take a little hit.

When it comes down to the auction announcements, I stand there holding my breath when the auctioneer comes on stage. People win paintings, a signed rugby and football shirts, holidays abroad and spa packages. Next up is the little cottage getaway. "Here we have a cottage break in the Cotswolds. A beautiful setting for a romantic break. The winning bid was a generous £25,000!" Everyone in the room applauds. You can buy a lot with that money. I feel a little disappointed, but I think of the children. "Congratulations to Miss Jessica Freeman!"

My heart stops. I didn't put down that amount. Oh my god, there's been a mistake. I can feel my heart coming up through my throat. Gavin places his arm around me and lowers his head to whisper in my ear. "Don't panic. I saw you put your bid down and wanted to make sure no one else got it. You looked so pleased with the idea. I've got this." He's not picking up dinner. He's just paid £25,000 for a weekend away. I forget about his wealth.

"Gavin, that was way too much. We could have just gone away for a weekend, you know? But the children will be benefitting." I wink at him, and he grips me harder, his hand slowly slipping down to my ass. I giggle, bumping him with my hip, bringing his hand back to my waist with a grin. God, I love this man.

Chapter Fifty-Nine

GAVIN

After Jess's near heart attack, the auction ends, and we go to the dance floor once more. When I dance with her, it feels like time stands still, and it's just the two of us. Her smile makes my heart stop. The love in her eyes makes me want to marry her on the spot.

As the evening draws to a close, I'm given the final figure of the funds we've raised for the hospital, and I take to the stage for my speech. "Ladies and gentlemen, I'd like to thank you all for being here tonight to support us in raising funds for Great Ormond Street Hospital. As you know, each year a charity is chosen by our own employees. This charity is one whose services are depended on greatly, and one of our own has a child under their care. It gives me the greatest pleasure to announce we have raised a staggering £259,000!" Applause rips through the crowd. "I cannot express properly how proud I am tonight. This money will change so many lives. And tonight, I am going to match this donation and round the total to £520,000. Enjoy the rest of the evening, and thank you all!"

Gasps can be heard throughout the room. There are tears and applause as I step off the stage and walk straight over to Jess, shaking people's hands on my way.

Jess stares at me with tears in her eyes. "You, Mr Andrews, are remarkable."

I hold her hand in mine. "Let's go home." I enjoy these events, but I want nothing more than to be alone with Jess.

We arrive back home, and as Jess shuts the front door, I push her back into it and kiss her gently, growing more passionate with each second. Dragging myself away, her eyes grow darker and hooded. I lead her to the bedroom and stand her in front of me. She still looks elegant and beautiful even after an evening of dancing, laughing and entertaining. I stop for a moment, drinking in everything about her. I know she has insecurities about her body, but I've honestly never met anyone as beautiful as her. Inside and out.

I slip her dress from her shoulders, and it pools down around her feet. I hold her hand as she steps out of it. Jess stands there in just her black lace knickers. The things I want to do to this woman. I lead her over to the bed and lay her down. I go to the drawers and pull out some silk restraints and a blindfold. I'm going to test her senses tonight. I tie her hands and feet to the bed, then place the remaining silk over her eyes, tying it at the back of her head and go back to the drawer for the vibrator I'd bought for her, and then nip to the kitchen for some ice.

When I return, she appears fully aware of the sounds around her, moving her head with the noises in the room. I want to bring her to a whole new level of pleasure. I move over to her and gently brush her side with the back of my fingers. She flinches, not expecting the touch. I sit beside her on the bed and lean into her. "Are you ready, my love?" I kiss her softly.

"Yes," she says, gasping already. I grab an ice cube and run it down her body from her collarbone, circling her nipples and over to her hip bone. Jess jumps at the coldness of the ice. I slide it over her stomach and place it in her belly button.

Grabbing another piece, I pop it into my mouth and kiss her nipples, then press the ice on them after making her squirm. "Ah, ah, ah. You'll lose the ice on your stomach." I giggle, letting her settle again before I continue my pursuit. I take the ice out of my mouth and lick her nipples, flicking my tongue over one whilst circling the other with the ice cube, then swapping. She's tilting her head back and letting out quiet moans. I continue with my tongue on her nipples and slide the ice down her body and into her lips, onto her clit. Her head shoots up as far as it can, and she gasps loudly. Chuckling to myself, I move my mouth down to her clit and start lapping up the cold water around her.

Jess arches her back, and the ice cube in her belly button is melting. A trickle of water escapes and slowly slides down her side, making her wriggle and laugh. While taking my tongue to her clit, flicking, circling and making her moan, I dip my fingers inside her with the small amount of ice left and feel her come almost instantly. I'm not done with her yet.

Moving back up her body, covering her with kisses as I go, I latch onto her neck and bite gently. My hand switches on the vibrator and moves it up her thigh and back down the other. Jess's breath is shallow with excitement. I circle her labia with the vibrator, dipping in gently now and then. She's bucking her hips, desperate for more, and I give it to her. I flick the switch to a throbbing vibrate and press it against her clit, then into her and repeat for a few moments whilst she's panting. I can't wait anymore and move between her legs. I position myself at her entrance and thrust in deep. My god, she feels good. I thrust hard into her and move the vibrator to her clit. I can feel her tensing and suddenly erupting around me. I don't want to come yet, so I slide out and lap up her juices, and whilst I'm down there, I tease her with my tongue and vibrator, knowing how sensitive she'll feel. I want to try something new with her and gently press the vibrator against her ass. She moves away but then relaxes into the feeling. I push a little harder on her ass, slowly dipping the tip in whilst working her clit.

"Oh God, Gavin," is all Jess can scream as she comes again. I turn the vibrator off and toss it to one side. I want to feel all of her. I slam into her, holding her hips. She has come numerous times tonight and feels so tight. I ride her hard, making her back arch. She has no words left, only sounds. I thrust over and over again until I feel my own orgasm building and come inside her. God, that's good!

I slowly pull out and untie her feet, then take off her blindfold. I bend down to kiss her as I untie her hands. I rub her ankles and wrists; I want to make sure she isn't sore. Moving beside her, I rest my head on my hand and throw my arm over her before asking, "How was that for you, Jess?"

"I'll be honest, it was a complete turn-on being blindfolded. I wasn't sure about the ass play, but again, major turn-on. Who knew?"

I chuckle. Most women find anal a taboo subject and dirty but done correctly, it can be a great experience. "I thoroughly enjoyed taking you to new levels." I smile, bringing her in closer to me as we drift off to sleep.

Chapter Sixty

JESS

Before we know it, I've been living with Gavin for three months. We've redecorated, seen some shows and generally lived our wonderful new life together. Everything is plodding along smoothly, and it feels like we've been together for years, but it's only coming up to a year. It suddenly occurs to me that we've been together nearly a year, and I don't know when his birthday is. I don't think he knows mine. I need to do some snooping.

I'm sitting at my desk and going through some proposals for new business, and I ping Anna. She's settled in really well to being Gavin's PA.

Me: Hi, Anna. How are you doing?

Anna: Hi, Jess! I'm well, thanks. How are you?

Me: I'm good. I need a favour. Can you access when Gavin's birthday is? Is there anything on his calendar?

Anna: Nothing in his calendar, but your name is in for next week with a present emoji next to it. Is it your birthday by any chance?

Me: Yes. Haha. Thanks for looking. Will see what I can find out.

Damn! He knows when my birthday is, but I don't know his. It suddenly occurs to me his mum absolutely loves me.

"Hi, Julia. How are you?"

"Oh, Jess, what a lovely surprise! I'm good. Thank you. How are you?"

"I'm good. Thank you! This is a little embarrassing, but I've just realised I don't know when Gavin's birthday is." I lower my head. I can't believe I haven't found this out yet.

"Oh dear. He doesn't really celebrate it, but his birthday is on April 19th. Only a few weeks away."

"Why doesn't he celebrate it?"

"When he was a child, he loved it, naturally, but when he went into the business world, he didn't want to celebrate and have the attention on him."

"Hmmm. I wonder why. But thank you for telling me. I've got a meeting to go to, but I'll let you know when we can come down for dinner."

"That would be wonderful, darling. Take care, and see you soon."

Excellent. I now know when Gavin's birthday is, but he doesn't like to celebrate it. I won't do anything other than a card and present. I don't want to upset him, but it is interesting that he knows when mine is. Speaking of which, I probably should get organising something. My mum loves a celebration. But first, an afternoon of meetings.

After a hectic day, I sit in the bath, waiting for Gavin to get home and start looking for a nice birthday present. What do you get someone like him? He literally donated a ton of money a few months ago without batting an eyelid.

As I'm scrolling, it suddenly occurs to me I've been living here for three months and haven't had a period. I check my app, and it's showing that I haven't had a period since December. Shit! I've been taking my contraceptive, and sometimes, they can mess up my periods. I jump out of the bath, get dressed and head to the shop to buy a pregnancy test just to be on the safe side.

Whilst I'm walking back home, my mind is racing. I'm too young to have kids. My career has only just started. We've not been going out for long. What will I do if I am pregnant?

I'm sitting in the bathroom, door locked, staring at the stick I've just peed on. Three minutes is a long time when you're watching something. I hear Gavin call for me from the living room. Shit, shit, SHIT!

"I'll be out in a minute!" My voice is all over the

place with worry. Three minutes are up, and the words become clear on the test: NOT PREGNANT. *Phew!*

I feel a little sad, but in reality, now is not the time. *Knock, knock.* "Jess, are you okay in there?"

"Yeah, I'm fine. Just coming out." I throw the test in the bin and put it in the back of my mind. We are still discovering each other. Now is not the time to introduce a tiny human.

"How was your day?" I say, my voice becoming more normal.

"Fine. Yours? You look a little pale."

"I'm okay. Not drunk enough today, that's all. What are you fancying for dinner?"

We go downstairs and decide to cook katsu curry for dinner. Whilst Gavin is cooking the chicken, I email the doctor for an appointment. I need to find out what's going on with my body,

We eat dinner and settle on the sofa.

Now that I'm out of my own head, I notice Gavin feels different, a little off. "Hey, are you okay? You seem stressed."

"Busy day dealing with some idiots. I also had to fire a couple of people today." He seems to relax a little.

"That sounds awful. Why did you have to fire them? And who?"

"I had to fire someone from admin, Aaron, and someone from finance, Zara. They had been accessing company information and feeding it to our competitors."

I sit bolt upright. "What? How is this the first I've heard of it? Aaron always seemed friendly."

"The information they were sending to our competitors was fake, so nothing got into the papers or around the office. We suspected for about a year that someone was trying to sabotage our new client list. We set up a fake folder on the company drive that anyone could access. With IT tracking every click into the folder and who opened files, we discover these two have been working together. The company is mine. It feels like a personal attack. When we questioned them, they both said it was about money. Both earn more than the market benchmark, but we don't know their personal finances."

I sit for a moment and absorb this information. I can't believe another company had our own employees spy for them and try to send them information. I have no words to comfort him. I pull him into me and hold him. I feel him physically relax more, and I love that he can be this way. This tough assed CEO, billionaire, philanthropist—the love of my life is so stressed because people are attacking his company. I know exactly what to get him for his birthday. A break is needed for both of us.

We carry on chatting about our days, and I'm silently planning our getaway.

Chapter Sixty-One

GAVIN

"We've secured the servers. We're okay, Gavin." I can hear Paul sipping his coffee over the phone.

I'm still wound up and angry, but we're handling everything here, and the solicitors are handling the company that employed the spies. He's right. We are going to be okay, and we can get back to normal. I don't know what I'd do without him or Jess in my life.

It's Jess's birthday this week, and her mum has organised a little party at her house. Apparently, this family loves birthdays, something I've not celebrated since I was younger. I used to love birthdays. The presents, the attention, the cake. But once I became CEO, people started using them as an excuse to try to get close to me. I've not even told Jess when my birthday is. It's in a few weeks. I have no doubt she's already spoken to my mother because Anna has blocked some time out of my diary and moved meetings without speaking to me. I won't let on that I've noticed. I sit back, stroking the stubble on my chin. I wonder what she has planned.

I check my drawer for Jess's present. I don't know why I'm nervous. I want to make sure she has a wonderful birthday. I'll do a little private celebration for her at home.

She's becoming sexually aware and enjoying experimenting, and she is very responsive. I love the way her body reacts to mine.

My mind is wandering, and my cock is responding to the thoughts. Just as I'm deep in thought about being deep in Jess, there's a knock at the door. "Come in." My voice sounds gruff. Anna strolls into my office with a grin on her face and a coffee in her hands. Jess picked well with this one. She doesn't need hand-holding, she gets on with everything, and I actually enjoy her chit-chat.

"Good morning, Gavin. How are you today?" She puts my coffee down and pulls some files from under her arm. "These are for signing, these are for your approval, and this is from Jess." She can barely contain her excitement. What's going on with her? "Thanks, Anna. Are you okay? You seem overly happy today."

"I'm absolutely fine. Thank you, Gavin. Simply having a wonderful Monday." She grins and walks out of the office. Now, I am suspicious. No one has ever said they're having a wonderful Monday.

I sit and read through the documents that need to be signed, approve the others, and then get to the documents from Jess. She's sent through a business proposal for a new branch of the company. This catches my attention. Jess is proposing we open a branch in Europe, not only for consulting but also buying firms, building them up and adding them to our portfolio. She's also outlined some businesses that we can potentially buy. Everything looks perfect, as I would expect from her, until I get to the person who will head up the Europe branch. I dial her number. "Jess, can I see you for a minute regarding the Europe proposal?"

"Of course. I'll be there in ten."

I sit back, looking at the name of the director: Lucy Donovan.

Ten minutes later, Jess enters my office with coffee from her favourite place down the road. She's trying to butter me up. She knows me too well. Sitting down in front of me, she smiles. "I know what you're going to say, but Lucy has more than proven her worth to this company. Yes, she brings in a lot of business for the U.K. side, but imagine what she can do in Europe. She's devoted and loyal, and I believe giving her this opportunity, she would run with it and prove me right. I also happen to know that Miles would move to Europe. I've done my research to make sure that this would be a good opportunity that she can't turn down."

I sit, staring at this beautiful woman in front of me. She was in admin before she applied to be my PA, and she smashed that job out of the park. We promoted her, and now she's proposing business ideas that will not only make the company more money but make us bigger across Europe. "Okay." I grin at her as I sign off her business proposal. "Go ahead and speak to Lucy. You two can work together with legal and anyone else to start the process to open the branch."

"Aren't you going to run this past Paul?" She blinks at me, grinning like the Cheshire Cat.

"Are you telling me you haven't already done that?" I raise my eyebrow at her, leaning back in my chair. I know her too well. She's covered all bases, and this will be a great move for the company. Jess gives me a kiss, grabs her document and skips out of the office.

I get up and lock the door. I have an important phone call to make. I sit down, drink my coffee and pick up my phone.

"Trevor. Hi. It's Gavin."

"Gavin! Is Jess okay?"

"She's absolutely fine. Sorry for worrying you. I have a question to ask you." I can feel my hand sweating. Never have I ever been so nervous about a phone call. I can hear Trevor laughing.

"Alison, I owe you a tenner!" he shouts.

"Sorry? Did I miss something?"

"Ha ha! Alison said you'd call asking for Jess's hand in marriage by her birthday. I said Christmas. I'm assuming that's what you're calling for?"

I sit back, smiling. This family is wonderful. They bet on us. "Well, now that you mention it, Trevor, I would love your daughter's hand in marriage. But she isn't to know we've had this conversation." I can hear Alison in the background, shouting in excitement. I hope Jess's reaction will be of the same level of happiness.

After speaking with Jess's parents, I sit back, feeling excited about proposing to her. I just need to sort out the arrangements.

Chapter Sixty-Two

JESS

It's my birthday tomorrow, and Mum's planned a little gathering. We're heading to their house tomorrow morning and will stay over. It's going to be fun. We love birthdays. I hope Gavin will be okay, as he doesn't really celebrate them. I'm working from home today so I can get us packed and ready. I've also been looking at weekend breaks for Gavin and me. I've used the holiday I won for a nice relaxing cabin weekend in the Cotswolds. It's rural and chilled, and although we're out of the way, there are plenty of shops and activities around if we want them. After booking that, I start to pack. I've scheduled a meeting with Lucy on Monday morning to discuss my proposal, and I want her to grab the opportunity with both hands. This will be an amazing chance for both the company and her.

After packing, I see I have a text from Gavin telling me he's going to be late. I've been cooking a curry in the slow cooker today, so it'll keep nicely for when he's home. I take the opportunity to tidy up some emails and take a pampering bath.

As I'm relaxing, my mum calls. "Hi, Mum!"

"Hi, sweetheart. How are you? We can't wait to see you tomorrow." She sounds giddy. Something has her excited.

"What's up, Mum? You sound chipper."

"Oh, I'm looking forward to seeing my favourite daughter tomorrow."

"I'm your only daughter. What's going on?"

"Honestly, nothing, dear. I'm happy, is all. My girl is happy, so I'm happy." Something is fishy with her, but I'm not getting anything out of her tonight.

"Fair enough! I'm in the bath. We're leaving at about nine tomorrow. We should be with you just after ten if that's okay."

"Wonderful, dear. We'll see you tomorrow."

I lie back in the bath, wondering what's got my mum all animated.

I'm so deep in thought that I don't notice Gavin leaning against the door frame, staring at me. "Hello there, Miss Freeman." He gives me a devilish grin. My insides spark alive at the twinkle in his eyes.

"Hello there, Mr Andrews. Fancy joining me?" Before I finish my sentence, he's stripping his clothes off. I appreciate his body. He's sculpted by the gods themselves. I'm gaining more confidence in my body. He's never made me feel anything but sexy and beautiful. Gavin is naked and sliding in behind me. As he wraps his arms around me, I'm flooded with different emotions. I feel safe, warm, and sexy, and my body tingles, reacting to him. We feel made for each other.

As I'm swimming around in my thoughts, he moves stray hair from my neck and kisses me. He has one hand around my waist and the other on my breast, fingers and thumb twirling around my nipple, snapping me out of my head and very much in the present moment with him. My head tilts back, leaning against his shoulder. I pant as he works me up. His arm moves from around my waist, and his hand dips between my legs and slips two fingers in, making me gasp and move on his fingers. He slides them in and out, making me wriggle around. Taking his fingers out, he grabs my hips, adjusts me and pulls me down onto him hard. I can't help the loud moan that echoes around the bathroom. I grip the sides of the bath and rock my hips on him. He tightens his grip and takes control of the rhythm. Within minutes, he has me coming hard right before I feel him throb inside me. We both needed that quick release.

I step out of the bath and catch my reflection in the mirror. I have always been curvy with lots of wobbly bits, things I hated about myself as much as I told everyone it's about having confidence. What I see in the mirror is different. I haven't changed much. My stomach overhang has reduced and moved up a bit, but I'm still wobbly and curvy. Yet, I feel different.

As I stare at myself, Gavin stands behind me and wraps his arms around me. "You are beautiful, Jess. Every single inch of you." It's as if he can read my thoughts.

I spin around and kiss him. I want him to feel my love for him. Right in the middle of what I want to be a romantic, passionate kiss, my stomach rumbles loudly, and it could have been mistaken for a 747.

"Haha. Hungry, Miss Freeman? Let's eat!" Rolling my eyes, we laugh and get dressed before going to the kitchen to finally have dinner.

I WAKE UP FEELING REFRESHED AND REALISE IT'S Saturday. My birthday! I leap out of bed and get ready so we can head over to my parents. I'm ridiculously excited. Even in my late twenties, I love birthdays. My mum also makes the best cakes, and I can't help wondering what she has made this year. I'm hoping for Devil's Food cake, my absolute favourite. When I'm ready, I walk downstairs to find flowers everywhere, balloons, presents, and a very handsome boyfriend making me breakfast.

"Good morning, birthday girl! Come, sit and eat breakfast." His smile is…I can't be a hundred per cent sure, but he looks amused. Is it just his birthday he doesn't like? Or is it because he hasn't had a birthday he's wanted to celebrate? I sit like a good birthday girl and gape at the amazing food in front of me. He made me a Canadian breakfast, one of my favourites. Pancakes, sausages, bacon and scrambled eggs cooked properly, of course. I can't do runny eggs.

"Thank you, Gavin. This is absolutely wonderful. You really didn't have to go through all this trouble.

The flowers are beautiful, by the way." I grin at him and eat my breakfast, side-eyeing the presents in the living room.

"Ah, ah, ah. They're for later!" He grins at me like a Cheshire Cat. I just roll my eyes at him and finish my breakfast.

After breakfast, we wash up and take everything to the car, ready to go to Mum and Dad's. "Are you seriously not going to even let me shake *one* present?" I laugh as he carries them to the car.

"Absolutely not. I've heard you're a nightmare with presents!" He's clearly been speaking to my mum.

As we drive out, we hold hands, and I'm lost in thought, staring out the window. Living in London, especially where I do now, I forget how beautiful the countryside is. The space, the fresh air, I immediately feel relaxed. I can't wait to surprise him with our weekend away. We will be alone, nothing but us and the countryside around us. I love being in the city, but this is what I grew up in, and if we ever have children, it's what I'd like them to grow up around, too.

"Penny for your thoughts?" Gavin grips my hand.

I hadn't realised I'd been quiet for so long. "I miss being out in the countryside sometimes, but I forget until we leave the city, if that makes sense."

He smiles and kisses my hand. "I get it. I grew up in the city, but I'd like to have a place out here somewhere. Close to the city, but our own little land of freedom." He really does get it. We drive the rest of the way in our own heads, and it isn't long until we arrive. It is only a forty-minute journey. Sometimes, it feels like a long trip, and times like today feel as if we walked here.

We pull up, and my mum opens the door with a big grin and open arms. I smile and jump out of the car to greet her. "Happy birthday, angel! You go in and see your dad. I'll help Gavin."

I go in, and when I look back, there is a look shared between Gavin and Mum. What are they up to?

Chapter Sixty-Three

GAVIN

Jess is a bundle of energy. I stand in the kitchen with Trevor, making coffee, and I can hear her chatting enthusiastically with her mum. "Are you sure you're ready to have this excitement for the rest of your life?" Trevor chuckles. "It'll be worse when you have kids!"

I'd not thought about children before Jess, I'll be honest, but it didn't scare me. Not with her. As I'm thinking about how beautiful and lucky our children would be, Jess floats into the kitchen, looking radiant. She has changed her outfit into a flowy dress. Her hair has been curled and is falling past her shoulders. The blonde is coming out now, and her hair has turned to her natural colour, a beautiful light brown with natural golden strands. I can feel my heart swell for her. She is the one. I didn't believe you could *feel* it, but when you know, you know.

Jess strolls over to me, and I wrap my arms around

her. "Are you ready for presents now?" I have to release her as she begins jumping with eagerness. I can't help but laugh. If this is what birthdays are like in this family, I may actually celebrate mine. It's relaxed, but there's this energy in the air that is infectiously happy. We practically run into the living room, where Julia has laid out the presents around a seat. I sit down in said seat, and Jess slaps my shoulder to move me. This is fun.

We spend the next half hour watching Jess open presents, everything from spa vouchers to a handbag. She saves mine until last. I've bought some openers for her, but her main present will be given to her later.

"Oh, Gavin. These shoes are AWESOME!" I'd bought her some Christian Louboutin shoes she'd been eyeing. I smile at her as she continues to open her gifts. She has a matching handbag for her shoes. She wants to look the part in her new position. I'd also gotten her a nice watch and a new travel mug. She smiles warmly and energetically after every present. "Gavin, you've spoilt me. Thank you for everything." I kiss her, knowing full well this isn't over yet. Julia gives me a little wink whilst we go back into the kitchen for drinks and snacks.

The afternoon goes by quickly, us putting out decorations and getting ready for the party. Julia has hired caterers for the food, so no prep needs to be done other than icing the cake, and Julia shoos us all out of the kitchen.

By the time people start arriving, the house appears to be party-ready. Balloons, presents, banners, we all make an effort to dress up, too. Jess walks over to me, looking radiant. She could wear a bin bag and look beautiful. Her hair flows down past her shoulders, and her breasts look outstanding in that dress.

When everyone has arrived, we are all having drinks and enjoying chatting amongst ourselves. Trevor looks over to me, and I nod. Seconds later, he taps his glass to gain everyone's attention. "Thank you all for coming today to share Jess's birthday. It's an absolute pleasure to introduce Gavin, Jess's partner, who would like to say a few words."

Jess spins around and stares at me with suspicion in her eyes.

I chuckle and walk over to Trevor. "Thanks, Trevor. I'm honoured to be spending the first of many birthdays with this beautiful woman. I also have one last present for you, Jess. Can you come and stand with me?"

Jess's eyes are wide. She walks over and stands by my side. I pull a box out of my pocket and present it to her. Her eyes well with tears. She's going to kill me for this trick. As she opens the box, her mum has her hands over her mouth, preparing.

When Jess lifts the lid, she frowns. "A fob?"

I chuckle as everyone gasps. "There's something on the drive for you, my love."

We all walk outside, and Jess gasps audibly when she sees what is sitting on the drive for her. "GAVIN!" she squeals. She practically runs over to the Jaguar F-Type in Firenze Red, just like she's always wanted. It sits with a bow on the bonnet and looks as divine as my woman.

When Jess opens the door, there is something on the driver's seat. I stand behind her and drop to one knee as she opens it. She whirls around with tears in her eyes and a hand over her mouth. "Gavin?"

"Jess, you are the most remarkable woman I've ever met. Before you, I could never see myself marrying. With you, I want it all. Will you marry me?"

Jess wobbles on the spot before diving down to kiss me. "YESS!" she shouts as we embrace. "I love you, Gavin! I want it all with you, too!"

I stand to slide the ring on her finger, and she wraps her arms around me before running over to her mum, who is crying so much, I fear there may be a flood warning.

Trevor strolls over and pats me on the back. "Thanks for your help, Trevor! I couldn't have pulled this off without you." It really isn't true, but he is a great man.

Kiera comes over to give me a hug and whispers in my ear, "Break her heart, and I'll kill you!"

"You don't have to worry there. She owns my heart, body and soul."

Kiera kisses my cheek and heads over to Jess to congratulate her. Kiera is fierce, but she's Jess's best friend. There's no stronger friendship than theirs, and I appreciate Jess has someone like that in her life.

The congratulations roll in, and we enjoy the rest of the evening. I feel Jess has more excitement about the cake than the car, but after tasting it, I understand why. It is the best cake I've tasted. Julia offers to make our wedding cake, which Jess is over the moon about. I go outside for a smoke, not something I do often, but I still enjoy it. I take the opportunity to call my parents to deliver the good news. They were so excited when I told them I wanted to marry Jess. I'm not as close to my parents as Jess is to hers, but she's changed that. I find myself calling them at least once a week now to catch up. I smile to myself, thinking about how she changed my life in a short space of time.

I go back in and enjoy the party with Jess and her loved ones. When it's time to retire, I take my wonderful fiancée to bed. "Gavin, you make me so happy. I love you!" Even tipsy, she can make my heart race. I help her get changed and into bed. Tomorrow, we will celebrate on our own without her parents down the hall.

I lay there, listening to her snore, thinking of the life we will build together. As my mind begins to wander, I think about the house we can live in, how many children we will have, what they will be like, what we will be like as parents. Before I know it, I drift off into a happy sleep.

Chapter Sixty-Four

JESS

I can't believe my birthday was a week ago. So much has happened. I was thoroughly spoilt, not to mention Gavin buying me my dream car, and of course, we can't forget that he PROPOSED! I'm going to be Mrs Jess Andrews. That sounds so strange in my head. I can't wait to get wedding planning.

As I'm considering where we can get married, my phone rings. "Hi, there. Is that Jess Freeman?"

"Yes, speaking."

"It's your doctor's surgery. Dr Woodstock would like you to come in for an appointment this afternoon at three o'clock if you're available."

"Of course. I'll block out my diary. Thank you."

In all the excitement, I forgot I'd emailed them for an appointment. I know the contraception I'm on can mess with my periods, but it's been four months since I've had one. Hopefully, we can talk about tests and the next steps. I never thought about children until the pregnancy test. Now, I wonder if I can have them.

Gavin is out of the office today in "meetings" with Paul. Apparently, golfing now classifies as meetings. I text him to let him know I'm going to the doctor later. I'm not expecting a reply because I know they'll be on the course. Therefore, when I get a call almost immediately, it makes me jump.

"Jess, are you okay? Why are you going to the doctor?"

"Hey! It's just routine. I want to check something with them. It's period related. Nothing to worry about."

"Call me as soon as you're out, and let me know how it goes. I've just realised you haven't had one for months. Are you….?"

"No, I took a test to confirm, which is why I wanted to speak to the doctor. Something doesn't feel right."

"Okay, love. Call me anytime. I love you."

"I love you, too."

I sit back in my chair. He didn't freak out when he realised I hadn't had a period in months. He also didn't sound panicked at the thought of pregnancy. But we'll wait until later for all that. I've got a meeting with Lucy in half hour to discuss the Europe proposal, and I need a coffee and a snack before then.

"What? You want me to head up a brand-new division in Europe? Why? We're not exactly besties."

"You're the best rep in our current business portfolio, which makes you the best candidate. No, we haven't been *besties,* but that doesn't mean you're not the right woman for the job. We'll have weekly check-ins for the first four months and then switch to monthly to make sure the business is running smoothly and talk about any support you may need. Other than that, this will be your baby to run."

Lucy sits back, sipping her coffee, deep in thought.

"This is a good opportunity for the company to expand and for you to gain the career progression you've been looking for." I am waiting for her reply. We've been over the finances, the set-up, and the office space the company bought and is having decorated. I've even shortlisted some apartments for her to review. "We've got a couple of months before this takes off the ground."

"Jess, when you first became Gavin's PA, I was jealous. I knew there would be something between the two of you. I didn't have what he was looking for, but you did. I am happy for you both, and don't think I haven't noticed that rock on your finger." We haven't made an announcement yet. Lucy grabs my hand and inspects my sapphire and diamond engagement ring. "Truly beautiful. He has always had good taste."

"Thank you, Lucy. So what do you think about Paris? Heading up our European division and being a Director?"

"I want to speak to Miles. We're in a good place, and I want to see if he'll join me. But as a gut instinct, it's a HELL YES from me." She is grinning from ear to ear, and I'm elated for her.

"That's wonderful news. I'll get contracts drawn up. Let me know when you've spoken to Miles, and we'll talk about dates."

After a brief chat, Lucy bounds out of my office, enthusiastic about her new role, and I couldn't be happier that my project is finally taking flight. I sit back and reflect on the last couple of years and how much has changed. I've gone from bored on the admin team to creating new divisions for the business and running with my projects. I'm proud of myself. Not to mention, I'm marrying the love of my life.

Just as I'm finishing some emails, I have a ping to remind me about my doctor's appointment. I close my laptop and walk the ten minutes to the doctor's office. I can finish my day at home afterwards and make a nice meal for the two of us tonight.

Once I check in at reception, I glance at my phone, reading emails and messages. There is one from Gavin wishing me luck. My doctor calls me in, and I sit there, suddenly nervous.

"Hi, Jess. I've had a look through your record, and you want to talk about your periods. Is that right?"

"Yes, they've always been all over the place, but I haven't had one for months now, and I've done some pregnancy tests, and they were all negative. I've recently become engaged, and I believe children are in our future, but I'm concerned something isn't right. I've not felt right for a few months now. Well, within myself, but something feels off if that makes sense?"

"Absolutely. Let's do the usual checks and see where we go from there."

After ten minutes of lying on the bed as the doctor pokes me, he checks my height and weight. I'm pleased I've lost a few pounds since my last visit.

"I can't feel anything abnormal at the moment, but I'd like you to do a blood test, smear test, and go for some scans to see if we can find out what's going on. I have a nurse available if you can do blood and smear tests now? Your scan appointment should be through in a few weeks."

"Thank you very much, Dr Woodstock."

I go through to the nurse and have my blood take and my smear done. I swear to god, these things are worse in your head than they actually are. But at least it's over in a few seconds.

After leaving the doctor, I take a cab home and try to work for the rest of the day. My mind is swimming with possibilities of what could be wrong. I text Gavin an update, start on the contracts for the Europe project and email Carol in HR for a new contract for Lucy. Once I've found my groove, I fly through the next couple of hours without a thought about my dysfunctional body. I don't feel like cooking tonight, so I text Gavin.

Me: Thai for dinner? Got my head into contracts and can't be bothered to cook.

Gavin: Sounds great. I'll pick it up on my way home.

Sorted!

Chapter Sixty-Five

JESS

Over the next couple of weeks, Lucy and I finalise the contract for the Europe project with legal. Miles is more than happy to go with her and work from Paris. He is completely in love with her. Lucy has put a deposit down on an apartment and organised her shipping. In a few weeks, she will be going over and starting up our new office. Excitement is flowing through us both as we organise the furniture to be delivered to the office. Lucy has picked out everything. This is her office, so she needs to put her stamp on it. Everything is moving along nicely.

I've had my scans and am just awaiting my results. I have an appointment with the doctor this afternoon to discuss the results of those and my blood work. Hopefully, we can figure out what's going on with my body. I've been doing my own research, which, let's face it, isn't a great idea! But there are a couple of conditions I may have, or it may just be the hormones from the contraception messing with my body. I've had both my mum and Gavin's mum messaging me about throwing an engagement party. Not my priority at the moment, but it'll be a nice distraction, and I decide to create a message group.

Me: Hi, both. I've created this group to throw some ideas around for an engagement party. Julia, this is my mum, Alison. Mum, this is Gavin's mum, Julia.

Mum: Hi, Julia. Trevor and I are so excited and happy that our daughter is marrying your wonderful son!

Julia: Hi, Alison. Daniel and I feel the same about Jess! Now shall we get planning? I've got some ideas I'd like your opinion on.

Me: I'll leave you both to it. Nothing TOO big please.

I mute the chat and let them catch up. Within five minutes, they've agreed to meet for lunch next week to discuss plans. I suddenly have visions of our wedding planning, and I wonder how much I will actually have to do. Chuckling to myself, I try work on some reports, and Gavin pops his head around my office door.

"Hey, handsome. What can I do for you?"

"Hey, beautiful. I wondered if you wanted me to

come with you to the doctor today. I had Anna clear my schedule in case."

This man truly is wonderful. "That would be lovely. Are you sure you want to hear about the gory details of my lady parts?" I laugh but hope he will.

"Absolutely! I love everything about you. Why shouldn't I know about the stuff you're going through? I want to help." He comes over to my desk, plants a kiss on my forehead and goes back out. Gavin is seriously one of a kind.

We're sitting in my doctor's office, waiting to be called in. I don't realise my leg is bouncing nervously until Gavin puts his hand on it. "It'll all work out the way it's meant to. We'll work through whatever is coming our way."

When the doctor calls me in, Gavin takes my hand. I'm not normally phased by doctor appointments, but I have a gut feeling this one isn't going to go well.

"Hi, Jess. Please take a seat."

Gavin introduces himself, and we sit down. I can see from my doctor's face this isn't going to be pleasant. I'm nervous about what he is going to say.

"Let's start with your blood tests. Those look okay, but you have elevated testosterone in your blood, and your HbA1C is also on the higher side. The HbA1C is what we use to track your glucose levels. Yours are currently sitting at fifty-one, which puts you in the diabetic range."

"What? I'm diabetic? That can't be right?"

"Unfortunately, you are. However, you're low on the scale. The normal range is below forty-eight, so you're not very high. This can be managed with medication. Your smear came back with no problems, so that's good there. However, your scans show that you have polycystic ovaries."

My mind is reeling. How? What? Why?

"With PCOS, polycystic ovary syndrome, your testosterone levels can become elevated, and this can reduce your ovulation and, in turn, periods. This could be the main cause for you missing so many periods. This also gives you a higher insulin resistance, which, if it isn't managed properly, can give you higher glucose levels leading to diabetes."

My ovaries are buggered?

"I'm going to refer you to the gynaecologist, who can go through everything in more detail and look at how we proceed. Do you have any questions?"

"Um, there'll probably be loads when I get home, but at the moment, I just have two. Will this affect my fertility, and do I have to go on a special diet to control the diabetes?"

I'm so embarrassed! Why did Gavin have to be here for this? My body is broken, and I have diabetes.

"Fertility-wise, I can't advise, but your gynaecologist will be able to help with that. As far as diet goes, I'm going to book you in with the diabetic nurse. Diet can help, and she will give you lots of information on what foods are better and how to help control your insulin levels. For the moment, though, I'm going to put you on Metformin. This will not only help with your PCOS symptoms but will also help with your insulin levels."

"Thank you, I'll wait to hear from you regarding the nurse and gyno appointment."

As we walk outside, Gavin pulls me into a massive hug. My emotions flood me, and I cry hard.

"It'll be okay, Jess," he whispers into my hair as I sob into his shoulder. We decide to take the rest of the day off and spend time at home together. Whilst Gavin is in the shower, I open Doctor Google. I look into PCOS and diabetes and write down so many notes my hand cramps. There are so many different websites to look at, but I choose to look at medical journals and the NHS site rather than any others. I don't want any false information.

When Gavin comes downstairs, he's on the phone. I smile at him as I'm reading. When he hangs up, he comes over to me, kissing me gently. "I know your doctor has referred you to a gynaecologist, but where your health is concerned, I'd rather not wait. It's up to you, but I have an appointment pencilled in for next week with a private consultant, who will have your notes emailed over in minutes to make sure we can get you the best care and answers possible."

I sit there, not knowing what to say. I mean, wonderful, I don't have to wait for an appointment, but private? That's expensive. Then I realise who I'm marrying. I agree to the appointment, and we decide on takeaway for dinner, but nothing too carb heavy. Diabetes and all.

Chapter Sixty-Six

GAVIN

Since Jess's doctor appointment, I've been doing research into PCOS and what it will mean for her. We've not had a proper discussion about kids, but we may encounter some problems having them. It's Saturday morning. Jess is sleeping in because she's exhausted. Unable to sleep, I've been up since six o'clock.

It's now seven o'clock, and I'm going for a run to process my thoughts. I can't do what I normally do and take charge. This is *her* body, so we need to do things at her pace. As I'm jogging, my mind races and my emotions are all over the place.

There's a lot of information on too many websites. How will this affect her mentally? What happens if we can't have kids? IVF? Egg donor? Adoption? What pain is this going to cause? She mentioned her periods are really bad when she gets them. It is probably this condition, but what will happen as time goes on? How can I fix this?

I stop running. I can't fix this. I lean against the nearest tree in the park. I didn't realise I'd run so far in a short space of time. I can't fix the problem, but I can certainly help Jess through it and process what it is that's going to happen next.... I run for another half hour, then head home.

When I get home, my thoughts are more organised, and my focus will be on Jess. We have an appointment on Tuesday to discuss options with the gynaecologist and go from there.

I sit at the breakfast bar with a nice Italian blend coffee after a hot shower, pouring through notes I've made when my phone rings. *Mum? Why's she calling at nine o'clock on a Saturday morning?*

"Mum, everything okay?"

"Good morning, dear. Everything is fine. Don't sound so worried."

"Well, it is early, and you don't normally call on the weekend unless we have plans. What do I owe the pleasure?"

"Alison and I have been talking and arranging an engagement party for the two of you. How does two weeks from today sound?"

Bugger! I don't want to go into everything with my mum right now since we are still wrapping our heads around Jess's news. But a party might be a good distraction. I check my calendar, and we are free.

"That sounds great, Mum. What did you have in mind?"

"Oh, I'll send you both the details. Alison and I have everything in hand. You two just show up looking lovely as you always do." I can't help the laugh that comes out. My mum loves a party, and from what I've heard from Jess, her mum loves to organise.

"No problem, Mum. Thank you very much for organising this."

"It's my pleasure, Gavin dear. You can repay me with grandchildren."

My body stiffens; we will need to tell our parents at some point. Since meeting Jess, I've become closer to my parents and don't like the idea of them not knowing. "Well, Mum, that's certainly something we can discuss. I'm going to go and wake my sleepy fiancée up and make us breakfast. We'll catch up in the week?"

"Okay, love. Speak soon!"

I'm not going to wake Jess up just yet; she needs some more sleep. Instead, I sit back down with my coffee and read some more. The more information I have, the better questions I will have for our appointment.

After Jess wakes up and has her shower, we have some breakfast and go for a walk to clear the cobwebs. We discuss our individual research and what questions we have for our appointment on Tuesday, we discuss the impending party our mums have organised, and we then sit in our favourite little coffee shop and start talking about the wedding and our future.

"What happens if it turns out I can't have kids?"

Her voice is a little shaky; she's clearly worried about this.

"Then we look at other options. We could look at IVF, egg donors, adoption...."

"I don't want IVF. Kiera's cousin went through it with her husband, and it ended with them nearly splitting up over it. The hormones alone are tough, not to mention scheduling when you can have sex."

I nod along. I haven't looked into IVF, but from what I understand, it sounds like an intense process.

"I'm not sure about an egg donor, either. Is that too fussy?"

"No, it's our future and our children we're talking about. Whatever we decide has to be agreed upon by both sides."

"How do you feel about adoption? Wouldn't you want your own children to inherit your empire?" I laugh and spill a little of my coffee. "I'm not Lord Vader! If we look into adoption, they will be our children. They won't be our DNA, but DNA isn't everything."

Jess sits back and looks at me with an enquiring expression on her face. "You really don't mind if they don't have your DNA? Your handsome genes?"

"Absolutely not. Our children will be loved and cherished no matter how they come to us."

We take a walk and return home, holding hands as we discuss different options. We've come to the decision that if we can't have children naturally, we'll look into adoption. This is a big decision to make over coffee, but it seems to be the easiest decision to make.

We are happy with adoption if we can't have natural birth children.

After that discussion, Jess seems a little lighter and less stressed. We have an afternoon of reading, catching up on some emails and cooking dinner. Jess has started a notebook with some wedding ideas, and we go through those. I haven't thought about weddings before Jess, but this is exciting.

After a simple dinner of tortellini, we curl up and watch a bit of Netflix. I sit there with my arm around Jess, reminiscing about the times I was here alone, wanting to have someone to share my life with. Now, I have her, and I couldn't be happier. Today was a perfect day of spending time as a couple in my opinion. I feel happy and relaxed. Before I know it, I've fallen asleep on the sofa with my girl, watching serial killer documentaries. There's something odd about finding these relaxing, that's for sure.

Chapter Sixty-Seven

JESS

Tuesday arrives. We've had a lovely weekend chilling at home and starting our wedding preparations, which is very exciting. We're looking at an autumn wedding, so it doesn't give us long to get ready.

Sitting in the waiting room at the private doctor's office, I glance around at everything. I've never been to a private doctor before. They have coffee machines, comfortable seating, and the walls are painted calming blues and greens rather than the stark white of my usual doctors. I actually feel relaxed before the doctor calls us in.

Gavin takes my hand and leads us into the office.

"Miss Freeman, Mr Andrews, thanks for coming in today. I've read your blood test results and gone through your scans. I can confirm the diagnosis of PCOS. I believe you wish to talk about treatment?"

The doctor speaks with a calm voice, which is nice.

"Yes, we've done some research and have some questions for you. Our main one is about fertility."

"That's a common question with this condition. With how erratic your periods are and going from your notes, I'm not ruling out the possibility of becoming pregnant, but it could be a struggle. Are you still taking your contraception?"

"Yes, I am for the moment. We haven't discussed when we'd like to start a family, but we know we want one. We just aren't sure when."

Gavin squeezes my hand. "The when can be anytime, but we're in no rush. We want to cover all our options," Gavin tells the doctor whilst running his thumb across mine.

We are in this together, and he is showing me he isn't going anywhere. I'm not going to lie. My biggest fear is him leaving me if I can't have children, but after our discussion of other options, I feel secure, supported and loved by him.

The doctor goes through some tests we can do, including the possibility of IVF, which we both say no to. However, he recommends I stop my contraception to ensure my body can return to its normal cycle. "It could take up to twelve months for the contraception to come out of your body and your cycle to return to its normal state, which could still be irregular, but you may notice more of a pattern. If you're worried about becoming pregnant sooner than you'd like, I'd suggest condoms as a way forward for now. Something for you both to discuss."

Gavin and I take a moment to take in what the

doctor has said. If I come off of my contraception, there's a possibility I could get pregnant. If I don't, then we know there's an issue. We thank the doctor for her time, and she gives us her card if we have any questions we want to email over. We book an appointment for a month's time for further discussions. We walk to the car in silence—not uncomfortable, but we are both processing our own thoughts.

"Jess, how do you feel about coming off of the pill?" We are nearly home when Gavin asks me.

"I'm happy to come off it. How do you feel about it?"

"Let's get you off the pill and your body functioning naturally. I'm not a fan of condoms, if I'm honest, and we can't have you on any contraception, and I'm sure as hell not taking a vow of celibacy."

I laugh out loud. I love him so much. He wouldn't survive two days without sex. "What happens if my body decides it'll take a child?"

"Then we'll have nine months to prepare for a tiny human."

We talk the rest of the way home about the what-ifs and decide that I won't take my pill from now on. We'll see what the universe throws at us and roll with it. It's exciting to think about having a tiny person now that we've actually discussed it. If, in a year, it doesn't work out naturally, then we're going straight down the adoption route. I don't want to be prodded and poked, I definitely don't want daily hormone injections, and I'm not interested in egg donors. It's not something I want to put myself through, and Gavin is supportive of that.

We spend the rest of the day working at home and making calls to venues we are interested in for our wedding. Two of them have slots available in autumn, and we make appointments to view them next week. I catch up on the chat group about the engagement party. I'm clearly not needed for anything, which is quite nice. At the end of our day, we have our dinner and go to bed, exhausted after an emotional day. Nothing beats lying next to the person you love, not cuddling, but our feet are touching to maintain that closeness. This is what I've been wanting, not a fairy tale, but a proper relationship with proper sleeping positions.

Before we know it, it's the weekend of our party. Julia and Daniel are hosting, and by the time we arrive at Gavin's parents, we are shooed upstairs for a few hours before the party begins. Plenty of time for a little nap, shower and getting ready. Gavin, on the other hand, has other ideas. He closes the door to our room before striding over and pulling me into him. I feel every part of his muscular body against my softer, curvy one. His hands are everywhere, like a teenager's. In my hair, down my back, my hips, breasts, face.... I pull away for a split second to ask him if he's okay. That is all he needs to pull me up so my legs wrap around his waist, and he pushes me back against a wall. He feels frantic, desperate to have me, the feeling swarms me, and I mirror those feelings.

We are like a couple of horny teenagers, trying to be quiet in his parents' house but bumping into everything as we go. I'm pretty sure they are too busy with the party prep to notice any sounds.

Gavin has ripped off my clothes and his, and we are on the bed, having a hot make-out session, when he pulls away. "I fucking love you, Jess." And with that, he opens my legs and plunges deep inside me whilst putting his hand over my mouth to muffle the sounds. This is hot, and I'm swiftly racing towards an orgasm. His pace quickens; this is going to be fast for both of us. Within minutes, we have climaxed and are out of breath. We haven't had a "quickie" before. He likes to take things slow, but I have to admit, I really enjoy it.

We both lay in bed, staring up at the ceiling. I have my head on his shoulder, and his arm is around me. "That was unexpected but amazing! Are you okay? I felt a lot of emotions…." I turn to see his face.

"I had the urge to have you. There were a lot of emotions, but mainly I wanted to see your come face!" He laughs. I've never seen my own orgasm face, but apparently, it's sexy. I highly doubt that!

We fall asleep for an hour, waking up to his mum softly knocking on the door, telling us we had just over an hour before guests arrived. We jump through the shower and get ready. I never need more than half an hour to get ready; I have no idea how it takes some women hours. I'm very low-key on makeup and hair, though. The last time I tried to contour my face, I looked like I'd been through a wildfire and come out with smoke damage!

We head downstairs to sneak a quick smoke in before guests arrive. We don't smoke much anymore, but still enjoy the odd one. *This is something that'll have to stop if you want kids!* I'm not wrong! We go back inside as the first guests arrive.

Chapter Sixty-Eight

GAVIN

Jess is looking elegant tonight. She is wearing a beautiful lilac dress with simple sandals. I'm in my usual trousers and shirt, but I have made an effort to match my tie colour to her dress. We greet guests, mostly family members, and answer questions about our wedding plans. My thoughts are straying back to earlier and our quick session. I felt this overwhelming desire to be close with her and have a raw moment with her. I don't know whether it's because of all the stress currently with doctor's appointments or the fact I just wanted it from a primal view, but it was exactly what I needed to get my head back in check.

After a couple of hours of chatting, mingling between guests and eating, my dad clinks his glass. "Thank you, friends and family, for coming here tonight to celebrate these two wonderful people getting engaged. Jess, we couldn't be happier that you are joining our family. You are everything we could have wished for and more in a daughter-in-law. Alison and Trevor, we welcome you into our family and look forward to getting to know each other more. Finally, Gavin, our only son. We have always supported and loved you, but we cannot express how thrilled and happy we are that you have found your other half. You two complete each other, and we wish you every happiness. Ladies and gentlemen, raise your glasses to Gavin and Jess!"

After a cheer and drinking, I go to stand next to my dad with Jess. "Thank you, Dad, for that lovely speech. Thank you, everyone, for coming to celebrate with us tonight, and thank you to my beautiful fiancée, Jess. You have made me the happiest man in the universe, knowing you'll be by my side for the rest of our days. We make a great team, and we will have our highs and lows, but if you've taught me anything, it's that together, we can accomplish anything." I raise my glass, not taking my eyes off Jess. "To us." I hear another toast and take a drink.

As glasses are being topped up, I have a couple of people come over to congratulate us and inevitably talk shop. Jess rolls her eyes, grins and goes to mingle. After half an hour, I go to find her but can't see her anywhere in the house. I walk outside and find her sitting on my favourite bench under an oak tree in the garden. She is a vision on a beautiful sunny day. Her expression, however, doesn't match the celebrations inside.

"Hey," I say softly as I sit down next to her. "Sorry,

I just needed some air and a little space." "What's wrong?"

"I don't want to go down the fertility route when it is only a maybe or possibility. I've been thinking a lot about it, doing research, and even if we do manage to get pregnant, there's no guarantee I will actually carry to term. It seems like a lot of heartbreak waiting to happen." She almost sounds panicked. "Then we adopt."

Jess spins around so fast she could have given herself whiplash. "What? Don't you want to try?"

"Not if it's causing you this much worry and pain whilst thinking about it. And you're right. What if it doesn't work? That's heartbreak we may not fully recover from emotionally. However, with adoption, we're in it together, and neither of us is going through physical pain."

Jess cuddles into me, her eyes welling with tears. We can't go through trying to get pregnant if it's going to be emotionally difficult. She knows others it has worked for, and it's lovely, but she also knows people who tried for ten years and had diddly squat. If we adopt, it'll still be hard emotionally, but not like losing a child through pregnancy.

"I love you, Gavin."

"Good job you're marrying me then, eh?"

She chuckles, and we sit for a while before heading back into the party. I can feel the weight lift from her. She seems brighter, too.

After a couple more hours, our guests start to head home. Jess has stolen some time to be with Kiera and have a good old catch-up. Kiera has a new job, so she has been travelling more with work, meaning less girly catch-up time. But they have some dates in the diary, which they are excited about.

Jess potters about helping both mums clear up. Jess's parents are staying at my parents' house for the night, too. It's not like they didn't have the space for guests, and it is nice we can all chill after the party. The minute the last guest leaves, Jess runs upstairs and changes into her PJs. I think it's because she's tired, but apparently, it's a tactical move so she can have more cake.

The rest of the evening is spent chatting around the dining table with coffee and cake and playing board games. Something hits me. I've never had this before. Yes, I've had nights in with my parents, but I have never been this close with them. This feels nice. Proper family time, and it's something I pin in my head to make sure we do with our kids. Jess notices my smile and reaches for my hand. I kiss the back of her hand. I can't wait to start a family with this woman.

THE FOLLOWING MORNING, MUM MAKES A HUMUNGOUS breakfast, just as if she's running a B&B! By mid-morning, Jess and I leave. Her parents are staying to go on a walk with mine—it's nice they're bonding. As we drive back home, we talk about when we'll start the adoption process and what we'll look for. Jess, of course, has done a lot of research and found that you rarely get a baby in this country unless it's private adoption or surrogate. We are okay with not having the fresh-out-of-the-oven baby experience. She mentions the universe already has a child in mind for us, and we'll know when we see or hear about them.

Jess sends an email to our local adoption agency, and we will go from there. We've got the wedding in a few months, and work is picking up, so there's no rush, but it's good to know what we're getting into process-wise. Of course, Jess has a dedicated notebook for her adoption research and has already been researching the process and adoption rates in the U.K.. Sometimes, I wonder if this woman could actually run the country with how organised she is.

By the time we get home, we have a light bite to eat and a long soak in the bath. When we get into bed, we cuddle; it feels intimate, loving and safe. It isn't long before we both drift off after our busy weekend.

Chapter Sixty-Nine

JESS

The next couple of weeks fly by. Gavin and I have made some life-changing decisions. I'm going to get a coil to help with my periods, and choosing the non-hormonal one means I shouldn't have any side effects, unlike the pill. We are going to an information evening next week for adoption, and I'm flying out to Paris to meet with Lucy tomorrow to see how the Europe Project is going. It's all busy and exciting. Especially as Kiera is flying out with me to have a weekend together.

I'm sitting in my office, absentmindedly twirling my engagement ring on my finger. I have finished my reports, done more research into adoption and have everything prepared for whilst I'm away in Paris. We've not done any wedding planning for a few weeks, so I start looking at venues. We both want an autumn wedding and are looking at October, so we'll have all those lovely colours around us.

After an hour of searching, I find something that I love. Botleys Mansion in Surrey. It has everything we've talked about, including grounds with lots of trees, a house with classic stone exterior, grand steps that lead to the entrance, and a huge beautiful interior that is colourful. I immediately send it to Gavin as well as send the venue an email to check on their availability in autumn. I have a great feeling about this place and really hope they have space for our wedding.

After a good hour or so of wedding planning, I pop into Gavin's office to see if he is free for lunch. We walk to our favourite coffee shop and have lunch before heading back to work. It's a quick break as Gavin has a meeting to get back to, but he loves the wedding venue I found, which is a bonus. When I sit back at my desk, my phone pings.

Kiera: Packed and ready for our Paris trip! Meet you at yours tonight. xx

Me: Excellent! I'm packed and will add the final few bits tonight. If you want, you come by work and grab my key. You're more than welcome. xx

Kiera: All access to the penthouse? I'll be with you in an hour! xx

I giggle at Kiera's reply; she loves coming over. To be fair, our home is a lot bigger than the flats we could afford in London. I text Gavin to let him know Kiera will be at ours by the time we get home and set about finishing my day.

It's only two in the afternoon, but I'm caught up and have nothing major to do. We're flying out first thing in the morning, so a relaxing afternoon with my best friend sounds too good to turn down.

By the time Kiera comes to work, I have packed up and am ready to head there with her. We get an Uber home, and whilst I'm packing my last-minute essentials, she's wandering around the penthouse. She doesn't feel comfortable doing it with Gavin around, but with me, she's totally relaxed.

"Jess, this place is humungous! Seriously, I could move in, and you wouldn't notice!" Kiera shouts from down the hall. It is an impressive house, I'll give her that.

She comes strolling into the bedroom, smiling broadly. "Literally can't wait to fly out in the morning! How long do you think you'll take at the Paris office?"

"I should only be there for a few hours, then the rest of the weekend is ours."

We spend the next few hours looking up where we want to explore in Paris. Kiera, of course, is focused on which shops she wants to go to. We order dinner in tonight, and by the time Gavin comes home, dinner is ready. Very fifties housewife.

"So what are you going to do whilst I steal your woman for the weekend?" Kiera asks Gavin whilst chomping through her Wagamamas.

"Well, I'm naturally going to be lost without her and mope around, waiting for her return." He gives a cheeky wink and grin. "I'll be spending tomorrow working, Saturday visiting my parents, Sunday golfing with Paul, then I will await your return on Monday."

"Sounds lovely. Send my love to your parents." I smile at him; I really do love his parents. They are so down to earth.

When we have finished dinner, we sit down in the living room with a cuppa. "So there's been a hiccup with the flights for the morning…." My heart jumps when Gavin speaks. I don't want any delays. "Unfortunately, I had to cancel the first class tickets we ordered."

I have a sinking feeling. After flying to Paris with Paul, I got quite used to the luxury of first class.

"You'll have to take the company jet instead." He winks at me and laughs. Kiera squeals in utter delight.

"WHEN did we get a company jet? And why?"

"Well, with an office in Paris, it made sense to have our own jet to fly out on rather than pay commercial airlines. And why not?"

I sit back. We have a jet! This is going to be the best weekend ever!!!

KIERA AND I SIT VERY COMFORTABLY ON THE JET AT seven o'clock in the morning. It is a beautiful plane. We have eight seats up front, four on each side of the aisle facing each other with a table in the middle, a sofa area in the middle, and at the back was a bedroom with an en suite! This is still bigger than my old flat!

Our pilot has advised we are taking off in five minutes. We sit back and enjoy the large comfortable seats. The flight is about an hour and a half, so we have time to chat and relax. By the time we land, we have a car waiting for us to take us to our hotel. We have a suite in the hotel, which has two bedrooms, two bathrooms and a seating area. If you had said to me a couple of years ago I'd be flying to Paris on a private jet and staying in a suite at an expensive hotel, I honestly wouldn't believe you. Yet here I am, loving life.

We unpack and freshen up before I go into the office to meet Lucy. Kiera is going to stay in the suite and catch up on some work whilst she has some downtime. She had changed jobs a few months ago from being an admin manager at a security firm to a finance manager in a software company. She loves the change of pace, but something isn't sitting right about the company for her. I might talk to Paul and see if there's anything we can offer her.

I walk up to our Europe office, and honestly, it's perfect. The exterior is clean, sharp and trendy, with flashes of colour. The interior, as I walk in, has plants and a nice waiting area. It looks completely professional. I head to reception and sign in. Lucy comes out a few moments later.

"Jess, come on through." Lucy is literally beaming; Paris clearly agrees with her.

"You look fantastic, Lucy. You suit Paris." I smile at her.

"I love it here. I can't thank you enough for this

project. It's turned my life around in an amazing way. Miles and I are really happy here."

I couldn't be happier for her. We talk through the numbers and how the office is doing, and honestly, it's booming. We have more than fifteen projects and have the budget to hire staff here in Paris for her. I couldn't be more proud of this project. This is MY baby. I thought of this and made it happen! I'm so proud of Lucy and how she's doing here, too.

"So, when's the wedding?"

"We're looking at autumn. You and Miles will be invited if you can tear yourselves away from this beautiful city."

"We'll be there. Honestly, Jess, I'm so happy everything has worked out for the both of us."

After a brief catch-up on our personal lives, we decide to go for lunch. Lucy takes me to her favourite lunchtime spot, and from there, I say my goodbyes. I want to get changed into my comfortable shoes for an afternoon of exploring. On my way back to the hotel, I receive a call from an unknown number.

"Good afternoon. I need to speak with Miss Freeman?"

"Hi, speaking."

"This is Anita from the adoption team. Is now a good time to talk?"

"Absolutely."

"We are looking at starting your prospective adopter's paperwork next week. Are you and Mr Andrews free on Wednesday?"

"We can be free. Send me the details, and we'll be there."

"Lovely, I'll email that over now and look forward to meeting you both."

"Thank you. You, too."

I hang up, feeling excited. My project is doing amazingly well in Paris, the wedding planning is going well, and our adoption paperwork is starting next week! And not to forget I have a weekend away with Kiera. I bound into the hotel room to find her completely focused on her laptop. I get changed, walk in front of her without her noticing and close her laptop.

"Enough now, let's go!"

Kiera jumps up, and off we go to explore this amazing city.

Chapter Seventy

GAVIN

Last night, being at home without Jess was strange. We texted a few times, but I wanted her to enjoy her time with Kiera. I spent time reading in preparation for our adoption meeting next week. From what I've read, the process is quite intense. I've mentally prepared myself and know Jess has all the forms prepared. She does love a bit of paperwork.

I grab a shower before having a light breakfast and coffee. I'm going to see my parents today, and that means arriving on a nearly empty stomach. My mum does love to feed people. Heading out, I have a pang of wishing Jess was by my side. Since we began seeing each other, we haven't spent much time apart. She'll be back on Monday, so there are only two more days though. I send her a quick text before driving to my parents' house.

Me: I miss you. xx

Jess: I miss you, too. Two more days and I'll be home! xx

When I arrive at Mum and Dad's, I can smell something mouth-watering coming from the kitchen. I walk in on Mum cooking a lamb dinner and apple tarte tatin. One of my favourites!

Mum turns round and grins broadly. "Hello, darling! How are you?"

Hugging her, I reply, "I'm good, Mum. You're looking well."

Dad walks in and pats me on the back. "Where's your better half?" He laughs.

"Paris with her friend. She's back on Monday." He isn't wrong; she really is the better half of me.

We spend time in the garden whilst dinner is cooking. Mum then works on finishing up the meal whilst Dad and I drink our coffees. "So, son, what's on your mind?"

"Can we talk about it over dinner? It's something I want to speak with both of you about."

"Absolutely. By the sounds coming from the kitchen, we should head in and wash up."

We sit down and start eating. Mum has cooked for a family of ten rather than the three of us. She's going to absolutely love having grandchildren to feed. "There's something I wanted to talk to you about." Mum and Dad look at each other but remain silent. "Jess and I have been to a couple of doctors. Unfortunately, Jess is unable to have children without severe medical intervention, which is something we want to avoid."

"Oh, bless her. Is she okay?"

"She's okay, Mum. We've talked about it a lot and have come to a decision. We plan on adopting."

Mum practically falls off her chair. "Adoption? That's amazing! Oh, you'll both be amazing parents."

"What are the next steps for you? Julia, remember to eat whilst you're internally planning our grandchildren's bedrooms!"

I laugh. I can literally see her going through colour charts in her head. I briefly explain the process and talk about our meeting on Wednesday.

"So we're open to sibling groups or only children. We just want a family to raise and love." By the time I've finished waffling on, we've finished dinner and have begun clearing the table, ready for pudding.

"Oh, Gavin, we're so proud of you both. You are doing a wonderful thing by adopting, too!" Mum is

still beaming.

After pudding, Dad and I clear up whilst Mum potters off. She comes back into the kitchen as we sit down with coffee.

"I know this may seem silly, but the moment you brought Jess home, I have been collecting bits for when you may eventually start a family." Mum puts down a huge box—seriously you could fit a house in this thing.

"Mum, what's in it? A house?"

"No, silly. That's on order. A playhouse that is. We wanted to be prepared for when you had children." She smiles, and I can feel the amount of love and acceptance coming from her. Whoever we adopt is going to be lucky to have her as a grandmother.

Mum goes through the box. No clothes, thankfully, but a few books, toys, and a few bits from when I was a child, the perfect set-up for any child. There are also catalogues for furniture ranging from nursery to teenagers! She really is prepared, just like Jess!

Dad sits back and drinks his coffee. I wonder how much he contributed to this box.

"Do you plan on staying in the penthouse with the children?" he asks whilst Mum is *still* showing us items she's collected.

"No, we both want to raise our children out of the city. With you guys being here in Surrey and Jess's parents living in Kent, it'd be nice to come back down this way to be closer to you all and be in the open air with the kids."

Mum and Dad look at each other and smile. "Well, my dear, there's something your dad and I wanted to talk to you both about. Since Jess isn't here, I feel bad about bringing it up, but it also seems like perfect timing." She looks at Dad, who sits up a little straighter.

"You know we originally bought this house to have a big family, but the universe thought you were the perfect son for us, and we couldn't have any more. So, we have this big house and just us living in it…."

No, they can't be?

"We'd like to downsize and for you and Jess to move into the house. We'd transfer the deeds over, and you'll have this wonderful house and space to raise your children."

I sit back and stare at them both. They've had this house since they got married. They have built so many memories here, and I can't believe they're giving that to us to build more. "Mum, Dad, we can't. This has always been your house."

"Yes," Dad interrupts, "but it'll be yours. You'll raise your family here and build many happy memories. When you want to downsize, you can pass it down to them."

I have been looking on the market for a perfect family house, and one has literally just been handed to us. "Well, in that case, we'll buy your new home." My mum is about to protest, but Dad stops her. He understands that I need to do something to show our gratitude. "And, of course, I'll speak to Jess when she gets home."

After that huge emotional bombshell, we talk for another couple of hours, and I drive home thinking about this afternoon. I wonder how Jess will feel about taking on my parents' house. It's perfect for raising a family.

It's perfect for raising our family.

Chapter Seventy-One

JESS

After two days of exploring Paris with Kiera, shopping until we dropped and eating everything in sight, we are ready to head home. It's at this point I'm pleased we have the jet rather than having to try to get everything onboard a commercial plane. A LOT of shopping has been done.

We sit in our seats, waiting for the pilot to carry out his checks. I look over at Kiera, who is tapping away at her laptop. I open my own and go through my emails. I find a response from the wedding venue I emailed.

From: Botley Mansion To: Jess Freeman Subject: Availability Message:

Dear Miss Freeman,
Thank you for your enquiry. I can confirm

we've just had a cancellation for October and would like to offer you the date. If you would like to call to book a walk around and appointment with our wedding coordinator, we can move forward with this date.

Date: 15th October Time: 13:30
We will have the entire mansion available for guests to book rooms. We look forward to your response.

Kind regards

I shriek in excitement. Everything is coming together. I immediately text Gavin to let him know and call the venue to book an appointment for next week before putting it in our calendar. It suddenly occurs to me that I haven't asked anyone to be my bridesmaid.

Kiera looks over at me with a quizzical expression on her face. "Something to be happy about, I assume?"

"Absolutely. I think I've just booked our wedding venue!"

"Oh, that's wonderful news and certainly something to celebrate." This is excellent timing as the air steward pours us some champagne.

"There's something I need to ask you, Kiera."

"Of course, I'll be your bridesmaid! I've already got ideas for the hen do, and I'm not wearing a terrible dress!"

We laugh as we drink our fizz and sit chatting

about the ideas I've had around colour schemes. I tell Kiera she has full licence on the dress she wears. I'd obviously be paying for it, but as long as it goes with the colours, she can wear whichever style she wants.

By the time we land, neither of us looked at our laptops again, as we were too busy talking about the wedding. Kiera has looked at dresses she likes, which doesn't surprise me. She is typically organised.

Gavin has arranged cars for us, and we say our goodbyes and head home. I can't wait to see Gavin. This is the longest we've been away from each other since we started dating.

I WALK INTO THE PENTHOUSE TO THE TABLE SET FOR two, candles, music on low and the smell of dinner. I couldn't be any luckier if I tried. I set my bags down and walk into the kitchen to see Gavin dancing along as he cooks. He turns around and smiles so broadly that I think his cheeks will fall off. He turns the stove down and walks over to me with such purpose, grabbing my head and smashing his lips against mine.

I can't stop my hands from roaming. I missed him so much this weekend. His touch, his voice, his smell.... He lifts me up moves me onto the countertop. His grip is strong; it's like he can't get enough of me. With one hand, he hitches up my dress, moves my knickers to one side, and plunges his fingers inside me, making me gasp. I can feel his desperate need. I fumble with his belt and undo his trousers. He edges me closer to him and pulls me onto him. It's rough, fast and oh so good!

Within minutes, we are both climaxing, breathing heavily.

"Hi, there, beautiful," he says breathlessly.

"I should go away more often if this is what I come back to."

"Not a chance. I missed you too much."

I jump down from the worktop and rearrange myself. I'm certainly glad to be home. Gavin wraps his arms around me and kisses me again, romantically this time rather than with the desperate passion from before. He turns the stove back on and carries on cooking what smells like a beautiful dinner. "You've got time to have a shower if you want to freshen up after your flight."

I smile and head upstairs; a shower sounds amazing right now.

Over dinner, Gavin catches me up on his weekend and the offer his parents have made. I'm in shock; their house is the sort of thing we were looking for but never had I thought about actually living there! We discuss the opportunity at great length. Money isn't a worry, so we can buy any property, but this one has wonderful memories for Gavin, and we can build our own memories there, too. We decide to take them up on their offer and will tell them over dinner this weekend.

We talk about the adoption meeting coming up this

week and the wedding venue. So much is happening at once. It's starting to feel a little overwhelming. The one thing we do agree on is that we will keep the penthouse and move into the house before we have children so that we can get it ready for when a child comes home to us if that suits his parents. The thought makes me tear up a little.

We spend the rest of the evening relaxing, talking over our potential futures, work, and the wedding. We have a lot to look forward to together. We go to bed feeling excited and happy.

Chapter Seventy-Two

GAVIN

Wednesday rolls around really quickly. We go to the adoption information evening, and it feels like they are giving us the worst-case scenarios for everything. Which, to be honest, is a good thing to hear, but some lighter stuff would have been appreciated. We come away feeling drained by all the information. Jess, naturally, has everything written down in her book in different sections. We fill out the "we're interested in continuing" form and expect a call from a social worker to start our stage one assessment soon. This is getting more real.

I always assumed I would have children and that they would be biological, but to me, it doesn't matter whether they are of my own DNA or adopted. They will still be ours to shape into little humans with my wonderful fiancée. We have all the wedding prep done —we are getting married in a couple of months—and have been talking to Mum and Dad about when they want to downsize.

My life was lonely before I met Jess, but I didn't realise it. Now it's full of fun, laughter, amazing sex and countless possibilities around our future. When I finally come out of my thoughts, it's nearly four o'clock in the afternoon. I shut down my laptop and head to Paul's office. His door is shut, so I knock.

"Come in." He sounds a bit gruff.

"Hey, fancy a pint?"

He looks at his watch, closes his laptop and follows me out. We walk the few short blocks to our local hangout and sit at our usual table.

"Out with it."

"I'm meeting her family this weekend. I haven't been in a relationship for years, and suddenly, I'm head over heels in love with a beautiful woman, who I'm sure is too good for me, and she wants me to meet her family. I'm useless at this stuff!"

"How do you know? You've never done it!" "Exactly!"

"Treat them like clients, small talk, chat, they'll get you to sit round a camp fire with marshmallows and…."

I laugh, but he just stares at me whilst drinking his draft.

"Not bad advice, apart from the hippy bit at the end."

We end up laughing, chatting about the rest of our lives. He's excited about the adoption; he's always wanted to be an uncle. He's already thinking of things he can buy our potential children to annoy the crap out of us.

After a couple of hours, we head back to the office to pack up and go home. I get a message from Jess to say we've got an appointment next week with a social worker. This is going a lot more quickly than I expected, and my nerves settle in a pit in my stomach. Am I ready? Are we? Have we had enough time together, just the two of us? We've been spinning so many plates with getting together, work, Jess's fertility, getting married, looking into adoption, and now moving house. My head starts to spin a little.

I walk through the front door to smell dinner is ready, the music is on, and my wonderful girl is in the kitchen plating it up. How she had time to cook this evening with the busy day she's had, I have no idea.

"Hey, you!" She looks chirpy. I wonder if she feels like the plates are spinning, too?

She takes one look at me, comes over and gives me a hug and kiss. "Bad day?"

"No love, just feeling a little overwhelmed."

She stands back and smiles. "Well, it's a good job we have a nice meal and a relaxing evening planned. I've been feeling a little dizzy with everything that's been going on and will be happening, as amazing and organised as I am. I thought we needed a night with just us, chatting, no paperwork, no phones…just us."

She gazes at me with those big blues. She is psychic, I swear. I instantly relax, knowing we're on the same page, and I cannot wait for our evening to start. I fire off a couple of emails before we sit down for dinner, and then my phone goes on silent, as does hers.

We spend the evening doing exactly what she has planned. Eating, having some wine and relaxing. Just us. We spend hours talking on the sofa, not just about everything going on but about our future. We get excited about putting a playhouse in the garden. Even though there are a lot of big things happening, there's always something to be excited about, and it feels a lot less daunting.

We head up to bed, and without realising it, we have a little routine. We'll brush our teeth, change and climb in. Jess will scroll through her phone, either on social media or her emails, and I'll be going through reports on mine. It's not that the sex has died out; it's just not as full-on as it was when we first got together. I do miss our "not being able to keep our hands off each other" phase, but I love this. We make love slow and sweet, have quickies in the shower, and have hard and fast times, too, but with everything going on, we've been exhausted.

Just thinking about Jess starts me stirring. She's lying on her front, reading in one of my T-shirts and her pants—I couldn't find her more attractive if I tried. I put my phone down and roll over to her, lifting up her top so I can kiss her back. She's humming in appreciation, which spurs me on.

"What's got you all riled up?" She chuckles as her head rests on the pillow, lapping up the kissing.

"Just thinking of you, how tired we've been and how much I haven't touched you like I used to," I say between kisses and nibbling her hip, making her giggle. *I love that sound so much.*

Jess turns over, and her eyes are on fire; she's feeling this as much as I am, which is making me want her even more. I kiss her slowly, wanting to take my time with her. However, when she throws her arms around my neck, lifting herself up to kiss me with such force and passion. I know I'll barely make it inside her before I explode.

Hard and fast it is! I pull her onto my lap, my mouth moving to her neck, then her magnificent breasts, whilst I push her knickers to one side and tease her. The gasps and moans coming from her sound like heaven! She's pulling down my boxers and grasping me. I'm already so hard it almost hurts.

Jess shifts in my lap and lowers herself onto me. She's more than ready. As she rocks her hips back and forth, I can feel her getting close already. *Damn, I'm nearly there myself!*

We're both breathing heavily, and I tilt my hips to angle differently, and Jess moans loudly. If I had any neighbours, they would probably wear ear defenders. It's the angle that sends her driving over the edge like *Thelma & Louise.* It's the feel of her spasming around me that gives me my own staggering release.

Jess finally comes down from her orgasm high, kisses me *much gentler this time*, and smiles. "Hey, you," she says, fully sated.

"Hey," is all I can muster.

We lay down, her head resting on my chest, and my fingers circling the soft pale skin on her back. "Let's book an off-the-grid honeymoon. Me, you, private pool, no clothes at all," I say. We need a break, some time for just us and no technology or working.

"I have a list of potential destinations on my spreadsheet." Jess giggles.

Of course, you have.

Chapter Seventy-Three

JESS

I finish my meeting and email some tasks to my PA. We are somehow in September, and with a month to the wedding, my nerves and excitement are building up. We've been through some really draining assessment meetings with our social worker. The last month has been a meeting every week, they want to know how you felt when your neighbour died when you were five years old, how your relationships are now, do you drink, eat well, did you get emotional when a bug hit your window screen?

I know they have to be thorough, but Jesus! I think they actually know more about us and our relationship than our parents do! Did we have enough time to grieve not being able to have children biologically? Yes! It wasn't an option. We can still be parents, but apparently, we have to go through a tough interviewing process, a thousand fiery hoops and then, maybe, we might be able to have children. Did I mention the training?

We could have fallen pregnant and had none of this, but this is our path. There are people out there that don't deserve children, and yet we do and can't have them. But we have the opportunity to change a child's life and ours.

My thoughts are a little negative, but after being grilled for hours, I kind of feel like I'm being judged. We know we'll be great parents, and that's what matters—well, that and the panel's approval. The fate of our parenthood lies in the hands of our social worker's report and five strangers who will say yes or no. I'm simplifying the whole process, but I've over-prepared for it and now I'm on edge. Speaking to other prospective adopters in our chat sessions, they feel the same, so it's not just us. Unfortunately, a lot of people drop out due to the intensity. Thankfully, I'm not judged for wanting to go back to work. I've already made a short list of nurseries and schools around the penthouse and the country house, depending on where we live when we bring our child home.

I push up from my desk and look out of my office window. I take a deep breath. Gavin is right. We've had a lot of conversations about how much we have going on around us. Work is normal, and everything else is being managed closely. Next month, we will be married, and after a couple of hours of researching, I've booked an amazing honeymoon in Barbados.

Private villa, pool, and room service. We have the

time booked off from work, and we'll be completely off the grid. Time for just us is definitely needed.

We're a week away from completing stage one of the adoption process. We're going to start stage two straight away and then have a couple of weeks off whilst we're on our honeymoon. We'll be moving into the house by the end of November, too. Julia and Daniel have found a wonderful three-bedroom cottage five minutes away. They are technically downsizing, but they wanted the extra rooms for "the grandkids." I'm pretty sure Julia has already picked out neutral colours for the rooms and furniture. I laugh, but they always wanted a big family. That wasn't in the cards for them, but they now have hope in their hearts for grandchildren. Apparently, they want as many as we can give them.

Probably to make their own rugby team.

THE NEXT FEW WEEKS FLY BY. WE'VE COMPLETED STAGE one of the adoption process and have geared up and started meetings for stage two. I'm tidying up my loose ends at work because the wedding is next week. Mum, Julia and Kiera came with me a few weeks ago to pick out my dress. I've never been one for shopping due to my size, so I didn't want a whole day of it. I picked two shops to visit, and the first shop had a dress I adored. It was simple, elegant and, more importantly, easy to wear for the dinner and dancing part of the day. Mum is picking my dress up tomorrow to keep at hers. Even though Gavin and I aren't spending the night apart before our wedding, she still wants something to be a surprise.

Just as I'm about to head out for lunch, I get a call from Anna, Gavin's PA. "Hey, Jess. Sorry to bother you. Have you heard from Gavin at all?"

"Hey, Anna. No, not since this morning. Everything okay?"

"I've just had a call from his one o'clock saying he isn't there yet, and it's half past. He's normally punctual."

Panic ripped through me. "I'll see what I can find out." I hang up the phone and log back into the computer to check his calendar. His last meeting was with Paul and a client. I call Paul.

"Hey, Jess, how are you doing? Getting ready for next week?"

"Hey, Paul. I'm good. Nearly ready. Thanks. Sorry to be blunt, but Gavin hasn't turned up to his one o'clock, and I'm a bit worried. Do you know where he is?

"He left me half an hour before the meeting to get there on time; I haven't seen him since. I'm near where his meeting is meant to be, so I'll walk over and see what I can dig up."

We say our goodbyes, and I hit the *Find Me* app on my phone. Gavin's phone is still circling, and no location has been found. I grab my bag to head out. The nerves in my stomach are beating against me like a flock of birds trying to escape.

I head down the street towards his last known location when my phone rings. It's Paul. My heart stops.

"Jess." His voice is fraught, my heart stops, and the emotions are in my chest, ready to burst. "There's been an accident…."

Chapter Seventy-Four

GAVIN

My god, my body hurts like hell! What happened? I think I'm lying somewhere. I can hear a distant chatter of voices. I try to open my eyes, but they're so heavy. By the time I've drifted back to whatever conscious state this is, I can hear Jess. I attempt to get up, but my body feels like I've been encased in cement.

"Gavin…." Her voice sounds worried.

Jess, I can hear you. I'm here, love.

I hear more mumbling in the background and feel something warm on my hand. That has to be Jess. She's shaking. Where am I?

I have no idea how long I've been lying here, but my body feels lighter than it did. I try to open my eyes. I can still feel Jess near me. My hand, I can feel it moving.

"GAVIN!" She sounds upset but happy.

I really need to open my eyes. Slowly they start to

lift. My vision is blurry, and my head hurts from the bright lights. *Are those fluorescent lights?* "Jess?" Why do I sound like I've smoked a pack of forty without a drink? My eyes are adjusting to the light and my surroundings. Am I in the hospital?

"Oh, Gavin!" She's sobbing. Have I been in an accident? "You're okay!"

AFTER DRIFTING IN AND OUT OF CONSCIOUSNESS FOR what seems like an eternity, I'm able to fully open my eyes. I'm alone in a very sterile room. *Hospital, I was right!* I can hear voices outside the door but can't hear what they are saying. I look down, and I have a hospital gown on. *Where are my clothes?*

Moments later, Jess comes back into the room. Her eyes are red and puffy, like she's been crying for hours. She stares at me and smiles, but I can see worry and pain in her eyes.

"You know, if you didn't want to get married, you could have just said." She chuckles, grabbing my hand. She lifts a glass of water with a straw to my lips so I can drink.

"What on earth happened? The last thing I remember is leaving Paul to head to my next meeting. Which I'm assuming I'm very late for."

"Well, it all seemed very dramatic, of course. The police officer took eyewitness accounts of what happened. You were happily walking to your next meeting, looking at your phone, emails, I presume...."

She gives me a little look—we've talked about not looking where I'm going before— "A shoplifter was running to escape security, knocked you into the road where you were run over."

I don't feel like I've been hit by a car or a bus. Am I paralysed? Are the drugs they're giving me that good?

Jess starts to laugh. I'm not sure whether it's hysterical or she finds my injuries that funny. "You were hit by a cyclist!" She bursts into uncontrollable laughter. The cheek. Her nearly husband is lying here on his death bed…or not.

"Well, I'm glad you find this amusing. I'm assuming there are no serious injuries, and I can go home?"

When she finally pulls herself together, she kisses me gently. "Yes, you can come home. They want to observe you for another couple of hours to check for any signs of a concussion, but other than that, you're absolutely fine." She swats my arm. "That's for scaring the life out of me!"

We catch up on the details. Apparently, my injuries are thanks to some young shoplifter who was stealing a bag from a shop. I still can't believe I got hit by a cyclist. This is London, after all, and there are no rules for them. I already know I'm not going to live this down. I shake my head, and Jess cocks hers at me.

"You're mocking yourself, aren't you?" she says with a chuckle. It's nice to see her laughing after the stress.

"Absolutely! Who gets knocked out by a cyclist?"

"At least you're not majorly injured. We are getting married next week, after all."

I smile. I'm marrying this wonderful woman. The lawyers suggest a prenuptial agreement, but there's not one ounce of Jess that cares about my money. What's mine is hers, and what's hers is mine.

It's been three days since I was in hospital. No concussion, thankfully, and not too banged up, either. It's also been three days of piss-taking from Paul, too. Aside from the embarrassment, there are no injuries, so that's good. Just a couple of cuts and scrapes. But with only a couple of days until the wedding, I must finish my vows. Jess has probably finished hers already.

Jess, there's been a connection between us only the universe can explain.

No, that sounds awful!

Jess, you are my light, my soul mate. What's mine is yours. Forever and always will I pledge my mind, body and soul to you.

Damn it. This needs work.

I'm still working on my vows when Anna knocks on my office door.

"Hi, Mr Andrews."

"Hi, Anna. What can I do for you?"

"Whilst you and the new Mrs Andrews are away, can I have a list of tasks to complete? I'd like to be able to keep busy and ensure everything is tidy for when you return." *Oh, how you remind me of Jess. Jess picked this one well.*

"I'll have that to you by the end of the day, Anna, and thank you for showing such initiative." She walks out smiling, and I continue with my current task.

Jess, there are no words to describe how I feel about you.

Literally none. I'm screwed!

Chapter Seventy-Five

JESS

Today is the day I get married to the man who has stolen my heart and made every dream come true. My nerves are fluttering, not because of the wedding, but because I can't wait to see him. We had breakfast together this morning, and I was then swiftly whisked away by Kiera to go to my mum's to get ready.

I'm standing in my old bedroom, my body is shaved within an inch of its life, moisturised to the point of drowning, and my hair is put up in a simple style as there isn't enough hair spray in the U.K. to hold any form of curl in this hair. Kiera is finishing my makeup. It is simple and elegant, yet it makes my eyes look amazing.

Mum bustles through the door, mumbling something about it's never too early for a drink on your wedding day. My mind is casting back to when I was sitting in the admin department, and I'd heard of Mr

Andrews, the scary CEO. I'm now getting ready to marry him. I chuckle, and Kiera hushes me whilst she finishes my eyeliner.

When my makeup is done, Kiera and Mum are getting themselves ready, and I pop into the garden for a few minutes of fresh air…and a cheeky cigarette. I haven't had one in a while and fancy one to steady the nerves. Autumn is my favourite time of year. There's a fresh smell in the air, the temperature is cool but not cold, and the sun is still warm on your skin. The leaves are dropping and turning orange. I pull out my phone to take a picture and see a text from Gavin. My heart smiles seeing his name.

Gavin: In a few hours, you will be my wife and make me the happiest man alive xxx

My heart dances. Will this feeling fade as we get older? I hope not. I take a picture of my view and send it.

Me: I can't wait to be waking up to a view like this, our children running amuck around us and us just sitting on the patio being with each other. You are my world, Gavin Andrews. xxx

Gavin: That is indeed a wonderful sight. The sight I want to see, however, is you on the bed later. ;) xxx

I laugh and send him a winking face. My dad comes outside with a fresh cup of coffee and a grin.

"Well, if you're having one then pass one here."

"Dad! I didn't know you smoked."

"I have the odd one now and then, just don't tell your mum."

We sit, having a cuppa and enjoying the view. I can hear my mum shouting my name, telling me I have an hour and a half before the car arrives. Even on my wedding day, it won't take me long to get ready. All I have to do now is to get dressed.

"Jess, if you don't get up here in the next ten minutes, you're going to be late!"

My dad chuckles and finishes his cigarette. "Well, best get up there, love, before she sends a search party."

My dad's eyes are tearing up. "Jess, you look truly beautiful." I grin, trying to hold it together. We're standing outside the mansion, waiting for our cue to go in. My dress is being shifted for pictures whilst we wait.

I'm glad I chose this dress. It accentuates my curves and hides the bits I want it to and I feel amazing in it. It's a floor-length white dress with silver and burnt orange leaf detailing on the short train. It's sleeveless with a sweetheart neckline and a corseted back. I used to hide my body and be ashamed of it, but Gavin has made me realise that I am beautiful. Accepting it was the best thing I ever did. I am standing tall with a wide smile on my face, ready to become Mrs Jess Andrews.

The registrar has come out to take us in. This is it!

We stand outside the room; my dad is holding me proudly as the doors open. Guests stand as they turn to watch us walk down the aisle, and I smile at them before making eye contact with Gavin. He has a tear in his eye, and his grin broadens as I get close to him. He looks exceptionally handsome today. His tie matches the orange detail on my dress. Our flowers are simple roses with a sprinkle of green leaves. I have no idea what they're called. Mum sent me a picture, and I said they looked pretty. With that, my job was done.

The music fades as the registrar starts talking. I haven't looked away from Gavin. My heart is hammering in my chest. Although my confidence has grown, standing here with my emotions heightened in front of a large room full of people is daunting.

I hear the words being spoken, and the time has come to read our vows. I wrote something quite beautiful but decided to "wing it" instead. I would stumble on my words if I had them in front of me. My mouth is suddenly dry, and I can hear my heart pounding in my ears.

"Gavin, I didn't imagine I could be as happy as I am standing here in front of you today. With you, I know I'll be eternally happy. I vow to love you fiercely, support you through highs and lows, and be yours forever and always." My eyes are welling up, and the look on his face is pure love.

"Jess, I never envisaged getting married, having a

family. My focus was purely on work. You have opened my eyes to the whole world, and suddenly, there in front of me was everything I would ever need. You. This is the beginning of forever. I promise to fall in love with you over and over again and be with you to climb every mountain and sit with you in every dark corner. You and me forever."

I couldn't love him anymore if I tried.

We exchange rings. Thankfully, no one bursts through the doors like they do in movies at the moment where someone can object. We kiss. In a room full of people, they melt away into the background whilst my *husband* kisses me.

We turn to our friends and family holding hands and smiling as we walk back down the aisle to a room where we can have five minutes alone whilst they head to the post-ceremony drinks area.

We walk into the room, I shut the door, and not even a millisecond goes by before Gavin pushes me against the door, kissing me passionately.

"Hello there, Mrs Andrews."

Chapter Seventy-Six

GAVIN

The band we have hired is on fire. Our guests are on the dance floor, and I'm standing against a wall with a scotch in my hand, admiring my wife while she dances with everyone else. I smile at that though. She is my wife.

Paul strolls over to me, my best friend and best man. "Shouldn't you be dancing or mingling instead of perving over your Mrs?" He chuckles.

"I should be, but I'm taking everything in. Thank you for today, Paul. I hope to be your best man when it's time."

"The woman has taken over my life, and I couldn't be happier. I am thinking of asking her to marry me next year. I didn't want to do it near your wedding or close to Christmas. I have an image in mind of us being at the top of the Shard."

I smile and throw my arm behind him, across his shoulders. We stand and watch everyone dance and talk. But in the moments we were talking, I'd lost sight of Jess. She's probably in the toilet or something. A moment later, I feel the hairs on the back of my neck stand up, and an arm wraps around my waist.

"Paul, love, do you mind if I steal my husband for a moment?"

He pushes off the wall and grins. "Can't wait until everyone leaves?" He laughs as he walks over to Sophie.

I turn to my beautiful wife. She's covered in sweat from dancing, but I couldn't care less. I pull her outside into the cool air and kiss her. She moans against my mouth, stirring every nerve-ending in my body. Surely, I don't have to share her for much longer? She pulls away, grinning as if she can read my mind. "We have an hour or so left, then I'm all yours." Turns out, she can.

We dance, talk with our friends and family, receive lots of hugs, and by the time the night ends, we are exhausted. The staff at the mansion are already taking the gifts to another room for safekeeping, and we make our way to the wedding suite, hand in hand.

"Right, get me out of this dress!" Jess laughs, but I sense a tone of urgency in her voice.

"Everything okay?"

"Yeah, Kiera tied me up like a pro, but after food and drink, I can no longer breathe."

I undo her dress and watch it fall to the floor. My body reacts at the sight of Jess letting down her hair, standing in just her white lace underwear and heels. I suddenly have a second wind of energy. She grins and walks over to me, helping me out of my wedding suit. As she undoes my shirt buttons, I kiss her neck, and her head tilts back as she pushes my shirt from my body. I grab her hips and pick her up. She swings her legs around my body and kisses me with both hands on either side of my face.

The bed is covered in rose petals, a beautiful touch, but I sweep them away as I lay her down. Jess leans up on her elbows, eyeing me as I undo my trousers and toss them to one side. I stand over her, drinking in the sight of her. She pushes herself up onto her knees and wraps her arms around my neck. "Penny for your thoughts?"

"I'm admiring the woman I love and taking the time to look at you."

"Well, that's lovely and all, but I want you now. Hard and fast."

That is all I need. I push her back onto the bed, pull down her strapless bra and free her nipples. I take one in my mouth whilst my fingers discover just how wet and ready she is. I plunge into her, which makes her gasp, moan and arch her back all at the same time. I grab her hips and drive myself deeper into her. She feels so tight and amazing; I'm not going to last long.

I pound hard and fast into her, lifting her hips slightly, which makes her go wild. I can already feel her clenching around me. She's close, and so am I. I take one hand off her hip and tweak her nipple slightly, and there she goes. I can physically see the orgasm go through her as well as feel her tighten around me. I last a few more seconds before finishing inside her and collapsing on the bed beside my sated wife.

"Well, that's our marriage consummated." She laughs, trying to regulate her breathing again.

"That it is. No going back now."

Jess turns to kiss me and wraps her arm and leg over me. "I'm not going anywhere, mister."

We lay there in bliss until we both drift off to sleep.

Day three of married life. We leave for Barbados tomorrow, so I'm going through my emails before my technology is confiscated. We'll still have our laptops and phones, but the majority of the time will be spent relaxing and having time together. Relaxing is something I'm not used to, although I have been a little better since meeting Jess.

The following day, I'm sitting in the executive lounge at the airport, and I'm not wearing a suit, either. I'm ready in my shorts, T-shirt and shades. Yes, it's October here in the U.K., and autumn is beautiful, but I'm not walking off the plane in Barbados sweating like a nun in a cucumber field! Jess is already relaxing, reading her book and sipping on a Sex on the Beach cocktail. I thought it was apt.

We get a call for our flight, and hand-in-hand, we walk to the jet—one of the perks of being rich is having your own plane. Nine hours in close quarters with my wonderful wife, heading to a lovely private villa that also has ‘room service’ is my idea of pure bliss.

“Here we go!” Jess almost squeals with excitement as the plane starts to take off. I hold her hand and lean closer to her.

“Once we get to cruising altitude, me and you in the back.” I wink and grin at her. Jess’s cheeks flush, and her smile widens.

Chapter Seventy-Seven

JESS

If I thought Gavin had a high sex drive before, I was mistaken. I've never been on a nine-hour flight with him alone. I can barely walk off the plane when we land. Even absolutely shattered, the feeling of the heat hitting me as the jet door opens is bliss, though.

We take a private car to the villa, unpack and have a nap which is much needed after no rest on the plane. It hit me earlier, between sessions, that I'm now a billionaire. Gavin didn't want to do a prenup, although I had no objections to it. I don't know if I'll ever get used to having money. Gavin knows it's not on my priority list, but having a private jet and villa? Absolutely amazing!

I wake up before Gavin and have a shower. Stepping outside in my towel, the heat hits me, and I feel myself drying in seconds. I nip back into the villa to grab a water and my book, slip on my robe and sit on a lounger. We are on a complex, but there are at least a few hundred yards between us and the neighbouring villas. I lay on the lounger, taking in the view of our private garden. It has colourful plants I don't know the names of, palm trees, a beautiful pool, and I can hear the ocean just on the other side of the garden. This is absolute bliss.

I'm a few chapters in before I hear Gavin padding across the patio. I lift my head up and see a towel wrapped around his waist and his hair messy from his shower. His body is glistening in the sunshine; he looks delicious. He leans in for a kiss and leaves me breathless, his hair dripping on my face. His hand cups my cheek firmly as he kisses me gently, which quickly turns passionate.

He leans in front of me with a devilish look in his eyes, and the towel around his waist drops as he nudges my knees apart with his. My book falls to the floor as my arms reach for his neck, drawing him closer to me. His lips drift down to my neck, kissing that sweet spot that makes my breath hitch as his hands pull apart my gown, revealing every inch of my naked body. His kisses trail down to my nipples, clasping them in his mouth one by one as his hand trails down my body to my parted legs. His thumb circles my clit, making my back arch off the lounger as he plunges himself into me at the same time.

Gavin moves closer and lifts my hips, allowing himself to get deeper as he increases his pace, hitting every spot inside, making me come hard and fast. Moments later, Gavin finds his own release and buries his head in my neck.

"Welcome to Barbados, Mrs Andrews." He grins at me.

"What a welcome it's been!" I grin whilst drinking some water.

We take a dip in the pool to cool off, followed by a leisurely stroll on the beach before we order in some local cuisine for dinner.

After a week of sex, swimming and relaxing, we decide to go out to explore the island. We spend the next few days snorkelling with turtles, looking through shipwrecks, and cave tours, and Gavin hires a boat to tour the island for the day, although not that much of the time on the boat is spent sightseeing.

We bought an underwater camera so we could document these experiences, and I'm going to start creating physical photo albums so our children and grandchildren can go through them like I did with my grandparents. So much of our lives is digital. It'll be nice to have something to flick through to reminisce.

Our last few days on honeymoon are spent much like the first few. Relaxing, swimming in the pool, eating and generally enjoying each other. I thought having two weeks off the grid would be difficult, but it's been wonderful not having my phone or laptop attached to me. We allow ourselves an hour a night to check emails, messages, and so on, but once that hour is up, it's back to us. We have talked about our pasts, presents and futures. We have so much to look forward to with the house, potential parenthood, and where we want to take different areas of the business. At first, I was confused when he said *we*, but now that we're married, *we* own the company. This is yet another something new I'll need to get used to.

During the hours we allow electronic devices, we have emails from social workers about our next assessment. We fire off forms, and when we get back, we already have meetings lined up. I'm glad we only allow an hour a night for this stuff because we could easily be overwhelmed and let it ruin our honeymoon, focusing on work, adoption stuff and everything in between. Outside of that hour, we enjoy our magical time, and I'm not just talking about sex.

It's our last night, and we promise each other no tech at all. Only us, dinner, and whatever else we decide to do. We eat on the beach, walk back to our villa and spend the night exploring every inch of each other. I will never get enough of this man. He's soft, kind, gentle, loving and makes love to me like we are made for each other.

By the time we're sitting on the tarmac in the comfort of our jet, I feel a little sad. It is time to go back to reality. The wedding was beautiful, and the only thing to deal with from that are the pictures. The honeymoon was complete bliss. I'm looking forward to the next chapters of our lives, but I will miss this time together. *Mental note: take more time 'off the grid' with each other, even when we have kids.*

The jet takes off, and we have nine hours until we land. I settle in with a movie and start making a mental list of things to do when we get home. I look across at Gavin, and he's thumbing through some papers.

Where did those come from? I move over next to him to have a peek.

"Whatchya doing?" I grin at him.

"Just going through some papers for the company. I want things in order before we return next week." His face is stoic, and his expression tells me where his concentration lies. He's sitting on one of the sofas, so I lay my head on his lap and pick up my book.

"Mrs Andrews, are you trying to distract me on purpose?" He looks like Sean Connery when he raises his eyebrow.

"Not at all! Just wanted to be close." I smile. He reads through the papers with one hand and drapes his other across my stomach.

I drift in and out of sleep whilst Gavin works. When I'm fully awake, he's smiling at me with a mischievous grin.

"Well, Mrs Andrews, I need you to sign on the dotted line to confirm you now co-own the company with me, and then...." His wink says it all. I sign, and off we go to the back of the plane for the last five hours of our honeymoon.

Chapter Seventy-Eight

GAVIN

My forehead feels cool on the glass of my office window; my migraine is slowly fading, thankfully. In the last three weeks since we've been back at work, Jess has been introduced to the running of the company, and we've had eight meetings with a social worker to go through every inch of our lives. I know they need to make sure they're not placing children with awful people, but seriously, do you need to know how I felt when I didn't win a race at age four?

We've got three more meetings scheduled with the social worker, and then on to a panel where a group of people decide whether we're good enough to be parents. Again, it's a necessary step, but it makes you feel so inadequate.

Paul is off on holiday with Sophie, so I've not got him to chat with about all of this. It has made me look at the people around us. We had to draw out our support network, and we both realised that we don't have many people we call close friends, which also isn't a bad thing.

The cold rain beating against the window is cooling me down nicely when I hear my office door open. Jess is the only person who comes in without knocking when she knows I'm alone. I feel her arms snake around my waist and a gentle kiss on my shoulder.

"Hey, you. Not feeling any better?"

"Yeah, but I also can't move."

"Come lay down on the sofa."

Jess potters about making me a coffee, prepping my migraine meds and laying me down. Hopefully, a little nap will help. As I doze off, I hear Jess leave and tell Anna to clear the rest of my day. What would I do without her?

I wake up thinking I've slept for hours; my head is clearer, and I can smell food. I've only been asleep for an hour, though, and Jess has left me some soup from the deli down the road on my coffee table. This woman knows me so well. I sit up and eat the soup—butternut squash today. The warmth of the food chases away the last remaining strain of my migraine, and I hop up to crack on with work. I ping Jess my thanks and make my way through some of these emails.

I see an email from my solicitor; I don't look forward to reading this. The last conversation we had didn't end well when I threatened to terminate his services due to pushing for a prenup. If I was marrying someone like Sacha, then yes, I would have gotten one without question, but this is Jess. She doesn't care about money and loves me for me and not my riches, which is why everything I have is now ours. I've already changed the deeds to the penthouse and a few other properties I own around the world.

When I delve into the email, it's regarding Mum and Dad's house. They're ready to move and have found a house we will buy for them, but it'll go in their name. Once that is completed, their house will be deeded in Jess and mine name. The solicitors can deal with the paperwork side. We should complete everything in a few weeks. There's no rush, though, because we plan to decorate the house to our taste, upgrade a few things and change a few of the rooms. Another exciting project my wife has fully immersed herself in.

With my emails done, it's now three o'clock in the afternoon. I decide to take off and work the rest of the day at home. Mainly so I can cook my beautiful woman her favourite dinner; you can't beat a tasty shepherd's pie on a grey day like this. I go through the Amazon fresh store and pick up the bits I need and head home. In the kitchen, I set my laptop up on the side so I can scroll through emails whilst I'm cooking and set about making dinner. We've both been so busy since we got back from our honeymoon we have barely eaten together. That changes now. We own the company and need to start practising what we preach about work/life balance. My eyes already sting from the onions.

JESS WALKS THROUGH THE DOOR WITH A LOOK ON HER face that matches the sky outside. I walk over to her with fresh coffee and take her coat.

"There's a bath ready for you upstairs. It might not be quite the temperature of Satan's armpit now, but it's the thought that counts."

She laughs at my joke, which makes me smile. "Hilarious, my baths aren't that hot."

She potters upstairs and emerges looking like a sexy lobster an hour later. *Her bath isn't that hot, indeed.*

I grin and think of Phoebe from Friends. *"She's his lobster."*

We sit down at the breakfast bar and demolish dinner, Jess expressing her gratitude through various "mmmm's" and "beautiful" as she eats.

We steal ourselves an "off the grid" evening, going through the proofs of the wedding photos and choosing which ones we want frames for and which will go in an album. Sitting with a coffee, cross-legged on the sofa, my wife is the picture of happiness. After the photos, we chat about our week and decide to take some time to ourselves over the weekend. Staying in bed, lounging around the house, which will no doubt end up in some form of project planning. Shortly after eleven o'clock, we head up to bed and cuddle as the rain continues to batter the windows. I find myself thinking of when we move into the house, what décor we'll have and how the rain will sound different on the windows. I'd like to have some time off to build the kids a play house, maybe build a little summer house for us to retreat to at the bottom of the garden. I can imagine Jess using it as a reading nook.

There are many plates spinning, but everything is under control, and there's an odd sense of calm that washes around us. I think about my manly projects and cuddle up with Jess as we drift off.

Chapter Seventy-Nine

JESS

I've redone my hair and outfit three times; we leave for our panel meeting in half an hour. I have never felt so nervous. This is where we find if we're approved to adopt, and if so, the age range and how many at one time. Gavin and I have spoken about adopting one as soon as possible and then another a few years down the line or adopting a sibling group straight off the bat and having our family start at once.

We're here. My heart is pounding in my chest, and my palms are sweating. I grip Gavin's hand and glance up at his face. He looks like he's about to enter a business meeting. He seems cool, calm and collected. Our social worker ushers us into a little room, where we wait to be called by the panel. I don't realise my knee is bobbing up and down until Gavin puts his hand on it to settle me down. There's a knock at the door. It's time. *I'm going to be sick!*

We sit in a big conference room. There are seven

people on the other side of the table, all smiling and giving off calm vibes, which soothes me a little. On our side is us and our social worker.

The chairman begins by talking through our report and asks questions about childcare, our careers, and how we see our futures. We answer every question with feeling and professionalism. We're used to running our own meetings, and this is like one of our meetings in some ways. I suddenly get the flutter in my stomach again. I feel sick, and I'm willing for this part of the adoption process to be over. Luckily, I don't have to wait long before we're back in the little room.

I start noticing the colours in the room, calming greens with gentle white swirls and potted plants on floating shelves. This room is made to give off soothing vibes, and it's working. The panel said they would discuss everything and come get us in half an hour. Thirty minutes is a long time when you're waiting. I look up at the clock, and only five minutes have passed. There is a soft knock at the door, and my heart sinks to the pit of my stomach. They can't have made a decision that quickly if it's positive. Can they?

We make our way back to the conference room. Gavin's grip on my hand is as hard as I feel tense. We take a seat and wait for the chair to talk.

"Gavin, Jess, thank you for your patience. I know it wasn't a long wait, but from experience, I know those five minutes feel like an eternity." He smiles at us, and we both relax a little. "Based on your social worker's report and our conversation today, I'm pleased to advise that the panel has unanimously approved you as adopters."

Your heart isn't beating. You're not breathing. BREATHE, WOMAN!

"Furthermore, you can adopt any age, from newborn and older, with no restrictions on how many children you can adopt. You have a strong support network around you, and we're confident you'll make fantastic parents. Congratulations!" The chairman and the others in the room grin from ear to ear.

I look over at Gavin, who's smiling broadly but squeezing my hand to the point it may break.

"Thank you all so much. This is wonderful news," we manage to say at the same time. As we walk out, a tear rolls down my cheek. We have a quick debrief with our social worker and then head to the car. We get in and sit in silence for a moment before we break into happy, nervous laughter.

"We're going to be parents!" Gavin grips my face, his eyes welling up.

"We may be giving your mum that rugby team she wants after all!" I laugh and kiss him.

We still have to wait a week for the final rubber stamp, but then we'll be in the matching phase of our journey. This is the bit that can take weeks, months or years. We can hear about a child and have them move in quickly, or it can take time. The unknown is what bothers me. I like to plan. We can't prepare room colours, furniture or clothes until we know if it will be a boy or girl, older or younger. But we can prepare space, make the colours neutral, and welcome a child or children into our family. For now, we celebrate being approved and await our future.

A WEEK PASSES, AND WE GET OUR RUBBER STAMP. THE house is moving along nicely. Julia and Daniel have moved into their new house, and we're renovating the kitchen and other rooms. We're making the guest bedrooms a little more modern and changing four of the bedrooms into potential children's rooms. We've knocked down walls to two rooms to make the master bedroom even bigger. Our offices are downstairs, and we have a playroom and family rooms, as well. I have someone managing the house project whilst we work and managing other projects. Being a control freak, naturally, I check in a couple of times a week to make sure it's running smoothly.

I'm just finishing up with Lucy; the European office is expanding quicker than we thought. I've gone through the budgets, and she's currently looking for a larger office to house the eight new staff members she's taking on. I'm proud of how this has come together and is progressing. I'll still be checking in monthly, but I know with Lucy in charge, I don't have to. She also told me that Miles proposed to her on the Eiffel Tower. So romantic! I also have a catch-up with Kiera tonight. She's been dating this engineer for a few months, and we've not seen much of each other. I know when Gavin and I first got together, we were with each other constantly, not that anything has changed much.

I head down to Gavin's office after picking up a coffee from the shop down the street. Anna isn't at her desk, so I let myself in. Gavin is lying on his sofa with a cold towel over his eyes. His migraines are back with a vengeance, by the looks of it. I place his coffee on his table and perch next to him.

"You okay, Gavin?"

"Mmmm, been better."

"I'm making you doctor and optician appointments; you can't keep going with your head like this."

He pulls me down into a kiss and doesn't let me go. I lay with him for a while before sneaking back to my office whilst he sleeps. I book his appointments for tomorrow and pack up for the day. I'm going to take him home to rest; I can work and check in on the house project from there.

We get home, and our social worker is standing at our front door. Odd. "Hi, Stacey. We didn't have a meeting planned, did we?"

"Sorry to just turn up, but I have an urgent case I'd like to talk to you about. I didn't want to come to your office. It's sensitive."

A case? That means there's a child looking for a forever family. I open the door, Gavin straightens himself up, and I can see him try to push his migraine aside. We head to the kitchen, and I put a pot of fresh coffee on.

Chapter Eighty

GAVIN

Stacey is sitting in our kitchen, Jess is putting on coffee, and I'm trying my hardest to get rid of this migraine. Whilst the coffee is brewing, Jess gets her adoption notebook. A few minutes later, we're refreshed and ready to hear what Stacey has to say.

"I have a sibling group. They're currently in emergency foster care, but the courts have already agreed they're best suited for adoption rather than going back to their birth family."

"What's the background? If it's emergency foster care, that can't be good for them." Jess looks worried for these children, and my heart aches for her.

"Birth parents are heavily involved in the drug scene. They had been receiving support from social services and were seemingly doing better for the children. We got a call from the police last night, advising that they attended the house after reports from neighbours. The birth mother had been stabbed multiple times by the birth father. The police believe it was a drug-fuelled rage."

What? I can't be hearing this correctly? You hear of this stuff happening, but you don't think it'll actually happen near you. "What about the children? Are they okay?" My voice is shaky. I want to bring them home and keep them safe, but we know nothing about them.

"The eldest is a four-year-old boy. He's suffered a fractured arm and is currently in hospital with the foster dad by his side. The youngest is a six-month-old girl. We were advised she has no external injuries. She was checked over in the hospital last night and seems to be okay."

I glance over at Jess, whose eyes are watering, already filled with love for these children. She looks at me, and I nod.

"When can we bring them home?" she asks Stacey, who appears shocked and stares at the two of us.

"Don't you want to read their file and talk first?"

"We will read their file, but we don't need to talk. I believe both Jess and I are currently having the same thoughts and feelings relating to these two children. What steps do we need to take to bring them home?"

It's been a week since we heard about Harry and Isabelle. Jess pushed for the house to be finished within two weeks. We have more contractors on site, and they are currently working to complete all tasks with their new deadline. We have had meetings with social workers, doctors, the foster care parents, and the more we hear about these kids, the more we want them in our lives.

Jess is buying furniture for their bedrooms and clothes as they left with nothing except what they were wearing. Our parents have already bought out the toy shops, too. We have a meeting later today with another panel group to "match" us with the brother and sister. We're both 'working from home' today, although not a lot of work is actually being done. We haven't had the official match yet, but we're preparing for Harry and Isabelle to come home. I'm currently reading up on feeding schedules for babies and how to help a four-year-old with emotions. We've decided that due to the violent situation they were removed from, Jess and I will work from home for a couple of days a week on reduced hours to spend as much time as we can with the kids to create a safe and loving bond with them.

Before we looked at kids, Jess had shortlisted the best nurseries and schools around us, so we'll take that step when we feel they are ready. For now, we'll be their safety and primary source of comfort until we feel they can take the next step.

Our meeting is in an hour, so we quickly freshen up and head over to the social office to meet this new panel. Before matching meetings, you normally have lots of time to prepare your answers, but we're going from the heart. Jess is the queen of research, and I've done my fair share of looking into what we can do to help these kids. *Gavin, Jess, Harry and Isabelle Andrews has a nice ring to it!*

Before we know it, we're sitting in the meeting discussing the plan for the children. Neither of us is nervous. We know we can provide the best care for them, and we are already excited to welcome them to our family. This panel is different from the first. They have the children's reports, police reports and a list of questions to ask us, and we're more than prepared for each and every one of them. Those are our children, and we want to bring them home.

We're sitting in the little green room, waiting for their verdict. If all goes well, we can meet the children this weekend and bring them home later in the week, which is both terrifying and exciting. We've told our parents we want two weeks with the kids alone to settle them into their new home and family before introducing them. They all understand, but I could hear their impatience at the delay in meeting their grandchildren.

There's a knock at the door. We're heading back in.

It's the beginning of December. We've moved into the house, and the frost lying on the grass makes everything slightly glittery and magical. I'm sitting at the breakfast bar going through emails with a coffee, and I hear Jess coming down the stairs on the phone, speaking in hushed tones. We're looking at decorating the house this week to get ready for Christmas, and Jess wants a real Christmas tree. Thankfully, we have cleaners as those things molt like no one's business.

"Morning, handsome." Jess kisses me on my cheek and heads over to the coffee machine.

"Morning, beautiful. Just getting some emails done before we start our day."

"No rest for the wicked." She chuckles and looks outside at the frost-covered garden.

"I thought today we could go for a walk, explore the grounds, and start looking at furniture for the summer house?"

"Sounds perfect." She's still a little sleepy, but it is only seven o'clock in the morning.

Before long, we hear the thunder of tiny feet upstairs. "He's awake!" I close my laptop and greet Harry at the bottom of the stairs, scooping him up into my arms and carrying him to the kitchen.

"What does my little man want for breakfast this morning." Jess beams at Harry whilst listening to the monitor. Isabelle is still fast asleep, so we make breakfast and wait for our sleeping beauty to wake up.

Chapter Eighty-One

JESS

It's been nearly two weeks since our lives have changed. We met Harry and Isabelle at their foster carers' house. Harry was really withdrawn, and I could tell he'd been hurt emotionally as well as

physically. Isabelle didn't seem to mind strangers cooing over her. It took two days before Harry would come and play with us, but even then, he was wary, and it broke my heart. We were given more information on the relationship between their birth parents, and I'm honestly shocked they weren't taken out of the situation sooner. I know there are rules and guidelines to follow, which is why I wouldn't make a good social worker. I'd want to take them and protect them all.

With their birth mother dead and their birth father in prison, there are no contact arrangements for us to look at. We will, of course, talk to them about their life story when they're of an age and we can work through their feelings about it all with them.

They came home with us after the fifth day of introductions. It was supposed to be a week, but after Harry had warmed to us, the social worker and foster care parents agreed that the introductions didn't need to go on any longer; the children needed stability.

The first night was awful. Harry had nightmares, and Isabelle wouldn't settle. It probably didn't help that we were on edge, too. So we brought them both into our room, had ocean sounds on in the background and cuddled them to sleep. We were told not to have them in our bed, but when children, *our children*, are hurting, we will do everything in our power to help them. If that's cuddling them to sleep, then that's what we'll do. The second night, we installed speakers in their rooms so they could have the ocean sounds in there. We also fixed Harry's favourite teddy bear, which made him feel better. The poor bear's arm was ripped off, and the head hanging. This was part of the emotional abuse he'd received. But we fixed it, and he slept much better.

By the third night, we were in a small routine of reading before bedtime. Isabelle loved cuddling up with Gavin whilst drinking her milk and listening to me read.

I still wake up some days not quite believing we're parents. We have eight weeks to go before we can apply for full adoption, but I already have the forms filled out and ready to go in my email drafts. We have spent two weeks making these children feel safe, happy and confident, but there are still days when memories come back, and that'll happen for years. Harry is of an age where he knows he's being adopted, and we've hired a counsellor who deals with PTSD in children through colour therapy. They come to the house once a week to help him through the emotions he's too young to understand.

The bonds have been building, and although Harry hasn't called us Mum and Dad, that's absolutely fine. We're taking everything at his pace. Isabelle is now seven months old, and we're discovering weaning. I'm very thankful I designed the kitchen with children in mind. Food gets EVERYWHERE!

Today, however, is not about us. It's about the children meeting their grandparents for the first time. We are having a nice lunch and plenty of space and play. All of the grandparents know that if the kids show any form of distress, then it's time to go, and we'll meet again another day. They understand their situation without knowing the details.

The kids are playing in the downstairs playroom whilst I'm pottering around in the kitchen. Harry appears beside me.

"May I have a snack, please?"

"Of course, you can. Those are excellent manners! What do you fancy?"

He looks up at me, and I have a feeling the manners were beaten into him rather than being natural, my poor baby.

Harry chooses some strawberries and eats at the breakfast bar whilst watching me cook. I can hear Gavin in the playroom with Isabelle, and it makes me smile.

"Why did you want me?" His tiny voice is barely audible, but I hear every heart-breaking word. I turn the stove off and give him my full attention. I get down on his level and look into those beautiful blue eyes.

"You are a wonderful boy with a laugh that will light up rooms, an imagination that could write books one day, and a caring heart that makes me smile." His expression doesn't change, and I'm not sure what I am meant to say, but I wait for him to respond.

"I'm broken. Dad told me I'm broken."

It takes me a moment to realise he remembers his birth dad. I scoop him up in my arms. The books and research have all gone out the window, and I'm following my instincts. "You, my beautiful Harry, are not broken. Bad things happened, but they were not your fault. I hope one day you will know how much I love you." With those last three words, he cries and cries. I wonder if he's ever been told he is loved? I hold him until he leans back a little to kiss me on my cheek. My tears won't hold anymore. I hug him and kiss him on the head. Gavin comes into the kitchen with Isabelle and stares at us for a moment. I give him a look that says, 'I'll tell you later.'

"Harry, are you helping Jess cook?" We decide not to push the mum and dad thing until he's ready. We're hoping by the time Isabelle starts talking, it'll be Mum and Dad rather than Jess and Gavin.

Harry nods at Gavin and climbs back down to his snack. I get back to cooking whilst Gavin prepares Isabelle something to eat. Since she's started weaning, she loves different foods and flavours.

By the time we are ready, the grandparents arrive. I check on the camera and see a horrendous amount of presents coming out of both cars. I roll my eyes and turn to Gavin and the kids. "Ready? Your grandparents are here to meet you!"

THE AFTERNOON GOES WELL. HARRY CLINGS TO MY side but is enticed away when he's told there is a room full of presents. He peers up at me as if asking for permission to go. I give him a grin and nod, and off he goes. Isabelle is in my dad's arms, trying to eat his T-shirt, which makes me giggle. The amount of presents is overwhelming, so we squirrel some away before the kids see. We'll bring them out bit by bit over the next few months. It's not like Christmas is a couple of weeks away or anything.

We hang back and let the grandparents play with the kids in the downstairs playroom.

The parents leave about five o'clock so we can have a quiet dinner and settle the kids down for bed. After their baths, reading and Isabelle's bottle, we tuck them into bed.

Harry hugs me tight, and I kiss his head. "Sweet dreams, handsome."

"Love you, Mummy."

My heart shatters into tiny pieces and reforms into a bigger heart. "I love you, too, my beautiful boy."

Chapter Eighty-Two

GAVIN

It's Christmas morning. Jess got the stockings at the end of the kids' beds last night, and we brought all the presents down early this morning. I put some flour footprints from the fireplace to the Christmas tree, so it seems like Santa has visited our house. We don't have snow, but he's from the North Pole, so he will have snow on his boots. Harry may only be four, but he's bright, and we want to keep the magic alive for as long as possible for them.

Jess and I are enjoying a coffee before the kids wake up. Jess is preparing the Christmas dinner, and I sit and think about how things have changed. A couple of years ago, I'd be sitting in my penthouse working, then heading over to Mum and Dad's for dinner and back home to work out and work. Then Jess came into my life, my world changed, and I saw more colour. This Christmas, we have two wonderful children who we love more than we could ever have imagined, and I woke up on Christmas morning excited to see their faces when they believe Santa has been here. More importantly, we were told the kids have never had a Christmas like we know it. No tree, presents, or dinner. Isabelle is too young to remember, but Harry has had four non-Christmases; this will be one for him to enjoy.

Before long, we hear a shriek of excitement, and Harry thunders down the stairs with even more shrieks when he sees the presents under the tree. With all the commotion, of course, Isabelle wakes up. We have breakfast, and the kids open their stockings from Santa. Harry has tears rolling down his face as he opens his little chocolate coins, a bouncy ball and a little Lego set. If this is his reaction to his stocking, then he's in for a hell of a surprise later. We want to spread joy throughout the day, so we open two presents each before we get dressed. Harry is outside playing with his football and net; Isabelle has started crawling and cruising now, so she's outside trying to play with her brother.

The day is wonderful, and as Jess calls for the thirty-minute warning until dinner, our parents arrive for the afternoon. Kiera, her partner, Paul and Sophie are dropping by tomorrow. They didn't want to overwhelm the kids. Harry runs inside to greet his grandparents. In the last week, he's started calling us Mummy and Daddy. We are honoured that he feels comfortable doing this.

Naturally, the grandparents have spoilt the kids rotten. There are bikes, Legos, and soft playthings for

Isabelle. We're going to need an extension to fit it all in.

After our beautiful Christmas dinner, prepared by Jess, we take the kids out for a walk whilst the mums stay at home to clean up for us. The dads, naturally, take to the living room with a cuppa and chat.

We enjoy our walk. Isabelle has fallen asleep in her pushchair, and Harry is happily riding his bike after only an hour of learning how. He has his stabilisers on, but it is still an amazing accomplishment.

Once we return to the house, we watch the kids open even more presents. Jess and I have decided that we will have a night to ourselves one night when the kids are comfortable with a babysitter as our gifts to each other. We leave a special gift for the kids until last. It is a picture of the four of us in a frame engraved with 'The Andrews Family'. They each have one for their rooms. Harry's face is a picture of sadness, happiness and something I can't put my finger on.

"Thank you, Mummy and Daddy. Can I have this right next to my bed, please?"

"Absolutely, love. We'll put it up now if you like?" Jess leads Harry to his room so he can choose where he'd like his picture. Isabelle tries to chew hers, so we're assuming she likes it.

Our little Harry and Isabelle have been part of our family for five months now. The adoption is approved, and today, we have our celebration hearing.

Naturally, our parents and best friends want to be a part of this special day. We all dress up for the occasion and meet at the local courthouse, where a judge will give us a certificate, and the kids get to see the judge's chambers. Harry picks out his own suit and tie for today and helps select Isabelle's dress. Jess is naturally stunning in her forest green dress to match my tie, and the kids look adorable.

We arrive at the court where our parents, Kiera and her new partner, Ed, wait with Paul and Sophie. We are lucky to have such a supportive network. Everyone smiles as we enter the courtroom. The celebration hearing takes about an hour and is an experience we have photos of to show the kids when they're older. We are going to go for a nice lunch, followed by Paul and me taking Harry to a trampoline park. I can honestly say I'm not sure who's more excited, Paul or Harry.

Our life as a family has merged so well with our busy working lives. We still run the company and have as much to do with projects as we did before, but somehow, we have a day or two off during the week to spend with the kids. Harry will be going to preschool for a few months to make friends before starting school next September. I sometimes have to stop and look at my life to see if it's actually real. I have everything I ever wanted and more, and it's all thanks to a wonderful woman who walked into my life a few years ago.

When we get home, Isabelle is crawling around and so very close to walking; it's scary. She's a year old now, and time is flying. We have a small bite to eat for dinner and put the kids to bed. Harry is exhausted from today but in a good way.

Jess is pottering about in the kitchen whilst I sit in my office and open my laptop. I'm not going to look at emails, but I want to do something wonderful for this woman. Then an idea hits me. I'm going to surprise her with a night away, just us, somewhere relaxing where we can spend some quality time together. Knowing Jess, she won't want anything extravagant, so I get my thinking cap on.

Got it! I make some phone calls and go online to get what I need. She's going to love it; I'm sure. A soft knock comes at my door, and there she is, dressed in shorts, a baggy T-shirt with no bra, and her hair up. I love her when she appears comfy and relaxed. She comes over with a cuppa, and I pull her down onto my lap after closing my laptop. We sit drinking our coffee, looking at the photos from the last six months, talking about how much we have all changed in that time.

"Take me to bed, Mr Andrews," she says in a husky voice. Who am I to argue?

I put the cups on my desk, stand and lift her over my shoulder, which produces the most delicious giggle, and take her upstairs.

Chapter Eighty-Three

JESS

The summer sun is coming in through the kitchen window as I sit reading my emails at the breakfast bar. It's six-thirty in the morning, and I can hear the birds chirping, the soft breeze rustling through the trees, and my husband walking down the stairs. He's been like an excited schoolboy for the last couple of days with secret deliveries and hushed phone calls. He thinks I haven't noticed, but I simply haven't said anything. He's planning something, and I'm sure I'll find out soon enough. He comes into the kitchen and wraps his arms around me whilst kissing my neck. God, he's sexy.

"What's got you in such a good mood this morning?"

"Nothing in particular! Are you heading out today?"

"Trying to get rid of me, eh? Mistress coming

round? As long as she prepares dinner and cleans the kitchen, I'll be back by three." I giggle as he bites my neck, making pleasure shoot down my body like an electric current.

"Now, now, you're not meant to know about her."

I get up and get another coffee, and he slaps my ass as I do. He's in a very playful mood today. I go upstairs to get ready. I'm heading into town today to get my hair done and get some clothes for the kids. Funnily enough, it was Gavin's idea for me to go out today. What is he planning? I shrug my shoulders and take a shower. My appointment is at nine-thirty, which means I've got time to get into town and have a cuppa before I sit in a chair for hours. I seriously have no idea why it takes so long to put some highlights in my hair. At the rate it's going, I'll look like Bruce Willis in no time!

I've spent a fortune for my hair to look mildly different from when I went in. I want to get some clothes for the kids, and I know the high street shops are not where some expect me to shop now that I have money, but I'm still getting the kids' clothes from there. They are not wearing expensive clothes to be trashed within seconds, and they last the same amount of time.

As I drive back home, I recognise my mum's car a few vehicles ahead of me and call her on hands-free. When she doesn't answer, I don't worry. She probably hasn't hooked her phone up to the car yet. I made her upgrade her mobile when she struggled to see the messages on her old phone.

I follow her all the way home, and I try to wrack my brain to see if I've forgotten her visit. Did we make plans? I get out of the car and grab my shopping. Mum comes to help; she knows full well what I'm like in the high street shops.

"Your hair looks lovely, dear. Just had it done?"

"Yeah, I'm not sure it looks any different, though. Did I forget we had plans tonight?"

"Oh, bless you, no. I thought I'd pop over and see the kids for a bit and maybe make some dinner. Your dad will be over soon. He's just picking some bits up." My Spidey senses are tingling.

We head into the house and are almost bowled over by Harry, and Isabelle is hanging onto her walker and coming towards us with the speed of a toddler on a mission. We scoop them up, leave the bags by the door to be rifled through later, and head to the kitchen, where Gavin is practically vibrating with excitement.

The kids go outside to play with Mum, and I turn towards him with a hand on my hip.

"Okay, out with it, mister. You have been giddy for days."

"I don't know what you're talking about. I'm very excited your mum is here."

I laugh. They get on and love each other, but he is a terrible liar, which I'm thankful for. I throw my hands up in the air. "Fine!" I grin and head outside with Mum. The kids are enjoying the new playhouse-come-swing set-come-climbing frame-come-everything you could imagine that the granddads built for them.

Dad arrives about an hour later, and I notice he's bought more than the few bits that he was picking up. I have an inkling my parents are staying over tonight. We're sitting on the patio with a cuppa when Gavin brings me an envelope. He grins, and I suddenly feel excited. I open it to find…a clue? Ooh, I'm going on a treasure hunt.

To begin your quest, you know where H hides best.

I down my coffee like it's a tequila shot and jump out of my chair. Harry loves to hide in the pantry, so that's where I'll go next. Another envelope.

I must warn you, you will want to stay warm.

Jumper? Coat? Not in this weather. Blanket? I head over to where the blankets were once neatly folded but now resemble some form of bird's nest, and there I find another clue.

Take this and stand where you were first kissed as Miss.

First kissed as Miss? Surely he can't mean my first actual kiss. It must mean the first time he kissed me here. The garden by the big old tree. Are we having a picnic? I saunter into the garden. The sky is turning to dusk, painting a picture across the sky with pink clouds, and as I get closer to the tree, I notice twinkling lights. Gavin grabs my hand as we walk down.

"I wanted it to be a surprise."

We get to the big old tree, and I stop and stare at the sight in front of me. There's a big white bell tent covered in fairy lights, two camping chairs out front with a blanket on one, and I remember I'm carrying the other. I place the blanket on the empty chair and peek inside. There's a nice comfy bed inside and petals strewn everywhere. I turn to look at Gavin, who is grinning like a Cheshire cat. "Do you like it?"

"I love it. Is there an occasion?"

"You. You are the occasion."

He pulls me into a kiss, arms around my back, pulling me closer to him, deepening his kiss. I throw my arms around his neck and practically jump up to lock my legs around his waist. He did this for me? I can't think of a reason why but I'm not complaining. We have a night to ourselves that isn't fancy, and I'm really hoping we can keep the tent. Camping in your own garden is amazing.

Gavin walks us over to the bed and lays me down with him on top. He's kissing my neck whilst his hands are riding up my leg under my dress. His fingers brush the lace edge of my knickers and move away, earning a disappointed groan. He kneels up and takes off his top with one swift movement. I wrap my legs around him and pull him down to me again, kissing him deeply and passionately. I manage to roll us, and I end up on top. I take off my dress and bend down to kiss him again whilst I'm rubbing myself against his jeans, feeling his hardening cock.

Chapter Eighty-Four

GAVIN

I wake up with Jess in my arms. We fell asleep at some point between sex, star gazing, more sex, eating, talking and more sex. Last night was everything I'd hoped. I was surprised by my stamina if I'm honest, but I am feeling a little sore this morning. I rearrange myself before pulling Jess closer to me.

"Good morning, sunshine."

"I love you, but if you're hoping for another ride, I'm currently out of service." She laughs, but I know exactly what she means.

"You and me both, sweetheart. Did you enjoy our night?"

"Absolutely, it was perfect."

We roll out of bed, and I notice the time. We've slept until nine. I can't remember the last time we slept in this late. As we get dressed, we glance at each other with a grin because we can hear whispering outside the tent. We sit very patiently, waiting for the tent door to open, and when it does, it's our little man with a tray of coffee, orange juice, bacon sandwiches and some strawberries. The breakfast of champions. He looks so proud of himself that he's carried it all this way without spilling.

"What do we have here?"

"Your breakfast in bed! Why are you dressed?"

We laughed and got back into bed with our clothes on so we could receive our wonderful breakfast.

"This is wonderful, Harry! Did you make it by yourself?" Jess beams at him.

"Almost! Grandma wouldn't let me do the bacon. Too hot, but I made the sandwiches and carried it down here all by myself!" He is so proud.

"Well, thank you very mu—" Before I can finish my sentence, he is off, running through the garden. Soon, we hear, "THEY LOVE IT! CAN I HAVE BACON NOW, PLEASE?" Jess and I grin whilst we eat.

Later in the day, we say our thank yous to Jess's parents and decide to head out for an afternoon at the park and to feed the ducks. When we get home, I make fajitas for dinner, and we sit on the sofa after and watch *Minions* for the five thousandth time in a week with the kids. Instead of logging in to work this evening, I run a bath for Jess, making certain her favourite candles are lit and she has a face mask to relax her. I bathe the kids, read stories and put them to bed. As soon as I'm done, I take some snacks and drinks up to our room, where Jess is just getting into her PJs. To relax and spend time with each other, we sit in bed and watch a film. A grown-up one, a much-needed change from the Minions.

Normally in life, when I feel a smidge of happiness, something happens to bring me down, but that hasn't happened. We are truly happy. We have wonderful kids, a great life, a lot of love, and although we both work hard, we play harder—*pun intended.* We have everything we could ever asked for.

During our snacks, we talk about taking the kids on holiday. Jess has already changed their names on their passports. She did it as soon as the adoption order was completed. It's merely a question of where to go. They're too young for Disneyland. We'd like Isabelle to be at least five or six before we go so she can appreciate it. We're thinking about taking a nice beach holiday, where we can explore a new place and start a wonderful journey with our children.

I lie there watching whatever is on the TV with Jess curled up beside me. She's drifted off to sleep, so I move everything off the bed and turn the TV off. I cuddle her tightly tonight; I never want to let her go.

A FEW MONTHS LATER…

We're woken up by the pattering of feet sneaking into our room, giggling as we pretend to sleep. I know Jess is awake because I can feel her trying not to laugh. The kids crawl into our bed and shout, "Raaaawwwr-rrr," as they wear their dinosaur masks. In response, we give them a well-deserved scream. This brings the biggest smiles, and when I check the clock, I'm even happier. It's gone seven-thirty on a Sunday morning. We're winning.

"Are we ready for breakfast, my little dino's?"

"Can we have dinosaur pancakes, Daddy?" Harry beams at me from behind his triceratops mask.

"ancakes!" Isabelle can't quite say it yet, but she's equally excited. We watched one of the *Ice Age* films the other week, and they've been obsessed ever since. Luckily, Daddy makes amazing dinosaur pancakes, with blueberries, strawberries and honey.

"Oh, if Daddy is making pancakes, does that mean Mummy makes milkshakes?"

Their eyes pop open. They run downstairs as quickly as they can. Jess and I laugh and follow them. Since Isabelle started walking, she's mainly been running. We miss the baby stage, but it's wonderful that she's finding her independence. Harry is in his element, teaching her lots of new things.

We head downstairs and start with our breakfast making. Jess, of course, heads to the coffee machine. Nothing can be done without coffee first thing in the morning. The kids sit at the breakfast bar whilst we prep. They're in charge of the fruit going on the plates, although judging by the giggles, there's more going in their mouths than on the plates.

After breakfast, we get ready for the day. My parents are coming over to spend time with us, and Mum is making one of her famous Sunday lunches. She's been itching to cook in the new kitchen again.

They're bringing over their new dog for the kids to meet. We haven't decided on getting a dog for ourselves yet. Although saying that, Jess wants one, so we'll probably end up getting one soon.

As we're heading downstairs, we can hear Mum and Dad in the garden with the kids. I thought Harry might faint going by the sound of his scream, but then I heard the barking. We're definitely going to end up with a dog. I grab my wife when we reach the bottom of the stairs, kiss her hard, leaving her breathless, and smile.

"So Mum and Dad are staying over tonight. Shall we head to the bell tent?" I wink, and going by the grin on her face, that'll be a yes. We walk outside into the sunshine to find our kids running around with a young Labrador and my parents grinning and taking a ton of photos.

Life couldn't get much better than this.

Epilogue

JESS

I stand in a large, open-plan space. Harry is sitting at a desk, doing homework, and Isabelle is trying to write her name. I walk around the space, planning where everything else is going to go. Gavin walks through the door in his suit, looking handsome as he talks business with someone on the other end of the phone.

We are opening our second foreign office. After the European office thrived, we decided to we need an office in Asia and have plans to expand into Africa in the next few years. A member of Lucy's team is taking the opportunity to head up the new office, and they're arriving tomorrow to set everything up. Naturally, I want to be a part of the set-up and opening. My forecasts have got us this far, and we're hoping to branch into the U.S. within ten-years.

The Hong Kong office is sleek in design, tastefully decorated, and we are recruiting ten local consultants to join our firm. Everything is moving along swimmingly. When the elevator door opens, my eyes nearly pop out of my head, and my feet start to move—the coffee machine has arrived. It's still the little things I get excited about.

Gavin finishes his phone call and checks on the kids, who are behaving impeccably, considering this must be boring for them. We are lucky that Harry likes his homework, and Isabelle is trying with her writing. She started school a few months ago and is doing well. Harry is now nine and acing all of his lessons in school. And we sometimes bring them on business trips. They enjoy seeing the world with us and learning what Mummy and Daddy do for work.

We have travelled the world with the kids. After the office handover tomorrow, we're going to Disneyland in Hong Kong, which they don't know about! We can't wait to see their faces walking into the magic kingdom! We went to the Paris one last year and looking at going to Florida next year. We wanted to get them all done before Harry gets 'too cool' for Disneyland.

Kiera is marrying Ed next month in Morocco, which we can't wait to attend. Naturally, I'm the maid of honour and wedding planner. Paul and Sophie got married last year and are expecting their first child in a few months. We're waiting until the baby has arrived to find out whether it's a boy or a girl, which is exciting.

Both of our parents are happy and healthy; they're hands-on grandparents, and the kids absolutely love it.

Eight years ago, I had no purpose. Bored at work, I couldn't stand dating and most of my meals were microwave or cheap. I lived payday to payday. Now, I'm successful, married to the most amazing man, have two wonderful children, and my life has passion, drive, purpose and love. That's what happens when you fall for the CEO, and he falls right back for you.

Acknowledgments

I'd like to thank my author friends Elouise East and Maria Vickers who supported me though this journey and helped me with my confidence in writing. My Mum, Dad, Sister and Mother-in-law who I couldn't have written this book without (thanks for the babysitting so I had time to write!), my friends Karen and Lynne who introduced me to Elouise and believed in me.

My sister Rebecca and author H.R.Lloyd, I thank you for being my beta readers, you provided valuable feedback and helped me make it the version it is today.

My husband believed in me and my passion to become an author. Without his unwavering support and believe, this book would just be a document on my computer, unfinished and unpublished.

Printed in Great Britain
by Amazon